I entered the vestibule and pressed the buzzer for the professor's apartment, waited ten seconds, and pressed it again. Nothing. I was about to buzz Mrs. Landsdowne when I noticed that the interior door was ajar. I let myself into the foyer and took the stairs to the second floor two at a time, pushed on by a growing sense of urgency I didn't fully understand. When I reached the professor's door, it too was cracked open.

"Professor?" No response.

Nobody invited me, but I went in anyway, treading softer than a sinner in a cathedral. The apartment looked the same as it had during my last visit: cramped, cluttered and empty. I crossed over toward the desk, then stopped short. The man I was looking for was lying on his side near the doorway to the kitchen, his head resting in a pool of blood...

"A clever...twist to the old mystery tale."
—*Kirkus Reviews*

"A thoroughly enjoyable trip on the St. Lawrence!"
—*Cleveland Plain Dealer*

THE ST. LAWRENCE RUN

STEPHEN F. WILCOX

ST. MARTIN'S PAPERBACKS

THE ST. LAWRENCE RUN

Copyright © 1990 by Stephen F. Wilcox.

Cover illustration by Michael Cassidy.

Library of Congress Catalog Card Number: 89-77949

ISBN: 0-312-92488-7

Printed in the United States of America

St. Martin's Press hardcover edition published 1990
St. Martin's Paperbacks edition/May 1991

10 9 8 7 6 5 4 3 2 1

FOR MY PARENTS,

Catherine and Frederick,
who said I could;
and for my wife, Pauline,
who said I would.

THE ST. LAWRENCE RUN

CHAPTER 1

CONGRESS was in recess and the president was in Maine pitching horseshoes with the king of Morocco. Out on the broad green Capitol Mall, the Beach Boys were pounding out old gold free of charge while a crowd of baby boomers hoisted their own babies onto sunburned shoulders and swayed to the tribal rhythms of summers long past.

It was the Fourth of July, the start of what the Washington press corps calls the dog days. Cars and tour buses choked the late-afternoon streets while low-flying jumbo jets screamed toward National Airport. Cadres of red-eyed tourists doggedly trudged the Mall from the Lincoln Memorial to the Hill and back. Waves of heat radiated from the sidewalks and rippled the air, lending an ethereal mystique to distant buildings. Even the Washington Monument, phallic tribute to the father of the country, seemed to lose some of its tumescence to the relentless humidity.

Meanwhile, two floors below street level, I found myself shivering slightly in a cold antechamber. I suppose I was fortunate to be there, in the stainless steel womb of the D.C. morgue.

"Janezek, Stefan T.," the lieutenant said.

"Right-o." An appropriately cadaverous attendant in a

1

stained smock dropped a half-gone liverwurst sandwich onto a square of wax paper, rose up from behind the gray metal reception desk, and motioned for us to follow. "Jes' came in a while ago. Got 'im in numbah two-three." The man's languid, shuffling pace matched his Virginia drawl. He led us down a long corridor of steel drawers set into white tiled walls and stopped before the drawer marked twenty-three.

"I heah it's a regulah sauna out they-ah, huh, lieutenant?" the attendant said, pulling open the drawer and turning back the sheet. "Nice and cool down heah, though. Best thin' about workin' the holiday."

The lieutenant grunted, then looked at me. "That him?"

I glanced at the corpse, turned away, and, unable to resist, turned back again and stared. Only that morning the face had been ruddy, the large body beefy and robust. Now the skin was sallow and slack, the lips blue, the eyes permanently shut. There was a small dark hole just above the right temple, marking the spot where a life had been extinguished.

"Yes, that's him. Professor Stefan Janezek."

"Autopsy hasn't been done yet, but cause of death is obvious." The lieutenant was a professional; he didn't explain, he gave testimony. "The victim was shot twice. Once to the abdomen, a second time to the head. The head wound was decisive. Cartridge cases found at the scene indicate a smallish automatic. They got his wallet but left his watch and a ring, scared off maybe. This sort of crime doesn't happen in broad daylight that often, not even here. The bastards are getting bold." I was still staring at the dead face, prompting the lieutenant to ask again, "You're sure it's Janezek? No question?"

"No question."

The lieutenant nodded to the attendant, who pulled up the sheet and rolled shut the drawer. "If you'll accompany me back to my office, Mr. Sheridan, I've got a few more questions."

2

The lieutenant's office was a ten-foot-square corner of a large common area designated as the squad room of the homicide division of the D.C. police. In penurious deference to his rank, a six-foot high partition of sheet metal and fluted Plexiglas surrounded the corner and lent the illusion of privacy. Like the rest of the squad room, the cubicle was done in someone's color-coordinated vision of bureaucratic chic. The beige walls complemented the chocolate brown partition, which complemented the burnt orange carpeting and the fake-walnut-veneer desk. The only thing that didn't conform to the overall color scheme was the lieutenant. He was ebony, a black so deep it appeared almost blue in the harsh glare of the fluorescent ceiling lights.

"Sit." He waved me to a brown swivel chair and lowered himself behind the desk. The brass name plate perched on the edge of the desk read Lieutenant LaVerne Bliss. The name fit in the same way it suits a bald man to be called Curly or a fat man Slim. He was built like a Volkswagen Bug, short and wide, designed for efficiency and endurance rather than speed. A bullet-shaped head perched on a stub of a neck. Shoulders broad and linear, as if he'd forgotten to remove the hanger before donning his jacket.

His expression was not blissful.

"Timothy Seamus Wolfe Sheridan," he read from a yellow sheet of paper. "Sounds like an Irish law firm."

"It isn't polite to mock people's names," I said, waiting two beats before adding, "LaVerne."

"Score one for the tourist," Bliss said, as he scanned the sheet. "According to the information you gave my men, you're a writer who specializes in factual crime stories."

I nodded.

"And you're in town to give a speech or something to, uh, let's see . . . a group called CHANA?"

"Crime Historians Association of North America," I supplied. "They're holding their annual convention. I'm being paid a fee to give a lecture and lead a seminar."

"Uh-huh. So you don't actually belong to this CHANA outfit, you're just a guest like?"

"Right. CHANA's membership consists mostly of academicians, college professors, and other assorted Ph.D.s who share a common interest in criminology and crime history." I paraphrased the wording from one of CHANA's press releases. My host wasn't impressed.

"I guess it beats stamp collecting," Bliss shrugged. "So what qualifies you to lead a seminar for these guys?"

"Eight years as a police reporter for a couple of different newspapers, five years as a free-lance investigative reporter, and dozens of magazine articles exploring specific criminal cases. And a book about a murder case I had a hand in investigating a while back, in upstate New York."

"Mmmm." Bliss again browsed through the yellow sheet. "I don't suppose you own a handgun?"

"No."

"Uh-huh. Ever owned a gun, Mr. Sheridan?"

"I had an M-16 once, on loan from Uncle Sam. He made me give it back before shipping me out of the country at Cam Rahn Bay." I didn't like the tone our conversation was taking, but it was his office and his city.

Bliss pulled a manila folder from the in-out basket on the desk and withdrew from it a slip of paper. After staring at it for a moment, he looked up at me and asked, "What can you tell me about the victim?"

"Not a lot," I said, settling back into the chair. "As I said in my statement, we corresponded four or five times in the past few months, since my book came out. In fact, most of what I know about him came from his letters. He taught history at Clampett College in Widows Cape, New York, up in the Thousand Islands. He was a bachelor, forty-six years old, I think, and a crime buff, which is why he began writing to me in the first place." I shrugged. "That's about it. I didn't even know what he looked like until yesterday morning, when I met him at the hotel."

"The Washington Hilton."

"Yes, that's the site of the convention."

4

"And you say Janezek was the one who got you the invitation to appear at the convention?"

"Pretty much. As an officer of CHANA, he was one of the people responsible for lining up guest lecturers. He suggested me and the organizing committee checked it out and made me an offer. A thousand dollars plus my meal and travel expenses and three nights lodging at the Hilton."

"A grand, huh? Maybe I should start saving up anecdotes and hit the lecture circuit myself. Anyway, when you showed up for the convention yesterday morning, that was the first time you met Janezek in the flesh. Go on."

"Well, we both had things to do, so we agreed to meet later over drinks at the opening reception."

"Things to do? Like what?"

"Like unpack, for one. Then I had to meet with Brunhide, the head of the organizing committee, to go over the convention schedule."

Bliss nodded, "Yeah, Brunhide. We contacted him already, he's coming in for questioning."

"Anyway, except for a brief hello at the afternoon seminar, I didn't see Professor Janezek until around six last night at the reception. We had a few drinks with a couple of the other CHANA members, and that was about it."

"Anything unusual come up during your conversation?"

"Mostly just shoptalk." I paused, putting it in focus. "There was one thing. The professor mentioned that he wanted to get together in the next couple of days to discuss something he was working on, a place called Castle House."

The lieutenant scowled. "What's a castle house?"

"Sounds like an oxymoron, doesn't it? I gather it's the name of a place up around Widows Cape, but I don't know for sure. There were half a dozen conversations going on at once, so I didn't get a chance to ask. You know how it is at a cocktail party," I said, adding, "we were supposed to get together at noon today to discuss whatever was on the professor's mind. Then all this happened."

5

"But you saw him again this morning?"

"Yes, in the hotel lobby, just as he was going out."

"Out where? Did he say?"

"The Watergate complex. He told me he was going to walk down and take a look at the place, now that it was a historical curiosity. He said he liked to take a good, brisk three- or four-mile walk every morning."

Bliss snorted, "That damn Watergate is more popular these days than the Smithsonian. The city tour buses even swing by there." He slipped the yellow sheet into the manila folder and pulled out a thin red appointment book. "I guess you're wondering why I had you singled out and brought in here for questioning."

"It had crossed my mind a time or two."

He tapped the little red book. "Your professor friend was fastidious. Had your name written down for drinks at noon in the mezzanine bar. Along with a little note to himself. 'Pump S. about C.H.' That'd be this Castle House deal, I take it."

"I suppose so, but, like I said, I don't know any more about Castle House than you do. I assume it has to do with some research he was doing, maybe for an article for the CHANA newsletter. Sometimes, in his letters, the professor liked to bounce his ideas off me, that's all."

The lieutenant considered me for a moment, then nodded, resigned. "We needed somebody to ID the body anyway. When I saw that reference in the date book, I figured I'd have my men bring in this T.S.W. Sheridan to do the honors." He smiled, his face crinkling up like a raisin. "Fact is, we already checked your whereabouts with the hotel staff and that Brunhide character. Lucky for you you stuck around the Hilton all morning. Too bad Janezek didn't."

"Where did you find him?" I asked.

"In Rock Creek. Looks like he was probably grabbed near the M Street overpass while on his morning stroll. That'd fit, if he was heading for the Watergate. Anyway, somebody hustled him down into the park along the creek and

6

ripped off his wallet. Maybe he put up a fuss, so the mugger shot him in the stomach, then decided to finish him with one to the head. Then he dumps the body in the creek."

"You have any kind of a lead, lieutenant?"

"We've got shit-all," Bliss grumbled, then rubbed his eyes wearily. "Christ, street crime is getting to be a joke anymore. We'll investigate, but unless we turn a witness, we're just blowing smoke. The department's already got enough unsolved muggings to fill up the Library of Congress, and those bastards just voted to cut our funding again."

"I'm afraid it's the same all over, lieutenant."

He slumped down in the chair. "The government spends billions of dollars every year to rim this country with nukes to protect us, right? Only sometimes I think they got those babies pointed in the wrong direction."

The phone on the ersatz walnut desk buzzed, saving me from having to respond. Bliss snatched it up, identified himself, and listened. After a moment, he said, "Just about. A couple more minutes, is all. We both know the feds'll step in anyway, so lighten up, okay?"

"Car bombing," he explained, as he recradled the phone. "We caught the initial squeal, but the FBI will take it away from us poor city cops quicker than you can say Jack Robinson. Only thing they'll leave us is a big hole in the ground over on Q Street."

"What happened?" I asked.

Bliss hesitated an instant, then shrugged. "What the hell, you're probably the only journalist in town that isn't already out covering the story. A limo got blown to smithereens over on Embassy Row, just as it was pulling up to some July Fourth shindig. Took out the governor of Puerto Rico and some midwestern congressman, along with the two men's wives and the chauffeur. A Puerto Rican leftist group with a name I can't even pronounce called up a local TV station to take the credit. So what else is new." He stood and came around the desk. "Listen, I'll

7

have a man type up your statement and you can sign it and take off. If we need you, we'll be in touch."

Thirty minutes later, I was back into the city's still-oppressive early evening heat. I jaywalked a diagonal across Indiana Avenue and tramped west on D Street, heading for Metro Center and a fast subway ride back to my hotel. My mind was still on Stefan Janezek—wishing I'd gotten a chance to know him better, wondering what kind of circus the CHANA convention had become since word of his death had filtered down, wondering what I'd say to his friends.

I skirted the FBI building and turned up Tenth Street, pausing to wipe my brow in front of Ford's Theatre. Across the street, the house where Lincoln died was closed for the day. It was getting late. Around me, tourists were hurrying back to the safety of their hotel rooms. Few were inclined to wander darkening streets in the capital city of the world's greatest democracy.

CHAPTER 2

THE gnome behind the counter smiled without enthusiasm. But then nobody likes working a holiday, especially Labor Day, with its unofficial status as summer's closing curtain.

"Welcome to the Thousand Islands," she said as she slid a three-by-five registration card and a Bic pen at me. "No pets, no cookin' in the rooms, no loud music or TV after ten o'clock. And no cleanin' any fish in the bathroom sink. Off-season rates don't kick in till tomorrow, but I'll give you a break if you stay at least three nights."

A black plastic sign mounted on the wall behind her said Velda Fuller, owner-manager.

"You have a weekly rate?"

"Two-ten for the week, same as the off-season rate—thirty a day times seven." Quickly, she added, "Comes to thirty-five off the summer rate, which is a good deal seein' as the best wall-eye fishin's just startin' up. You come by a week from now, you won't find a room anywhere along the river, 'less you stayed down the road at the Starlight, which is run by a couple of Pakis." She wrinkled her pug nose. "They keep goats."

I stared down at the woman and thought about asking to see the room first. She was short and stocky; her face re-

9

sembled a bowl of oatmeal, lumps and all. A Brillo pad of gray hair was penned in with an industrial strength hair net. Like the motel office itself, she was shopworn and tired, but clean. I experienced a sudden leap of faith and began filling out the card.

"You'll be stayin' the week then?"

"Probably. Three or four days, at least."

She tossed a room key onto the counter. The metal tag on the key ring said, 'If lost, please return to the Clearview Motel, Rte. 12E, Widows Cape, N.Y.' It should have said 'If found,' but I decided not to point that out. Instead, I handed over my Visa card.

Five minutes later, I carried my travel bag and briefcase into room number ten and dropped them beside a sway-backed double bed. The room and its furnishings would've been right at home in the 1940s; an Art Deco bedroom suite in laminates of maple, wide white venetian blinds on the windows, a faded green and brown rag rug covering two-thirds of a speckled linoleum floor. Remove the small TV bolted to its metal stand and you could easily picture John Garfield and Lana Turner nestled like spoons in the bed's depression, colorized version courtesy of Ted Turner.

Spartan but neat and scrubbed, I decided as I sniffed the air and caught the mingled scent of Lysol and Murphy's Oil Soap. I spread open two slats on the venetian blinds and peered out across the narrow parking strip and the two-lane highway and its steady drone of minivans and large sedans with roof racks; the exodus of families heading back to city jobs and the new school year. Beyond the highway, ranks of silver maples and blue spruce and scatterings of shingled roofs hid all but a sea green bite of the St. Lawrence; one isolated frame of a great commercial waterway that stretched a thousand miles, from Lake Ontario through the Thousand Islands and the Seaway Locks along the Canadian border, jogging north past Montreal and Quebec City before continuing on to Labrador and the Gaspé Peninsula, where icebergs floated down from the Arctic to make navigation an adventure.

I stretched out across the spongy bed, letting the tensions of the three-hour drive north drain away, and ruminated on the circumstances that had drawn me up here to my own little adventure.

I wish I could say it had begun nobly, that I had come to Widows Cape with some nagging sense of unfinished business concerning the late Professor Stefan Janezek and his tragic death. But, in all truth, the impetus for my trip some two months after the professor's demise in Washington came out of a more basic—and selfish—impulse. I was bored.

The fishing stinks in late August. Every decent angler and his brother knows that. The high summer sun warms the lake and drives the big ones—the lake trout, the largemouth bass and pike—down into the deepest nooks and crevasses of the lake where they sulk and brood and ignore every manner of bait, be it worm, minnow, or lure. Ralph Cramer, the old fellow who ran the diner in Mohaca Springs, claimed pork rinds would do the trick, but his stringer was as empty as my own.

We were in my aluminum skiff near the middle of the lake, a few hundred yards out from the dock. It was a sleepy late morning, the quiet lap of the water against the bow and the distant buzz of an army of cicadas the only sounds.

"Know what I think it is?" Ralph said, as he gave a few gentle tugs on his rod.

"What's that?" I was stretched out near the stern, my Yankees cap pulled low over my eyes.

"It's this ozone deal."

I lifted the cap a notch. "Ozone?"

"Whatchamacallit," he said, scratching at the thinning gray brush of hair atop his head. "This greenhouse effect business. How the ozone's being ate up by car fumes and hair spray. My theory is the fish got some sixth sense about stuff like that, see. They can sense somethin's screwy, like mice and things do just before a earthquake.

11

So they get all nervous and go to ground, so to speak." He spit over the side. "Only reason I can think of the lunkers aren't hittin' on these rinds."

"Uh-huh."

"Well, I don't know what else it could be."

"It's the heat, Ralph. It's been over ninety for three weeks now. The fish are smart enough to lay around where it's cooler, even if we aren't."

Ralph flashed the sort of perfect smile you see only on denture wearers and television personalities. "Well, that proves my point, Sheridan. Why'dya think we got all this heat anyhow? It's that damn greenhouse effect."

"I've got a theory, too," I said, as I sat up and began reeling in my line. "I contend that if we stay out here much longer, you're gonna start blaming it on the Loch Ness monster. Anyway, it's almost noon. What would you say to a tall, cold iced tea and a BLT?"

We packed up our gear and putted back toward my dock and the modified A-frame cottage I call home. The cottage was a bit of serendipity bequeathed to me by my uncle, Charlie Dugan, who'd died suddenly at the wrong end of a knife. He'd left me the place along with the several prime acres surrounding it there on Seneca Lake, second largest of upstate New York's Finger Lakes. He also left me smack in the middle of a murder investigation that, with a bit of luck, I'd had a hand in solving. I wrote a marginally successful book about the case, sold off the property's excess acreage to a local winery, and moved into the cottage more or less permanently. All of which left me with a comfy piece of change tucked away in a mutual fund, an enhanced reputation as an investigative reporter, and, not least of all, a measure of justice for my uncle's killer.

Serendipity.

And that was part of the problem. I'd never had any financial security before, particularly since I'd gone freelance. I was used to having to hustle for assignments, then hustle to complete them on deadline. But things had changed. I now owned an unmortgaged home and my own

12

little slice of Wall Street. What's more, the alotted fifteen minutes of fame that the book had brought me had also brought a deluge of story assignments. Now that I no longer needed steady work, it seemed every magazine editor in North America wanted a piece of my byline while it was still warm. And old habits die hard. In the past six months I'd taken on every decent assignment that came my way. Straightforward stuff mostly; retrospective pieces that could be handled with a few visits to libraries and newspaper morgues and a few phone calls.

And now I was profoundly bored. Bored of having a phone pressed against my ear and my fingers poised over the keyboard of my word processor, bored with rehashed where-are-they-now stories about ex-safecrackers and once notorious gangsters. It was time to say no, to kick back from my desk and stretch my legs.

But the fishing stinks in August. And there is nothing so boring as a slack line on a dead calm lake.

"Mail lady just swung by," Ralph said as we stepped onto the entrance deck to the cottage.

"How 'bout bringing it in for me while I get started on the sandwiches?"

"Will do." He hopped down to the gravel parking area, still spry despite his seventy-plus years and arthritic knees, and double-timed down the drive. By the time he got back, I was in the kitchen opening a can of goo for the cat, William of Orange, while waiting for the fry pan to heat up on the stove.

"Anything there besides junk mail?" I asked, setting the cat's bowl on the floor.

"Copy of the *Sporting News,* somethin' looks like a bill from some magazine, and this here." He held up a large gray envelope and perused the return address label. "Huh. Says it's from the history department at Clampett College up to Widows Cape. Isn't that where that professor friend of yours was from, the one got killed in D.C.?"

"Yeah." I took the envelope from Ralph and studied the

13

Clampett College logo. "Put the bacon on, will you? While I take a look at this."

I carried the curious envelope out to the vaulted great room and dropped into the morris chair beside the fieldstone fireplace. Ripping open the legal-size envelope, I shook out the contents; a couple sheets of notebook paper and a sheet of erasable bond clipped together under a memo-size piece of paper bearing the letterhead of the college's history department. A terse message was scrawled across the memo sheet:

"Forwarding the enclosed to T.S.W. Sheridan, at the request of Mr. Betz."

The note was signed Catherine Witherspoon, department secretary.

Curiouser and curiouser. I didn't know a Mr. Betz or a Catherine Witherspoon. I removed the paperclip and fanned out the other papers on the coffee table. The two sheets of lined notebook paper bore the familiar, pinched handwriting of Stefan Janezek—I knew his style well from the several letters he had sent to me. The first sheet contained little more than the doodles of a preoccupied mind leaking out bits of information. There were a square with the word FELLOWSHIP written all in caps inside, a circle containing a large question mark, and a rough triangle from which leapt out the words "Castle House." Immediately below the triangle, the professor had scratched in a short list of surnames: Johnson, DuPree, MacKenzie, and Dougherty. Again, no bells went off.

The second sheet of notebook paper was badly crinkled, as if someone had balled it up, then tried to smooth it out again. Across the top of the page, the professor had written "Preliminary Interview—Howard Johnson, Riverside Nursing Home." The notes scratched onto the page were choppy, difficult to decipher. There was a reference to Legs Diamond, the notorious gangster who had made his start running bootleg whiskey across the river from Canada during Prohibition. This Howard Johnson character apparently claimed some association with Diamond back in the thirties. Under the heading "The St. Lawrence Run," Professor Janezek's crabbed shorthand recorded how the Diamond gang used open boats to move the whiskey from near Kingston on the Canadian side, skirted Wolfe Island, one of the largest of the Thousand Islands, crossed the main shipping channel marking the international border, and unloaded its contraband at various sheltered coves and private docks along the U.S. side, where it was packed onto trucks and hauled south to the big cities.

Pretty basic stuff, as far as I was concerned. Apparently, the professor had been researching a paper, probably an article for the CHANA newsletter. But he changed directions suddenly in the last two lines at the bottom of the page, where he had written and underlined a new heading; "Castle House Holocaust—1937." And under that, 'H.J. on J.R. and C.H. tragedy.'

That was all there was on that single, crumpled sheet. I reread the page, finding nothing new, and set it aside for the piece of erasable bond. Neatly typed in the upper left corner of the sheet were the same four names that appeared on the first sheet of notebook paper, except that here Christian names and occupations had been added: "Howard Johnson, ex-merchant seaman; Maurice DuPree, Fellowship founder; Rodney MacKenzie, attorney; Liam Dougherty, English professor, Clampett College." The rest of the sheet was blank.

"BLTs are ready," Ralph announced as he carried two plates from the kitchen to the old oak pedestal table that graced the dining half of the great room. "I knew I'd get suckered into some shortorder cookin', even on my day off. Think you can manage to pour the beverages yourself?"

"Oh, yeah, sorry." I pushed myself up from the chair and went into the kitchen for the pitcher of iced tea and a couple of glasses.

"So what's with the envelope from Widows Cape," Ralph quizzed me as I came back to the table. He was already well into his sandwich—bacon, lettuce and tomato

15

thickly packed between two toasted slices of wheat bread, slathered with mayo and a touch of hot mustard.

"I'm not sure. Somebody I never heard of sent me some of Professor Janezek's notes and a list of people I've also never heard of."

"Hmmph. Somethin' to do with your friend gettin' himself killed in Washington, y'think?"

"I don't see how there could be a connection," I said between bites, adding, "Anyway, Janezek was more an acquaintance than a friend. I barely knew the guy."

Ralph took a long pull on his iced tea and smacked his lips. "Needs more lemon. So you gonna head up there?"

"Up where?"

"Widows Cape. The college. Find out what's what."

"Why the hell would I bother to drive all that way?"

Ralph grinned, a dab of mayonnaise clinging to the corner of his mouth. "Jeez, I wish I could get away from the diner for a few days, I'd go with you."

I stared at him. "What makes you think I'm going anywhere? Some wild goose chase to the Thousand Islands."

"'Cause you've had cabin fever for weeks now and this ozone thing's killed the fishin' and you got nothin' better to do." He pushed his empty plate away, his grin expanding to shit-eating proportions. "And because you're a crime writer and maybe there's a story waitin' for you up there."

"No way." I scarfed down the last of my BLT and chewed thoughtfully. "But maybe I'll make a couple of phone calls."

From somewhere outside my motel room a truck horn blared angrily, followed by a feeble answering bleat from what had to be a small economy car. The mad holiday rush was building toward a critical mass.

I rolled off the cupped mattress and checked my watch. Twelve-forty p.m. My interview with Howard Johnson was set for one o'clock, the end of the lunch hour at the Riverside Nursing Home. I clicked open my briefcase and rummaged for pens and a fresh notepad.

That had been the second call I'd placed from the cottage a few days earlier. I'd spoken with the home's director, a Dr. Knox, who had reluctantly agreed to let me call on Johnson. My first call had been to Clampett College, where, after several aborted attempts, I was able to reach Catherine Witherspoon. A somewhat addled Miss Witherspoon was able to tell me very little, except that Mr. Betz—Alan Betz, associate professor in the college's history department—had asked her to forward a few of Stefan Janezek's papers to me. Betz, she informed me, was out of town just then, not due back until the following Tuesday afternoon.

The last of my three calls had gone to Lt. LaVerne Bliss. The Janezek case file was still open, he told me, but there were no fresh leads. The only interesting new information had come from the FBI lab, which had identified the cartridge cases that had been found near the body as an uncommon brand of 7.65-mm ammunition manufactured in Italy and commonly available only in Europe. The feds had also concluded that the murder weapon had probably been an expensive Swiss-made automatic called a SIG P-201. Unusual for a D.C. street mugging, Bliss admitted, but not without precedent.

So there I was, standing in room ten at the Clearview Motel, about to begin an investigation into a story that I couldn't define and I didn't even know existed. But it still beat drowning worms on a placid lake.

I'd begin where the professor had begun, I decided as I slipped into my herringbone jacket.

The St. Lawrence run.

CHAPTER 3

"PROHIBITION! Hell, yes, some kinda days those were. Rich sonsabitches was still all over them islands back then. Not so much anymore. And the mob was around, too. Bootleggers used to come rippin' right through Widows Cape here, with Treasury goosin' their tails, right on through town along the St. Lawrence Pike, which is what we used to call the main stem. Now it's just Route 12E or F or some fuckin' thing. Arrr-hmm!"

The old man cleared his throat violently, then paused to gaze out the dayroom's picture window at the river. Clearing the mind was more difficult.

"Well, now. You asked about Legs Diamond and the St. Lawrence run. He was one of the big fish. Used to ferry hootch 'cross the river and on downstate to Albany and the big city regular. Canadian blend, bonded scotch, French bubble juice, all top drawer stuff. Not that bathtub shit you hear about. Him and his brother and some other fellas, they had this big Chris-Craft with them huge Merc inboards. Used to run it over from Canada and unload down the road at Currens Bay late at night, put it on trucks and haul ass. 'Course, that's back when Currens Bay was just a quiet little spot with a roadhouse and a buncha sugar maples. Real cozy. Mostly just trailers along there now, I understand."

He hawked into the hanky he held in his gnarled fist, then winked at me, if that's possible for a one-eyed man.

"Hell, yes, I can tell a story or two about Jack Diamond. That's what everybody called him then. This Legs stuff come along later, prob'ly from some newspaper man. He was pop'lar with them newsies, right up until he got hisself killed, down there in Albany. Arrgghh, um, um, um."

I waited for the old merchant marine to recover again. It was a long tale for Howard Johnson, one that took him back fifty years to a time when he had two eyes, both clear blue, and two solid legs to stand on. He stared down at the coarse wool blanket draped across his lap, perhaps remembering a young man's legs and puzzling at the withered stumps fate had left him. Then, slow as the freighter just now making its way up river outside the dayroom's window, he rolled the wheelchair closer and began again.

"I tell you somethin' for free, boy. Jack Diamond, he was a big name around these parts, no denyin' it. He had the big city rep and all. But you want a story that ain't never been writ up, you wanna know about the other Jack."

"The other Jack?"

"Jack Rose, that is," he said, his face puckering into a grin. "Hell, boy, Jack Rose was just the ballsiest son of a bitch ever born in this burg. Built himself a rep in the early thirties. Rumrunnin', smugglin', thievin'. Used to swipe the rich folks' boats in the summer and rob the antiques and silver outa their mansions in the winter, when they was all closed up. Got hisself locked away in Dannemora for a couple years. Did some work for Diamond, too."

The garrulous old seaman's breathing was coming in shallow gulps now. He pressed against the side of his neck with a heavily calloused hand, the fingers yellowed with nicotine stains.

"Doc says it's some kinda chronic pulmonary disease," Johnson rasped. "Bullshit! It's that damned pneumonia from back in '43. My ship caught a fish from a U-boat—put

19

me and my mates into the North Atlantic with nothin' but our Mae Wests to keep us afloat. Goddamn ocean's cold enough to freeze the nuts off a polar bear, boy, let me tell you. Specially when you're already bleedin' outa half a dozen wounds. That's when I lost these." He tapped the blanket where his legs should have been. Then he pointed to the black patch covering his left eye socket. "I give this up back in '59, while I was down at the seamen's hospital in Massachusetts. Some sorta tumor," he added indifferently.

He was a mess, there was no denying it. The missing legs and eye, the greasy tufts of hair unevenly distributed over a bone white scalp, thin bloodless lips covering a dwindling rank of teeth that resembled tiny yellowed tombstones in a long-neglected cemetery. Yet I could find no trace of self-pity in the single milky eye. I glanced down at the two breast pockets on the old man's blue cotton work shirt. A pack of Kools in the right pocket and a small, hand-held inhaler in the left. Maybe forty-some years of living in a succession of state-supported hospitals and nursing homes was enough to make a fatalist of anyone.

I nodded sympathetically as Johnson continued to recite his long and daunting medical profile, but my mind was somewhere else: Professor Janezek's scribbled interview notes; the passage "H.J. on J.R. and C.H. tragedy." When the old man wound down, I said, "I seem to remember the professor mentioning this Jack Rose, Mr. Johnson. I wonder if—"

"Call me Howard."

"Right. Howard. I wonder if you could repeat for me just what you told Professor Janezek about Jack Rose."

"'Course I can. Like I said, Jack did some work for Diamond back in the early thirties, roundin' up good boats to use on the St. Lawrence run, sometimes trucks if they was short." He grinned slyly. "Jack was good at whatcha call procurin' transportation, if you get my drift. Anyhow, ol' Jack did some of that for Diamond but, like I tell the perfesser, all that petered out after '34, when they called off

20

Prohibition. It was the deal in '37 that really got his juices flowin', the perfesser, I mean."

"What happened in 1937?"

"What happened in '37?" Johnson's cloudy eye grew cautious, scanning the dayroom like the lens of an antiquated movie camera. I followed its sweep around the brightly lit room. An old woman was hobbling around aimlessly behind a walker. A youngish nurse in starched whites and crepe-soled shoes sat along the rear wall and pored over a magazine. In the far corner, a blue-haired grandmother rocked sedately, a colorful scrap of crewel work lying dormant in her lap. Hunched over a card table beneath the large bay window, a Methuselah with a green and orange tam perched on his head studied a chess board while his venerable opponent fought the urge to doze.

Satisfied that there were no eavesdroppers about, my host swiveled his wheelchair back to face me.

"Let me ask you this." He reached over and tapped my arm. "Didn't the perfesser tell you about the Castle House murders?"

I said, as casually as I could, "He made mention of Castle House, but I don't recall anything about any murders."

"Shit, boy, if you don't know about the murders, you don't know nothin' about Castle House."

"Well, why don't you enlighten me, Howard."

He glanced around the somnambulent dayroom again. "Yeah," he croaked. "I think maybe I will."

"The thing you got to remember," he began, "is how things were around here back in the thirties. In those days, there weren't no trailer parks and state parks and such all along the river. In the old days, you had two kinds of people here; your regular working man types—dairy farmers and pisspoor little store owners and the like—and the rich folks, them bein' the only ones had the dough and what you call the leisure time to enjoy it, y'know? I mean, this was durin' the Depression, when if you had a job at all it meant six-day work weeks to earn what a good pair of brogues would cost you today." He paused. "In those

21

times, what with there bein' so many poor people and so few filthy rich types, well, it was only natural that some folks took to thievin', bein' as it was the only way to get ahead. You follow me?"

I nodded that I did.

"Anyway, ever since way back before the turn of the century, the islands were crawlin' with private yachts and big fancy mansions. Summer homes, they called 'em," the old man growled scornfully. "Christ, most of 'em had more rooms than the goddamn White House.

"Well, by the thirties that began to change, what with FDR's goin' after these rich bastards to start payin' taxes, and with a lot of 'em losin' their shirts in the crash and all. Some of 'em cleared out entirely, but some didn't. Anyhow, one of these mansions belonged to a fella named Ernest Castle. A bachelor or widower or some such, made his millions in the lumber trade. Bought Coffin Island back in the twenties. Built this big house out there and used to have lots of parties. Called it Castle House."

I looked up from my notepad. "Where's this Coffin Island situated, Howard?"

"Out on the goddamn river, where else?" he grumbled, irritated at being interrupted and disgusted that a person could be ignorant of any one of the nearly eighteen hundred islands that make up the modestly named Thousand Island chain. "She sits about a half mile offshore of Widows Cape, just to the northwest, in U.S. waters. Can't see it from here," he waved toward the big bay window overlooking the river, "but it's plain viewin' from the docks in town. Middle-size island 'bout three-quarter mile long by a quarter-mile wide. Got a old dairy farm on the east end and this here Castle House down to the western half."

"Got it," I said as I scribbled in the pad. "So where do the murders come in?"

"I was gettin' to that, wasn't I?" he snapped, then settled back in the chair. "New Year's Eve, 1937. As I hear it, this Ernest Castle was up this way on business, so he decides to open up his summer place for a big New Year's shindig. Invite up all his high livin' friends from Boston and New York. The river was already froze over, but that was fine. Castle decides to have everybody drove over across the ice from Widows Cape to the island. Back in them days, before they had a bridge up at Alex Bay, the only way you could get across to Canada in the dead of winter was to cross the ice. That's still the only way to get out to most of the islands durin' the bad months. Usually, you had to wait till January for the ice to be strong enough, but we had a early winter in '37. Arrghhhh-hmmmmm!"

This latest fit hit the old guy like the San Francisco earthquake. He fought to regain control, then threw his head back, fumbled the inhaler from his pocket and took a couple of hits.

I started up from my chair. "Are you okay, Howard? Should I call a—"

He waved me back down, a ghoulish grin gradually spreading across that catcher's mitt face. "I'll live. Maybe not for long, but I'll live. So, where was I?"

"You were explaining about the New Year's party."

"Right. All them rich folks decked out in their finest clothes and jewelry, headin' over to Coffin Island. Never expectin' the Castle House to become their tomb."

"What happened?"

"Place went up in a blaze that'd give Lucifer hisself the sweats. Flames you could see for miles up and down the river. And Castle and his friends, nineteen souls in all, locked up in the wine cellar, went right to hell with it." He stopped to make sure I was taking it all down. I was. "See, they was locked away down there by a coupla robbers who come sneakin' across the ice, figurin' to rob all them folks and hightail it for Canada. But somethin' went wrong and the robbers decided they couldn't leave no witnesses. So they torched the place to cover their tracks. Only the fire didn't quite get the job done."

He leaned in close again and I could smell peppermint and the sour odor of decay on his breath.

"See, when the state troopers dug them poor burnt bodies outa the cellar the next mornin', they come across a name scratched into one of the foundation stones with a tenpenny nail they found lyin' next to the body of Ernest Castle." Johnson, his lone eye squinting, smiled at me. "You like to guess whose name it was, boy?"

I didn't have to guess.

"Jack Rose," I said evenly.

Howard Johnson nodded. "Jack Rose."

CHAPTER 4

"LET'S see if I've got this straight, Howard," I said skeptically, pushing aside my notes. "You claim this Rose character and an accomplice, in the course of a simple armed robbery, deliberately set fire to the Castle House and incinerated, what? Nineteen people?"

"That's exactly right."

I frowned at the old man. "I have to tell you, Howard. I've spent a dozen years covering crime stories and it just doesn't jive. From what you say, the guy was an experienced thief with a long history of burglary and housebreaking. So why would he resort to mass murder?"

"'Cause he didn't think he had no choice in the matter," Johnson said petulantly. "Least ways, that's how the state troopers figured it. See, when they dug out them bodies, they found one with a thirty-eight bullet hole smack in the middle of the forehead. The troopers, they identified the body from dental records or somethin' and found out it was Tommy Trevain, Castle's caretaker. Y'see, Tommy lived on the island full time, him and his daughter, workin' that little dairy farm on the east end of the island. Castle owned it, but they had some sorta deal where Tommy got to lease the farmhouse and keep the profits from the dairy operation in exchange for takin' care of the main house and the estate grounds. You follow?"

I indicated that I did. Johnson lowered his chin to his chest, cleared his troublesome throat with a fierce growl, and continued.

"The way it figures, Castle didn't have none of his regular house staff available, it bein' outa season. So he commandeers Tommy Trevain and the daughter into helpin' out at the party. The coppers figured it this way: Jack Rose comes bustin' into the party with some other guy—prob'ly Big John Cawley, who happened to be damn near a moron but was big and scary lookin'. They prob'ly wore masks, but that wouldn't make no difference to Tommy, who woulda known Big John by his size and Jack Rose by his voice. Likely what happened is, Tommy recognizes Rose, yells his name out in front of Castle and the others, and then tries to take ol' Jack's gun away. Jack shoots him in the head. But now he's got a real problem. He's just kilt a man in front of eighteen witnesses and they all heard Tommy call him by name. So, Rose figures they can only fry you once for murder—"

"Since he was already on the hook for killing Trevain," I said, "Rose decided his best bet was to eliminate all the witnesses. He herds them all down to the wine cellar, locks them up with Trevain's body and then torches the place."

"That's how it got writ up in the papers."

"What about Rose and his accomplice?" I asked. "Were they ever brought to trial?"

"Nope. After the robbery, they got in their car and headed across the ice for Canada. Only they never made it."

Johnson saw the quizzical expression on my face and rolled his wheelchair closer. "Understand now," he said, talking low. "Coffin Island lies in U.S. waters. The border between the States and Canada follows the main shipping channel up the river. Anythin' lyin' north of the channel is in Canada and anythin' south is in the U.S. Got it?"

"Yeah, but what's that—"

"Hell, boy, what I'm sayin' is, Jack figured he'd make his getaway across the ice to Canada. But he made a mistake in his thinkin'. See, the channel is the deepest part of the river, naturally. And anybody with half a brain knows that the last part of a river to freeze solid is the channel, on account it's so deep and the current runs so strong." He sat back, smiling like a deacon on Judgment Day. "Now you follow me?"

"His car broke through the thin channel ice?"

Johnson bobbed his head enthusiastically. "Takin' Jack and Big John straight to the bottom. The coppers followed the tracks out onto the ice the next mornin' and them tracks led right to a big damn hole in the middle of the channel."

"But they must've dredged for the car," I said. "To recover the bodies and the stolen merchandise."

"Nope. Couldn't do it then, in the winter. Wasn't safe to take any heavy dredgin' equipment out there. And by the time the spring come and they got a Coast Guard salvage boat out to the spot, they couldn't find nothin'." He reached out and tapped my knee. "You gotta remember, boy, the channel's over a hunnerd feet deep, with tricky currents. Coast Guard mighta missed it with their grappling lines, but more likely the car already drifted down river on 'em."

"Then they never recovered the bodies?"

"Well, not at the time, no. But later, back in '63, I think it was—I left these parts to go to sea in '38, didn't move back here 'til '69, so I got the story sorta thirdhand—in '63, a coupla scuba divers run across a rusted out '32 Oldsmobile in the channel down off Birdsnest Island. That's a little postage-stamp-sized island about three-quarter mile downstream from Coffin. Arrr-hmmm!"

Johnson fell into another coughing fit. This time the young nurse at the back of the room took notice. She seemed on the verge of coming over, then changed her mind and turned her attentions back to a dogeared copy of

27

People magazine with a picture of Tom Cruise on the cover. Maybe she had developed an ear for serious distress and knew this was a false alarm, or maybe she was simply more concerned with the life-styles of the rich and famous than the death rattles of the old and infirm. In either case, after a few moments of serious wheezing, Johnson managed to get control of his lungs again and I, halfway up from my chair and feeling helpless, sat back down.

"You okay, Howard?"

"Yeah, yeah. Sorry about all the goddamn fuss." The old bird was tough. I could see the fatigue working its way onto that leathery face.

"If you'd like to take a break—"

"Nah, no need," he cut me off. "We only got a few minutes till I gotta go for my treatments. Might's well use it." He inched the chair forward again. "Anyway, what I was sayin', those two scuba divers found that '32 Olds down along Birdsnest Island and that ain't all. The windshield was broke out and the doors were open, but there was still a skeleton on the front seat. So the divers called in the Coast Guard or somebody and they raised that Olds outa the water. Besides that skeleton, they found some jewelry—a few rings and a watch with Castle's name inscribed on it—but that was it. They figured the other body and the rest of the loot probably got washed outa the car. Most likely still lyin' in the silt at the bottom of the St. Lawrence, but who knows where? Could be halfway to Montreal by now."

"Did they manage to ID the skeleton?"

"Figured out it was Big John Cawley judgin' by the teeth, I guess. They dug out some old DMV records and found out the car was stole down in Watertown back in '37."

Johnson stopped suddenly, his gaze settling on something beyond my left shoulder. I half-turned and found myself facing the young nurse of modest literary taste.

"Excuse me, Howard, but it's almost three. Time for therapy." She said it with the tone some people reserve for house pets and infants. Then she looked at me and added, "You'll have to go now, sir. No visitors after three."

I tried on my most ingratiating down-home smile. "Gee, I did have just a few more questions for Howard—" But she wasn't buying any. Tom Cruise I'm not.

"I'm sorry, but there's nothing I can do about it," she said testily. "I don't make the rules."

"Goddammit, Lisa, it ain't three yet!" Howard jumped in. "Not for another four minutes, which you're cuttin' into with all this crap about rules." He shooed at her. "You hustle that pretty tail of yours on outa here, now, leave us alone. Christ on a cross," he turned back to me. "This place got more bullshit than a rodeo."

Nurse Lisa gave Howard a withering stare and then squeaked away on white orthopedic shoes.

"So," Howard said after she'd gone. "You had a couple more questions for me?"

I nodded. "Just a few names I'd like to throw at you, to see if they ring any bells." I consulted my notebook. "Liam Dougherty? Maurice DuPree? Rodney MacKenzie?"

I said each name slowly and studied the old seaman's battered face for his reaction. Nothing on the first two, but there was a slight glimmer on the third.

"Don't know any Dougherties or—what was it, DuPree? Don't know no DuPree, either." He scratched at a scaly patch of scalp. "I don't recall a Rodney MacKenzie, either, but there was a fella named Angus MacKenzie in these parts. I remember him from way back, before I left. He'd be about my age now. His people were in real estate."

"Rodney MacKenzie is an attorney, I think."

"Shit," he muttered. "I don't think much of them, either. Sons a bitches are what's screwin' up this country, lawyers and real estate men."

"Can't argue with you there, Howard," I said, sneaking a peek behind me. Nurse Lisa was at the dayroom doorway, helping an old lady negotiate her walker over the threshold. The rest of the room was empty, but for Howard and me, and I could detect dinner smells starting up—something featuring boiled cabbage.

"One last thing, then you better go," I said. "What about the Fellowship?" I dropped it in fast and offhand and watched the milky eye. Nothing. Not a tic, not a blink, not a glimmer.

"The Fellowship? What's that?"

"Just a notation I ran across in the professor's notes," I said. "I don't know what it is."

"Well, that makes two of us, boy. Anyway, listen, before you go, I wanted—" He grimaced. "Ah, shit, here comes Nurse Goody-Two-Shoes again. I better get a move on or she'll have the head harpy down on my neck." He began backing the wheelchair away from the table. I stood up and shook hands with him.

"Listen," he whispered urgently, his grip tightening in mine. "You'll be back again soon, huh? I got somethin' else I want to tell you about. Somethin' on that Castle House deal I wanna cut you in on."

"I'll be back," I assured him.

"You just be sure. I got things to tell you." He released my hand. "Meantime, see you in the funny papers."

"Mr. Sheridan?"

I was halfway across the front foyer, heading for the visitors' parking area and my car, when a voice caught me from behind. It belonged to a dark-haired man in his mid-forties wearing a white smock over an oxford shirt and striped tie. The black name tag affixed to his breast pocket read James C. Knox III, M.D.

"I'm Dr. Knox, Mr. Sheridan," he said, offering his hand. "We spoke on the phone."

"So we did," I said, letting go of his hand. "You're in charge of the place."

"The medical director," he corrected, adding, "And the chief administrator, for that matter."

"That sounds like an arduous combination, doctor. You must like to keep busy."

Knox smiled wistfully. "It comes with the name, I'm afraid. My father was the founder of the facility, back in 1952. He wore both hats and, now that I have majority ownership, the same responsibility falls to me."

30

"Well, you certainly seem to be up to the task," I said, glancing around. It was more than polite small talk on my part. The Riverside Nursing Home was impressive. Unlike the Clearview Motel, the nursing home actually had a clear view of the St. Lawrence across a broad, sloping lawn dotted with rose of Sharon bushes and dogwoods. The dayroom was clean and bright and the residents' rooms, from what I could see when I had passed down the main corridor earlier, were spacious and reasonably homey.

"I, uh, wanted to speak with you about Howard," Knox said. "Over the phone, you said you were an aquaintance of Professor Janezek. I take it you're an academician, too?"

"I'm a free-lance writer, specializing in factual crime stories."

"Oh." My admission put a slight dent in his professional demeanor. "Then you're probably connected to the late professor through the Crime Historians group?"

"Correct."

"The reason I ask . . . well, you see, Howard is a very old and very sick man. I explained all this to Professor Janezek when he first began his interviews here. As I understand it, he was researching an oral history on the Prohibition era, wanted to interview various of our residents to record their recollections. But when he began to concentrate on Howard Johnson, I, uh, felt I should warn him about Howard's condition, as well as his tendency to, um, well, exaggerate, so to speak." The doctor smiled. "Like many elderly people, he sometimes builds up the characters and desperados he remembers from his youth into something heroic, fanciful. The Jesse James syndrome, I call it."

"Are you saying Howard is senile?"

"No, not really. He just isn't very, mm, dependable."

"He seemed lucid enough when he told me about Jack Rose and the Castle House tragedy."

Knox flushed slightly, washing away the smile. "That's exactly the sort of thing I'm talking about. Howard is very ill, Mr. Sheridan. I'm afraid he has very little time left. Despite the fact he has COPD—that's chronic obstructive

31

pulmonary disease—he continues to smoke. He's very self-destructive."

"So why don't you take his cigarettes away?"

"This is a medical facility, Mr. Sheridan, not a prison. Our philosophy is to help our clients preserve their dignity, not lose it."

"I'm not sure what you're trying to tell me, doctor."

Knox exhaled. "Look, I'm just telling you to take it easy with Howard. He can't take long visits; they're bad for his lungs and he develops severe pressure sores on his buttocks if he's in that chair too long. And, anyway, you have to take anything he says with a grain of salt." He studied me with somber brown eyes. "This is a pleasant little community, Mr. Sheridan. We're proud of it. Old news like the Castle House affair . . . well, those sorts of memories aren't apt to do anyone any good. Least of all a sick, excitable old man."

"I'll remember that, Dr. Knox."

"I'd appreciate that," he nodded.

"And I'll keep my next visit with Howard shorter."

CHAPTER 5

A LASER beam of sunshine streamed through a gap in the motel room's venetian blinds. Tuesday morning had come to call.

I blinked myself awake, fending off the intruder with a forearm while I groggily surveyed the room. The radio on the nightstand was still on. So were my shirt and pants. The unused side of the bed was strewn with colorful pamphlets. On the carpet beside the bed, lined up like toy soldiers, the gaping mouths of four empty beer bottles stared up at me accusingly. Guilty, your honor.

After leaving Howard Johnson and the Riverside Nursing Home, I had stopped off at a tourist information kiosk at the corner of Route 12E and the main drag into Widows Cape, where I picked up half a dozen free brochures extolling the local recreational and historical attractions. This was followed by an uninspired dinner of roast beef, mashed potatoes and gravy, and rhubarb pie at a small eatery called Floyd's, located just down the road from the motel.

The remainder of my evening was spent in my room at the Clearview, browsing through the brochures and a complimentary map of the Thousand Islands, studying my notes from the Johnson interview, half-listening to an Expos game on a station out of Ottawa, and demolishing two-thirds of a six pack of Molson's I'd picked up at a 7-Eleven. So much for the romance of travel.

I groaned, scratched myself, and crawled from the bed, shedding my crinkled shirt and slacks as I moved toward the bathroom. The side of my brain that controls the pleasure zones urged me to crawl right back in the sack for another hour or so of REMs. A week earlier, I'd have done just that. But things were different now, thanks to a hoary tale told by a decrepit old sea dog. I still didn't know how much of what Howard had told me was true, or why Castle House was so important to Stefan Janezek. But I did know one thing; I wasn't bored anymore.

Joe Jackson pulsed from the Bronco's cassette player. The morning sun hinted at a warm September day. I could make out snatches of the blue green river off to my left as I cruised east along the tortuous two-lane highway.

I turned off Route 12E and drove under a giant banner that spanned the main drag into town—Welcome to Widows Cape, Gateway to the Thousand Islands. Traffic was minimal the morning after Labor Day, typical for a summer resort. Every third car I passed was compact and rusted and driven by someone too young to remember black and white TV or Beatlemania—college students returning for the fall term.

Main Street began with stately Victorian houses with gingerbread trim and Tourists Welcome signs on the front lawns, then abruptly devolved into a series of low-slung motor lodges and, finally, the downtown business district with its two-story brick storefronts. On the east side of the street, dominating a small village green, was an imposing cut-stone Presbyterian church.

Main ended at River Street, where yet another solid line of brick storefronts obscured any view of the river. I parked the Bronco at a meter with twelve minutes left on it and went into a nearby cafe for coffee and directions. I was served up both by an obese counter jockey who sported a two-day "Miami Vice" beard on his chins and half a pack of cigarette ash on the front of his bib apron. The town library, he informed me as he absently ran a damp rag over the Formica countertop, shared space with the Clampett College Student Resource Center on College Street.

His directions led me to a shaded avenue and a scattered group of neoclassical buildings that were slightly overdone with fluted columns and ivy. These proved to be the various lecture halls and dormitories for Clampett College. The Widows Cape Public Library was itself housed in an old Greek revival mansion with white clapboards, a pillared portico, and ornate pediments surmounting tall, multipaned windows. I pulled into the adjacent parking lot and grabbed a spot designated for noncampus vehicles. From the parking lot, I could see that the rear of the mansion was joined haphazardly to a boxy two-story addition. A modern entrance of tinted glass and brushed aluminum was indented into the side of the addition. A sign over the entryway read Clampett College Student Resource Center.

I strolled around to the front of the converted manse and entered the public half of the library.

"Good morning. May I help you with something?"

I was standing with my back to the book checkout, surveying the various rooms that led off the library's rotunda and considering my options, when a soft female voice came across the counter. It belonged to a diminutive brunette, about five-two, with forest green eyes, short brown hair, and a chest that she must have inherited from a much larger woman. She smiled expectantly in the manner of a conscientious public servant and I smiled back.

"I'm looking for the local history section," I said.

"That's to your left, in the back, just behind U.S. History. There's also a local section in the Clampett College Annex," she pointed in the general direction of the back of the building, "which the public is welcome to use, although materials can't be loaned to anyone without a student or faculty ID."

"Do you have a newspaper morgue here?"

"We keep copies of the *Thousand Islander* weekly on

35

file, backdated for one year. We also have the Watertown dailies available on microfiche in the college library annex, dating back to 1960. For anything earlier, you'd have to drive down to Watertown."

"Maybe I'll run down there later in the week." I caught myself staring, and not at her luminous green eyes. "Well, I guess I better get to it," I said, reddening. "Thanks for your help."

"I'm here to serve." She nodded curtly and slowly turned away.

"Saints preserve us," I mumbled, and went off in search of knowledge.

An astute Englishman once said that real history doesn't get written, because it isn't in people's brains but in their nerves and vitals. I'm still not sure where real history comes from but, after two hours of digging, I knew it didn't come from the Widows Cape Public Library.

I had spent the time commuting between the public library's local history section and its twin in the Clampett College half of the building. The sum total of my efforts looked impressive, but there was no meat. It was as if every detail of Widows Cape's past had been carefully weighed by the local contingent of the Moral Majority, with the neat and tidy and heroic going into the books and the rest being glossed over or ignored entirely. History according to Walt Disney.

I learned that the region used to be fought over by the Algonquins and the Hurons and the Iroquois, until the "civilized" Europeans came along. At that point, it evolved from Indians fighting other Indians, to Indians fighting Frenchmen and Englishmen, to Frenchmen and their Indians fighting Englishmen and their Indians. It finally came down to upstart American Colonials fighting Redcoats, and we all know how that turned out.

Thanks to a thin green paperback titled *Our Town; A Look Back*, I learned that Widows Cape had been founded in 1798 by Scottish immigrants, who originally named the town Cape Caledonia. During the War of 1812, the male population of the town was wiped out while launching an ill-conceived river attack on a British frigate that had sailed down from Montreal. By the time the New York City newspapers wrote up the story, it had been dubbed the Battle of the Widows' Cape. Patriotic fervor being what it was, the name stuck and Cape Caledonia became Widows Cape.

According to the sanitized reporting of the local historical society, Widows Cape had gone on to an idyllic existence that had continued uninterrupted up to the present. In the mid-1870s, a large salt deposit had been discovered just south of town and mining became, along with dairy farming and fishing, one of the economic mainstays of the community. In the late 1880s, the first wave of business tycoons began adopting the region as a summer playground, thus adding tourism as an important profit maker. In 1904, one of the wealthier summer residents, a railroad car manufacturer named Josiah Elwood Clampett, founded a small liberal arts college in Widows Cape, named it after himself, and, upon his death in 1913, endowed it with nine million dollars. That was about it, as far as the historical society was concerned.

I stretched my arms and yawned. Not a word on smugglers or Prohibition era rumrunners or a killer named Jack Rose and an anomaly called the Castle House murders. Frustrated, I packed up my paperwork and adjourned to the rotunda. Widows Cape's comely librarian was still behind the checkout counter, Dewey decimaling a pile of index cards.

"Well," she said, "how do you like our little library?"

"Oh, great," I lied.

"Did you find what you needed? I notice you made several trips to the Xerox machine."

I smiled. "I'm sure I could ace a history exam at Widows Cape High right about now, but, to be honest, I didn't find much that can help me with my article."

"Oh, you're a writer?"

"Yes, I free-lance for magazines. I guess you could say

37

I'm up here on a sort of working vacation." I filled her in on my connection to Professor Janezek and Castle House and my interview with Howard Johnson. I decided to leave out the part about the enigmatic list of names.

"Hmm," she murmured, tapping her fingers on the countertop. "So you're more or less digging around in the dark, looking for the story angle. Is that it?"

"Exactly."

"Well, personal interviews with some of the elderly residents of the town sounds like a good way to go. You can't beat oral history, after all. I've heard the stories about this Rose character and the Castle House incident, of course. Everyone who's lived here awhile has. But I've never been sure where fact leaves off and fiction begins."

"I know what you mean," I said, leaning forward to rest my elbows on the checkout counter. "If it was just the old sea dog, Howard Johnson, telling the story, I wouldn't waste my time on it. But Professor Janezek's credentials as a historian suggest there must be something to it."

"I think you're probably right. I don't know Mr. Johnson, but I did know the professor and he wasn't the sort of man to waste time chasing fairy tales." She crinkled up her brow. "Your best bet is the old newspapers on microfiche at Flower Memorial Library in Watertown."

"I plan to drive down there in a day or so," I said. "Any other suggestions?"

"You'll want to see the original police files on the case, provided they're still available. I doubt that the Widows Cape constable's office has much, but maybe the state police will be able to help. Oh! I almost forgot. I assume you'll want to get as much background on Castle House as you can—its history, the architecture, and so on?"

"It couldn't hurt."

"Well, I know someone involved with the Midstream Fellowship who should be able to help you there—" She paused, noting the look of surprise on my face and interpreting it as confusion.

"I can see I've lost you," she said, laughing lightly. "The

38

Fellowship is—let's see, how would I describe it?—a cross between a highbrow social club and a think tank, I suppose. They help promote the college, sponsor a few guest lectures every year, and hold an occasional symposium."

"But what does this Fellowship have to do with the Castle House?" I asked.

"That's where the group holds most of its official functions. It's the headquarters, actually, although the administrative work is handled here in town at the college. At any rate, a friend of mine named Liam Dougherty—he teaches English Lit at the college—he's a member of the Fellowship. I'm sure he'd be willing to help if you mention that I gave you his name." She blushed, a charming anachronism. "Liam and I date once in a while."

"Uh-huh. So this Midstream Fellowship," I said, taking out my notebook, "is a private social organization affiliated with Clampett College, and the Fellowship owns the Castle House?"

"Not exactly. The Fellowship has use of the house and grounds from its owner, a French-Canadian businessman named DuPree, who also happens to be one of the college's wealthiest benefactors and a founding member of the Fellowship."

"Maurice DuPree?"

"Yes. You've heard of him?"

"The name rings a bell, but faintly."

"He owns a fleet of freighters that operate out of Montreal. Also the Islander Tour Boat Company here in Widows Cape, a couple of quarries south of town, and a resort hotel across the river in Kingston. He bought Coffin Island about ten years ago from the state, which took possession years ago in lieu of taxes owed by Ernest Castle's estate. Supposedly there were plans to develop the island into a bird sanctuary, but that never materialized. At any rate, Mr. DuPree ended up buying the property, restoring the house and grounds, and eventually using it to help establish the Fellowship."

"About this DuPree," I said, still scribbling.

"Whoa." She held up her hand, then motioned at the clock on the wall behind her. "I'd be happy to do all I can to help you with your story, but as of now, I'm on my lunch hour." She reached below the checkout counter and came back up with a plum-colored purse. "And I'm famished."

I can take a hint as well as the next guy, so I said, "The least I can do for all your help is to buy lunch. And by the way," I added, "My name is Sheridan."

CHAPTER 6

HER name was Rita Tonelli.
She was twenty-nine, a graduate of the library science program at the State University of New York at Geneseo, and, for the past four years, head librarian at the Widows Cape Public Library. She grew up in Buffalo, along with a younger sister and an older brother who had come back from Vietnam a paraplegic. She was single, but hoping to correct that condition as soon as "the right sort of man comes along."

All this I learned over lunch at a shamelessly trendy restaurant on Main Street called the Glass Gazebo. It was one of those places where the college-aged waiters told you their first names and then rattled off the day's menu offerings in one breath. The fare was heavy on broiled fish, artichoke hearts, and kiwi slices, not to mention pita breads and unlikely pasta concoctions. In the center of the room, housed in a lattice-work gazebo, was a salad bar that quite literally contained everything from soup to nuts.

"When were you over there?" Rita asked as she picked at a leaf of endive. The topic was Vietnam.

"Toward the end, early seventies," I said between bites of something called the Great Gazebo Sirloin Patty Melt, which is what you call a cheeseburger that sells for $4.25.

"My brother was there in the late sixties," she said quietly. "He was serving his second tour when it happened. The jeep he was riding in ran over a mine. He hoped to make a career of it—" She let the sentence trail away.

"I was a draftee," I said. "Two months after I dropped out of college, the Selective Service Board picked my number. It's the only lottery I've won."

"Well, at least you were able to come back in one piece, finish your education."

"Yeah, I have to admit, the G.I. Bill came in handy."

"Not to change the subject," she began.

"Please do," I said. Vietnam was a conversational minefield I didn't feel like traipsing through, especially not with the sister of someone who had come home with a severed spine.

"Well, I just thought of something that might be useful to you in putting together your article on the Castle House." She popped a cherry tomato into her mouth, chewed a moment, and continued.

"Professor Janezek's personal papers should be helpful, since you say he was researching the subject. He must have more extensive notes filed somewhere. You'd want to go over to the administration building at the college, to the history department office. Professor Janezek was head of the department, you know. I hear his replacement is a new man, a Dr. Alston. He may or may not be able to help you. Anyway, the department secretary is Miss Witherspoon. She's been around for ages. I'm sure she can help."

"I've spoken with her," I nodded. "In fact, I'm planning to go over there this afternoon. What about your friend, Liam Dougherty?"

"He's with the English department. I doubt if he'd be familiar with Professor Janezek's research project."

"Still, if they were friends—"

"I never said they were friends." She laughed. "Friendly adversaries is more like it. They used to argue politics and books and things—quite heatedly at times." She blushed for the second time that day. "Liam is a bit of a Socialist

42

rabble-rouser and Professor Janezek was conservative. Oh, some of the rows they used to have!" She leaned forward. "Liam can be difficult sometimes, with his opinionated manner. But he's really an interesting man. Extremely well read."

She pronounced him well read with the licentious fervor a nymphomaniac might employ in calling a man well hung; a fetish peculiar to librarians, perhaps.

"He sounds interesting. I'd like to meet him, even if he can't help me with the professor's research papers."

"Well, his office is in the administration building, too. I'm sure he'd be glad to speak with you if you dropped by," she said, then glanced at her watch. "Oh, look at the time! I've got to get back to work."

I paid the check and followed Rita out of the restaurant. It had been a worthwhile lunch. My chance encounter with Widows Cape's head librarian had provided me with more information than I had gathered in two hours of foraging through the library's shelves. I now knew the basics on the Fellowship, if not its significance. And I had some background on two more of the names on the list, Liam Dougherty and Maurice DuPree. What any of that had to do with Professor Janezek or Howard Johnson or the fifty-year-old Castle House incident, I hadn't a clue. But it wasn't a bad start. When you added to that a full belly, a sunny September afternoon, and the company of a pretty young woman, I was beginning to feel downright optimistic about the whole enterprise.

We were strolling down Main Street, chatting about the change of seasons, gradually working our way back toward College Street, when Rita stopped suddenly in midstride and squeaked out a tiny "Oh!"

I tore my eyes away from her mesmerizing profile and followed her gaze down the sidewalk. Three men were approaching us. One was tall, sturdy, and at least seventy years old. He wore a well-cut blue pinstripe suit and a politician's patronizing smile. He was flanked by a small middle-aged businessman type in a dark brown sportcoat and checked pants and a medium-tall sinewy guy wearing a tan double-knit cop suit. The lawman appeared to be around my age, mid-thirties.

"Miss Tonelli, how nice to see you," the old guy said, his voice going off like a sonic boom. He bowed from the waist, then lightly shook Rita's hand. The businessman type merely nodded his head, but the lanky cop mumbled, "'Lo, Rita," and then glared at me out of wideset, hostile eyes, the way a cobra stares at a mongoose.

"Good afternoon, gentlemen," Rita said, recovering from her momentary fluster. "This is Timothy Sheridan, a free-lance writer. He's in town to research a magazine article. We were just discussing source materials over lunch," she added, obviously for the edification of the stringbean in the police tans.

"Judge Robert Burns Dunleavy, Mr. Sheridan," the old guy introduced himself, pumping my arm like it was the last well between Widows Cape and Taos, New Mexico. "So named by my dear mother, who was a poetic soul in her own right!"

The judge was one of those gregarious glad-handers who seemed to speak in capital letters, the type who never learned how to whisper at funerals and movie theaters. Not unlike a few of my relatives, whose antecedents can be traced to the land of the Blarney Stone. Which may or may not explain why I broke into spontaneous verse.

"'Farewell to the Highlands, farewell to the North, The Birthplace of valor, the country of worth!'"

The judge released my hand and finished off the recitation. "'Wherever I wander, wherever I rove, The Hills of the Highlands forever I love.' By God, I don't believe it! A youngster who knows the work of Robbie Burns. You've restored my faith in America's educational system, Mr. Sheridan." He gave me a firm pat between the shoulder blades, nearly recycling my Great Gazebo Sirloin Patty Melt.

"Actually, I learned that piece from an Irish uncle of mine who admired the Scots for their whiskey and their early resistance against the English."

The other three had been following our exchange with varied reactions. Rita seemed impressed, which was probably the real reason I had spouted Burns. The diminutive businessman looked bored. The cop was peeved.

"Judge Dunleavy is the town justice, Sheridan," Rita explained. "And this is Rodney MacKenzie, our mayor and one of the area's leading attorneys." Bingo. The fourth and final name from the mysterious list. Sometimes it's better to be lucky than good. I shook hands with the little man.

"Nice to meet you."

"A pleasure," he said, although it obviously wasn't.

"And this," Rita indicated the cop, "is Ellis Turnbull. Ellis is chief constable for the town of Widows Cape."

Turnbull nodded curtly and turned to give Rita a proprietary stare. "I was planning to drop by the library later to see you. About tonight."

Damned if lovely Rita didn't blush again. Liam Dougherty, Ellis Turnbull. I was beginning to wonder if beneath that demure facade of hers lay a smoldering Mt. St. Helens. Before I could mull over the inherent symbolism buried in that thought, the judge asked, "What is the nature of your article, Mr. Sheridan? A travel piece?"

"No, sir. I concentrate on crime stories mostly. I'm up here to get in some fishing and, while I'm at it, I thought I'd check out the local history back during and immediately after the Prohibition era. The Castle House murders, for example."

"Castle House?" The stoic Mayor MacKenzie grew animated for a beat or two, then receded back into a pose of boredom. "Rather old news, isn't it? Why would you—or anyone, for that matter—be interested in that?"

"A friend of mine got me hooked on it. Professor Stefan Janezek."

"Ah, I see. The late professor, our local crime buff."

"The professor and I were attending the same convention when he was killed. I was called in to identify the body."

"Tragic," the judge said. The good-natured bluster of a moment ago was gone now, the old man's fleshy face seeming to sag with melancholy. "It pales, however, when compared with the tragedy at Castle House."

"You have some personal connection to the case, judge?"

"The judge was in one of the first cars to make it out to the island after the fire was spotted," MacKenzie said. "My father was with him, along with a couple of others."

"It was so long ago now," Dunleavy cut in, talking more to himself than to the rest of us. "I was a young man, come home from college for the holidays. I'll never, ever forget that terrible night."

"I'd appreciate it if I could talk to you about it sometime, at your convenience," I said.

The mayor butted in again. "It's not the kind of thing we care to see exploited, Mr. Sheridan. Having the community's dirty laundry hung out like that." He turned to Dunleavy. "Bad publicity for Castle House can't help but reflect back on the Fellowship and the college. And what's bad for the college is bad for the whole town."

The judge laid a heavy paw on MacKenzie's shoulder and gave it a paternal pat. "You're right. The Castle House story doesn't do much for our image, does it, Rodney." He focused his watery brown eyes on me. "You'll have to excuse Rodney his protectionist instincts, Mr. Sheridan. Not only is he our mayor, but he serves on the Clampett College Board of Trustees and he's very active in the Fellowship. He tends to be a little overzealous at times."

"What about you, sir?" I asked. "Do you think the story should stay buried, or will you give me an interview?"

"Yes on both questions. I'd prefer that chapter of local history be forgotten. On the other hand, I suspect you'll pursue it with or without my help. So, in the interest of fairness and accuracy, I'd be willing to tell you what I know of the Castle House incident." He glanced at his wristwatch, a paper-thin Piaget. I had him figured for a pocket watch on a gold fob. "I'm afraid we have to hurry along now, but if you'll stop by my office in the municipal building or call my secretary, we'll arrange an interview."

"I appreciate it."

46

"A pleasure, Mr. Sheridan." He grabbed my hand again and jerked it up and down a couple of times.

We watched them go, the large and imposing judge and the small, severe mayor. After they rounded a corner and disappeared from view, Rita broke the silence that stood like a stone wall between Turnbull and me.

"Well, I'm late, I have to get back to the stacks. Thanks for the lunch, Sheridan." She squeezed out a herniated smile. "Listen, you two should get together on this Castle House thing. Ellis, I'm sure you could dig out some old police reports that might help." Turnbull said nothing. "Well, anyway, I have to run. I'll talk to you later, Ellis, about tonight." Then she, too, left us, walking briskly back in the direction of the library.

"Nice lady," I offered as we watched her go.

Turnbull stared at me with those cobra eyes.

I tried again. "You two an item, as they say at the beauty parlor?"

Nothing. I figured I'd give it one more try and if he didn't respond, I'd switch to sign language.

"I bet you don't like Liam Dougherty much, either."

"Dougherty's a flake." He had the softest voice I'd ever heard on a cop.

"Maybe so," I said. "But well read."

Things were looking up. He almost smiled. "Rita does go for the bookish type. Over lunch, anyway."

"Uh-huh." I decided not to touch that one. "So, how about it? Those old police files could be a big help."

The Widows Cape chief constable sighed. "What's left of the old files are stored in the basement of the municipal building. I'm not sure it would be in the public interest for me to be digging them up, like the mayor says."

"Well, chief, look at it this way. The sooner I get the information I need, the sooner I leave Widows Cape."

This time he did smile.

CHAPTER 7

THE constable's office is on River Street, just across a narrow strip of green from the Widows Cape Municipal Building. The large plate glass windows that front the place suggest it was once a grocery or a general store. The interior had been neatly remodeled to accommodate a small office for the chief, a squad room with three desks and a dispatcher's station, and, partitioned off in the back, a washroom and two empty holding cells.

Next door is the more impressive municipal building, an antebellum mansion that, according to Turnbull, had been converted for public use back in the twenties. It housed the offices of the town clerks and the mayor, the chambers and court for the town justice, and a handful of cubbyholes reserved for various lesser local government functionaries.

I spent half an hour trailing Chief Turnbull, first from the constable's office to the town clerk's office, then down into the musty bowels of the municipal building and back across to the constable's office. Our efforts turned up one badly mildewed cardboard file box with a faded gum label that read "Town Marshal's Official Records—1930-1939."

"Back in the old days, the only law officer around here was the town marshal," Turnbull explained as I settled in

48

behind an empty desk in the squad room. The box of old records sat before me amidst a profusion of dusty civil defense handouts and blank arrest report forms. "The state troopers handled most of the crime in those days. Then, in the 1950s, what with the college enrollment picking up and tourism taking off, the town board decided it might be a good idea to hire a small regular force to keep an eye on things firsthand, so they started the constabulary." He frowned. "Of course, the troopers still get most of the real police work. With only myself and two constables working under me, I can't do much more than rattle a few doorknobs and make sure the college kids don't get beat up too often by the local toughs."

"I guess you've seen your share of panty raids and Halloween pranks," I said. "How'd you come to be Widows Cape's head cop anyway?"

"I was with the Jersey City Police. A ten-year man, the last three working vice." He shrugged. "I got so I wanted out of all the sick shit that was going down. So, when I heard about this job, I applied. It sounded like just what I was looking for." He smiled, and the velvet voice that had seemed so menacing before took on new shadings. "I've been here two years and, although it seems like two hundred sometimes, I don't regret the move. I sure couldn't take much more of Jersey City."

"If it's anything like Newark, I can understand your reasoning." I pulled the top off the file box and began rummaging through the old records. They were brittle and badly yellowed, some typed haphazardly, others printed out in longhand. The signature at the bottom of each was the same.

"Orbis Younger?" I asked, holding up a report on the capture and subsequent execution of a rabid dog.

"He was town marshal in those days. I think he was a game warden originally. Died back in the forties, they say."

"Not from job stress," I said, as I skimmed through several of the reports. Eviction papers served, lost children returned, the town drunk picked up one night and released the next morning. "This stuff reads like a script from 'The Andy Griffith Show.'"

"What'd you expect, Sheridan?" Turnbull bristled. "If you want the Sam Spade crap, go out to Los Angeles. You won't be missed here." There was a short silence, during which Turnbull managed to calm down a little and I managed to resist telling him that Sam Spade's milieu was San Francisco.

Eventually I said, "No offense, chief. I live in a small town myself, down in the Finger Lakes."

"Then those file reports shouldn't come as a surprise," he said, hitching up the belt on his tan double knits. "Police work's a whole different thing in these little burgs. You take Widows Cape. We got maybe sixteen hundred permanent residents. During the school year, you can add another thousand or so college students. In the summer, we get a few hundred seasonal residents, retirees mostly, up from Florida. The trailer parks and cottages are full of 'em. They're a pretty quiet bunch, which is okay with me. I wanted to get away from all the bullshit you run into doing police work in the city and I did. All except for the politics. That seems to be the same everywhere."

"Speaking of local politics," I said. "What's the story on your mayor?"

"What d'you mean?"

"I mean he strikes me as a bit churlish for an elected official. I was wondering what his—"

Turnbull cut me off with a scowl. "I thought you were here to go over some old files on the Castle House case."

"Right." I turned back to the cardboard box on the desk. "Ah, here we are. 'Ernest Castle Investigation, January 2, 1938.'" I read the report out loud, with Turnbull following along over my shoulder.

"'Arrived at scene of Castle House fire approx. 11:45 P.M., 31 Dec. 1937, with members of W.C. Vol. Fire Dept. Assisted firemen in losing battle to save house until arrival of state police unit under Captain Lester Tinderlay.

"'1 Jan. 1938, approx. 7 A.M. Troopers locate bodies of E. Castle, T. Trevain, Alice and Victoria Spicer, and fifteen others in cellar of burnt Castle House. Preliminary investigation indicated Trevain was shot once, others probably died of suffocation or smoke inhalation.

"'1 Jan. 1938, approx. 9:30 A.M. State police assume full responsibility for investigation. Note: Capt. Tinderlay requests this office forward to his attention all local files on Jack Rose. Request completed as of 2 Jan. 1938.'"

It was signed Orbis Younger.

I laid the report on the desktop. Behind me, Turnbull said, "Well, he sure writes reports like a game warden."

"Mm. I guess I'll have to try and track down the state police reports by this Captain Tinderlay if I want to find out the details. Like who were Alice and Victoria Spicer. You got any ideas on that?"

"A couple of local girls who were guests of Castle's the night of the fire. A pair of real beauties, to hear the town's old-timers tell it. It was those two dying that hit everybody around here so hard. The other guests were all outsiders, so I guess they didn't count as much."

"Guess not," I mumbled, making a mental note to check out Alice and Victoria Spicer more thoroughly when I could get around to it. I was busy pawing through the file box as I spoke, not really expecting to find anything of interest, but pleased when I did. "Hey, here's something on Jack Rose from April of 1933."

It wasn't much. A handwritten summary of Younger's attempts to track down Rose at the request of the state boys, who wanted to question him about a robbery involving an antiques dealer from downstate. According to Younger, he called off his own efforts when the troopers reported picking up Rose in Alexandria Bay, twenty miles or so downriver.

"According to Howard Johnson, this Rose character did a stint at Dannemora back before the Castle House fire," I said. "Maybe this was the rap they nailed him on."

"Wouldn't know," Turnbull said. "Far as I can figure

51

from the stories I hear, Rose was just a second-rate punk who got his moment of glory after he torched a bunch of innocent partiers at the Castle place. Of course, the same was probably true of Dillinger and Billy the Kid until some money-hungry writer made heroes out of them."

I looked up at him. "I'm not interested in creating any new legends, chief. I just want to find out all I can about the Castle House and its history. What happened out there on New Year's Eve, 1937, and what's happening today."

"What's happening today is that a bunch of eggheads show up out there every once in a while when the Fellowship has a big confab. They 'theorize' and 'conceptualize' for a few days—just an excuse to party, if you ask me—and when they run out of breath, everybody goes home." Turnbull made a Warner Bros. production out of checking his watch. "You about through there, Sheridan? I gotta walk down to Smitty's garage and pick up my cruiser, providing Smitty's done putting in the new head gasket."

"Don't let me hold you up, chief. I'll just sit here and finish thumbing through this file. When I'm done, I'll run it back over to the clerk's office."

"Uh-uh. I signed 'em out, I have to bring 'em back. That's the procedure. Fact is, I shouldn't leave you alone here with public files anyway."

"It's not exactly like you're leaving me in charge of the Pentagon Papers. This stuff hasn't even seen daylight since before you or I were born."

Turnbull checked his watch again. "Well, I guess." He crossed over to one of the front windows and looked out at the street. "Smiley oughta be back in a few minutes anyway. That's Smiley Chase, one of my constables. He's on his lunch hour." He turned back to me. "Okay. Finish up with the records, Sheridan, and mind the phones for me. But don't dawdle. I wanna get that stuff back where it belongs."

I watched him go out the front door, then moved myself and the file box to a desk with a phone on it. After a few minutes of combing through Orbis Younger's rudimentary reports and coming up with nothing more on Jack Rose or the Castle House case, I pushed the box aside, put my feet up on the desk, and waited for the phone to ring. Ten minutes crawled by and I was still waiting. It was a long way from Jersey City to Widows Cape. A cop could grow old gracefully here. Or go crazy waiting for something to happen. I passed the time by counting the desks and chairs, then counting the floor tiles. I was about to start on the drop-in ceiling panels when the door opened.

"Hello, stranger. What can I do ya for?" He had a high-pitched voice with an upstate accent trapped halfway between Grandpa Walton and Eleanor Roosevelt. His tan double knits fit him like the skin on a butternut squash. Underneath a gray flattop haircut that needed pruning, a bulbous nose hovered above a wide-open grin.

"You must be Smiley Chase."

"Must be." He belched. "Goddamn! Let that be a lesson to ya. Never mix chili and root beer. And you are?"

I gave him my name and a brief explanation of why I was sitting with my feet propped up on his desk.

"Well, that's dandy," he said, the grin never leaving his face. He looked to be about fifty-five, with at least fifty of those years spent outdoors in the wind and sun. He was straight from central casting for every B Western I'd ever seen, as if the director had called down and said, "Send me a marshal's sidekick type." Andy Devine, Slim Pickens, Chill Wills, Smiley Chase, take your pick. "Any calls?"

"Not a one."

"Well, that's the way it goes. Next week things'll pick up, once the college kids get back to classes. I just love those peepin' tom calls over to the sorority houses."

I laughed. "You been around this town long, Smiley?"

"All my life. Used to run a digger out at the salt mine until the company cut back. Then I got lucky and hired on as a constable back about fifteen years ago. Ellis inherited me when he come on board. We get on just fine."

"That's more than I can say. I don't think your chief constable likes having me around." I explained about my

53

lunch date with Rita Tonelli and our encounter with Turnbull.

"Yeah, that'd do it all right. Ellis usually is pretty easy-goin'. Kinda quiet even. But he's got a real case for that little librarian. She got a way of stringin' a man along, if you get my drift, and it about drives Ellis crazy." He tugged at his drooping pants. "Fine-lookin' little thing, though, ain't she?"

"Not to change the subject," I said, "But seeing as how you've been in Widows Cape all your life, I wonder if I could throw a few names at you, get your comments. Strictly as background for my piece on Castle House."

"Like who?"

"Like Professor Stefan Janezek. Did you know him?"

"Sure. I seen him around town once in a while. Real nice fella, for a professor."

"Did he ever speak to you about the Castle House case?"

"Not that I can . . . oh, wait, yeah." He cocked his head to one side. "Come to think of it, sometime last June, I think it was. I run into him over at the diner one day. We got to talkin' and he asked me did I remember Jack Rose from when I was a little kid. Well, hell, I was just a tyke when the Castle House went up, but I heard all about it and Rose and everything while I was growing up."

"Did he say what he was after specifically?"

"No, just that he was researchin' the story, like you are. I told him, from what I always heard, Rose was just a small-time thief. That's about it."

"What about Rodney MacKenzie?"

"The mayor?" Smiley lost his grin for the first time. "What's he got to do with the price of tea in China?"

"Nothing, I was just curious. Turnbull made a comment to me, how everything's different in a small town except the politics. I thought maybe he was referring to the mayor."

"Well," Smiley nodded grudgingly. "Could be he was. See, Ellis and Mayor MacKenzie, they've had a few run-ins, mostly over security for the doin's this Fellowship outfit

54

puts on now and again. They have these whatchacall symposiums and cocktail parties and such—invitation only stuff. Ellis don't like havin' to keep the regular town folks away from these uppity bigwigs when they come around." He threw up his hands. "'Course, the mayor runs the council and the council runs the constable's office, so what ya gonna do?"

I was about to follow up with another question on MacKenzie when Turnbull marched through the front door.

"Well, I see you managed to live through another lunch special at the diner," he said to Smiley. "I hope to Christ you didn't order the chili again."

Chase patted his distended belly. "Don't worry, Ellis, the old digestive system is clickin' on all eight cylinders ever since Louise got me eatin' more roughage."

"Let's hope so." Turnbull zeroed in on me. "You still here, Sheridan?"

"I was just leaving," I said, rising. "Thanks for the use of the hall."

He grunted, then added optimistically, "Leaving my office or leaving town?"

"You must be kidding," I said as I made for the door. "Who'd ever want to leave a nice, friendly burg like this?"

CHAPTER 8

THE Clampett College Administration Center was easily the largest building on campus. Maybe Reagan was right: America's problem is too much bureaucracy. Still, it depends on which paper shufflers you favor and which you don't. After all, the Pentagon is said to be the world's largest office building.

I found the door I was looking for tucked away on the third floor of the building's west wing. The frosted glass in the door's upper panel read History Department, Professor Stefan T. Janezek, Chairman.

"Good afternoon, how may I help you?" An older woman with a chirpy voice greeted me as I came into the reception area. Her rich henna hair seemed out of place surrounding her deeply lined face, but then, perhaps she had a few Reagan genes of her own. The nameplate on the desk said simply Miss Witherspoon.

"My name's Sheridan. We spoke on the phone last week."

"Oh, yes!" She trilled. "Professor Jan's friend. You've come to see Mr. Betz, haven't you? I'm sorry, but he called this morning to say he wouldn't be in today."

"That's unfortunate," I said. "I did want to speak to him about the materials he had you forward to me."

"Yes, I explained that to him, but he said it couldn't be helped. Oh!" Her hands fluttered the air like a pair of wounded doves. "He did say he could meet you tonight around eight at Lord Jim's, if you're so inclined."

"Lord Jim's?"

"That's a tavern on River Street, down by the public docks." The hands lighted on the desk top. "I do hope Alan—Mr. Betz, that is—calms down by tomorrow. We have so much to do before classes begin next week and, what with Professor Jan gone, God rest his soul, and his replacement not due until Friday—"

I cut in. "Excuse me. You said you hoped Mr. Betz calms down. What's he upset about?"

"Did I say that?" she said, her voice dropping from thrush to pigeon. "Dear me, I'm afraid I've let my mouth get ahead of my brain again."

"But Mr. Betz has been upset about something?"

"Perhaps I've overstated the situation," Miss Witherspoon said after a moment, her brow furrowing. "I mean, Alan has been a bit, mm, annoyed, certainly. Not that I can entirely blame him. After all, it wasn't very considerate of Professor Dougherty to exclude Alan from the selection committee for the new history department chairman. Alan was Professor Jan's assistant." She lowered her voice to a conspiratorial whisper. "Frankly, I think Alan may have had some tiny hope that he'd be considered for the department chairmanship. Not that he really had a chance, of course. He's only twenty-eight, and still a few credits short of his doctorate."

"Why did Professor Dougherty exclude him, I wonder?"

"Oh, they've never gotten along." Miss Witherspoon shrugged daintily. "Alan is a very intense young man and Professor Dougherty is very, er, outgoing. A personality clash, if you will."

"I see." At least, I was beginning to, and I didn't like what I saw. Alan Betz, the person who had so cleverly whetted my interest in coming to Widows Cape, had his own ax to grind, perhaps using me somehow to get even for

whatever petty slights he'd endured from Professor Liam
Dougherty.

"I hate to waste the visit, and I did want to review more
of Professor Janezek's notes," I told Miss Witherspoon.
"Would that be possible?"

"Oh, dear. I'm afraid I'll have to disappoint you again,
Mr. Sheridan. You see, the board assigned Alan and Professor Dougherty to gather up all of Professor Jan's personal
papers and send them along to his brother in Chicago. I'm
afraid everything is gone."

"Do you have an address for the brother?"

"Yes, I do, somewhere here." She pulled open the desk's
file drawer and began rummaging. While she searched, I
posed another question.

"Did it really take two men to clean out the professor's
files?"

"Well, there were a couple of boxes' worth just here at
the office," Miss Witherspoon explained, still searching.
"Alan took care of those. The rest were kept at Professor
Jan's apartment off campus. Professor Dougherty volunteered to take care of those, since he lives in the same
apartment house. Ah, here we are!"

She read off the name and phone number of Professor
Janezek's brother in Chicago. I wrote it down in my pad
and, as an afterthought, asked her for the address of the
apartment building where the professor had lived and
wrote that down as well.

"You know, I believe Professor Dougherty is in today,"
Miss Witherspoon said. "You may want to speak to him
about the papers, so that your day won't have been a total
loss."

A flight of stairs later, I was standing in front of another
frosted glass door panel, this one reading Literature Department; Liam X. Dougherty, Chairman. I stepped into an antechamber much the same as the one in the history
department office, but with no Miss Witherspoon to welcome me.

The reception area's central adornment was a large portrait poster of Walt Whitman. There was also a framed recruitment handbill from the Lincoln Brigade, which may have aggravated J. Edgar Hoover but didn't do a thing for me. I was about to knock on the door to the inner office when the rumble of discordant voices held me back. I stood there with my fist poised in midair as snatches of conversation filtered out like the word puzzles in the back of the Sunday paper.

". . . Jamie, so don't think for one . . . There are certain limits—"

". . . hypocritical bullshit, man. That fascist son of a bitch—"

"I don't want to discuss it any more!"

The door swung inward, leaving me face to fist with a red-bearded man. He was of medium height, pug-nosed and ruddy-faced, with a surfeit of curly hair that was beginning to retreat from his forehead.

I lowered my clenched hand. "Professor Dougherty?"

"Yes. What can I do for you, Mr.—?"

"Sheridan. I was a friend of Stefan Janezek. I wanted to see you about some of his research notes."

"Janezek's research notes? Hang on a minute." He turned to his debating partner, a thin dark-haired youth wearing a U-2 T-shirt and a sour expression. "Jamie, I think we'd better continue this another time," Dougherty said smoothly. "As much as I enjoy polemics, I'm really too busy today, as you can see."

Jamie glanced from Dougherty to me, then shrugged. "Sure, professor. I'll get back to you in class next week."

The kid slipped past us, giving me another appraising glance in transit, and left. Dougherty motioned me into his inner sanctum and sat me in a high-backed wooden chair, the sort used by high school principals and Nazi interrogators.

"I like to encourage an open give-and-take with my students," he explained as he settled behind a cluttered desk.

59

He was grinning, but his heart wasn't in it. "Some of them, like Jamie there, tend to get carried away sometimes."

"Yeah, kids say the darnedest things," I said. "Which fascist son of a bitch was he talking about anyway?"

"Huh?" The professor fidgeted with the knot of his broad paisley tie. It looked like something Sonny Bono would wear to a love-in. "Oh, uh, he's doing a paper on Jack London. Having a problem reconciling London's prose with his politics, you might say. What was that you said about Professor Jan's notes, Mr. Sheridan?"

I gave him the *Reader's Digest* version of my relationship with Janezek and my interest in following up on the professor's Castle House research. I credited Miss Witherspoon for sending me in Dougherty's direction.

"She said you helped pack his stuff off to Chicago," I said. "I thought you might recall if there was anything in his files that I could use."

Dougherty dug his fingers into his beard, frowned, then picked up a pipe and a tobacco pouch from the desk. "I'd be happy to help you out, of course," he said as he packed the pipe with shreds of dark tobacco. "Problem is, there were no references to Castle House in Jan's papers."

"Nothing at all?"

"Not that I recall, and I read through them fairly carefully." He torched the pipe with a stick match, the office suddenly filling with the cloying scent of burnt cherries.

"Why?" I asked.

Dougherty blinked. "Why what?"

"Why did you carefully read the professor's notes?"

"Well, it comes with the job, doesn't it?" He exhaled a cloud of nicotine across the desk. I didn't mind. I was used to people blowing smoke in my direction. "Much of Jan's papers were just pointless scribblings—much of any academic's papers are a waste, my own included. No point in paying shipping charges to send scrap paper halfway across the country, is there? Anyway, I think you're on a wild goose chase with Castle House, Mr. Sheridan. I can't believe any first-rate publication would be interested in a rehash of an incident that happened half a century ago." He grinned wryly. "There are so many bloody atrocities to choose from in the here and now."

"I guess I write for a lot of second-rate publications," I said. "I thought I might do a then and now thing. You know, contrasting the Castle House's hedonistic origins with its current role as headquarters for a benevolent, scholarly organization like the Fellowship."

This time he blinked twice. "Well, I don't know about that. As a member of the Fellowship, I have to tell you that we're not really interested in seeing the organization touted to the general public—and particularly not in the same context with some fifty-year-old dime novel crime spree." He shrugged his regrets, then added, "Please understand, Mr. Sheridan. Our goals are to help enrich the academic life at Clampett College and also to enhance its prestige, which we try to achieve by holding occasional symposia and guest lectures and publishing a few papers. We're a small, contemplative-oriented group and we like it that way. The sort of publicity you propose to bring us just isn't the sort we want."

"It sounds like you people don't particularly like any kind of publicity, Professor Dougherty."

"Call me Liam, please," he said, shifting gears. "I didn't catch your first name."

"Timothy."

"Ah. Any ties to the Kerry Sheridans?"

"No, County Mayo, as far as I know. I'm fourth-generation American, so it's hard to keep up."

"I know what you mean. I'm a second-generation Yank myself. Granddad caught a boat right after the Easter Uprising. But an Irishman never completely abandons the old sod, does he?" A trace of a brogue had crept into Dougherty's voice, which often happens when those of my breed wax nostalgic. Usually on St. Paddy's Day over straight shots of Old Bushmill's. But I wasn't about to let blarney sidetrack me.

"Getting back to the Fellowship," I said. "I'd never even

61

heard of it until I came up here. Seems odd to me that the board hasn't done more to cultivate a reputation."

"Excuse me for saying so," Dougherty said, a condescending smile seeping through the bushy beard. "But I doubt you'd be interested in the type of papers we do, or the scholarly journals we publish in." He smacked the pipe hard against a large glass ashtray, like a judge bringing down the gavel at the close of a session. "We do encourage publicity, Mr. Sheridan. But aimed at a specialized audience."

Dougherty began shuffling papers, just to make sure that I got the message; the interview was over. But I didn't take the hint.

"Nevertheless, professor, I'd like to arrange a trip out to see Castle House, maybe set up an interview with the owner. Maurice DuPree, isn't it?"

Dougherty stood. "Castle House isn't a tourist attraction. We don't give tours. As for Mr. DuPree, he's rarely at the facility, except for official functions. He resides in Montreal, where his company headquarters is located."

"Could you give me his number? Maybe he'd feel differently than you do about—"

Dougherty cut me off. "I doubt it, Mr. Sheridan, I really do." He shook his head, then exhaled slowly. "Tell you what. I'll relay your request to Mr. DuPree and leave it up to him. But don't get your hopes up. Now, I really have to get back to work."

"Right," I said, rising. "I'll get back to you later."

"Just don't get your hopes up," he repeated.

CHAPTER 9

LORD Jim's looked like a gritty sailors' hangout that had been gentrified by yuppie rehabbers. The weathered gray exterior sported touches of plum trim; the post and beam interior had stenciled friezes and polyurethaned brass ceiling fixtures. A small outdoor dining deck, cantilevered off the back of the building, jutted out over the water like the bowsprit on an old clipper ship.

There were only a half dozen people in the place, most of them spread out along the bar—three old-timers nursing glasses of draught at one end and a middle-aged dandy and a girl huddled close at the other. The girl was thin and bleached blond and wore a denim miniskirt below a black tank top. Her companion was fitted out for yachting in a blue blazer and a pair of crisp white ducks. Seated at a corner table was a young man wearing wire-rimmed glasses. He was hunched over a book, gnawing on a sandwich.

I ordered a bottle of Molson's Golden at the bar and went over to join the bookworm. The glasses covered intense hazel eyes. His hair was brown and shaggy, hanging down across a high forehead. The black crew-neck sweater he was wearing hung on his lanky frame like a graduation gown.

"Alan Betz?" I asked, taking a chair.

He stared at me for a moment, then dropped the sandwich onto the plate and wiped his hand on a paper napkin before offering it to me. "You must be Mr. Sheridan. I heard Jan talk about you so often, I feel like I already know you."

"You can drop the mister. Most people just call me Sheridan." I released his hand and glanced at the book he was reading. *Washington Goes to War*, by David Brinkley. I was expecting something arcane. "You using that in one of your classes?" I asked.

He smiled. "No, this is the last of my pleasure reading before the term begins. Actually, I feel a little guilty about it. I'm supposed to be home putting together the syllabi for my courses. If I don't get those in by tomorrow, Miss Witherspoon will have me drawn and quartered. I'm not the most organized—" He stopped, the smile receding into a sheepish grin. "I'm rambling, aren't I? I do that sometimes when I'm nervous. You want to know why I sent you those scraps of notes from Jan's files."

I nodded. "And why you included that list of names and occupations you so carefully typed up."

"How'd you know I did the list?"

"An educated guess. The professor was a pad and pen type of guy."

"That he was." Betz contemplated the sandwich for a moment, then sipped from his glass of beer. "This is a bit awkward to explain. It was just an impulse, really. I wanted someone . . . Let me start again." He picked up the sandwich and took a bite, chewing over his story along with the ham and cheese. "Okay, let me give you the chronology. First, do you know anything about the Fellowship?"

I nodded. "From what I can tell, it's sounds like a small-time, insular group of eggheads with delusions of grandeur."

Betz laughed. "Well put. That's what most of us who haven't been invited into the group believe. Except for Jan.

He didn't buy the idea that the Fellowship was merely an ego massage for Maurice DuPree and Liam Dougherty and a few others. He had this inkling, this intuition, that it had some other purpose. Of course, Jan was a crime and mystery nut."

"Did he have anything to back up his suspicions?"

"Not much. I mean, there's the fact that the Fellowship doesn't promote itself very hard in the academic community. And the board of governors is odd. You've got DuPree, of course, a millionaire French-Canadian businessman, and Mayor MacKenzie, who also handles DuPree's legal business on his U.S. holdings. Neither of them is particularly qualified to run a group that's supposed to be dedicated to academic achievement and international policy studies."

"Still, it sounds like an ego massage to me," I said. "A rich man trying to buy himself some prestige. He brings his attorney in to make sure all the tees are crossed."

Betz shrugged. "That could be, only the rest of the board doesn't add up, either. The only other board members are Dr. Stevenson, president of Clampett College, and Liam Dougherty, head of the literature department. Stevenson is a nice enough old guy, but he's no intellectual giant. He's been simply a small college administrator for the past thirty years. And Dougherty? A literature professor with radical Socialist leanings. What qualifies him for the board?"

I took a swallow of my ale and stared across the table. "Are you sure this doesn't have more to do with other people's egos? Your own, for example?"

Betz bristled. "I'm giving you Professor Janezek's impressions, not my own. Sure, I've maybe got an ax to grind with Dougherty. I don't like the way he manipulated Dr. Stevenson to keep me off the selection committee for Jan's replacement and I don't like his condescending attitude around me and the other junior faculty members. But I don't believe I've lost my objectivity, if that's what you think."

That's exactly what I thought, but I decided not to press

the point just then. "So Professor Janezek had doubts about the legitimacy of the Fellowship. How does that connect with Howard Johnson and the Castle House tragedy?"

"That's just it. I don't know that it does." Betz shook his head in frustration. "Look, last May Jan started researching local history from the 1930s for a book he wanted to write, an oral history of the Prohibition years. He did some preliminary work in local archives, then began doing interviews with some of the town's oldest citizens. That's when he met Howard Johnson and diverted his attention to the Castle House incident. Something about that tragedy back in 1937 caught his imagination. This was in late June, just a week or so before Jan left to attend the CHANA convention."

"He didn't tell you what piqued his interest?"

"He was very secretive. Most academics are. It's publish or perish in this business and some people aren't above stealing other people's ideas and research. We're all a little paranoid on that subject." As if to drive the point home, Betz leaned over the table and spoke with the hush of a priest in a confessional. "All he told me was that the Castle House incident had 'greater dimensions than anyone realized.' And that what happened out there fifty years ago just might—and I emphasize might—have a direct link to what's happening in Widows Cape today."

Betz sat back, looking quite pleased with himself. I was less sanguine. "And that's it? That's the whole basis for trying to entice me up here with a few scribbled notes?"

"That and the fact that Jan said he wanted to discuss his ideas with you at the convention before going any further. He did talk to you about Castle House, didn't he?"

"He mentioned it at a reception. Unfortunately, he was killed before we had a chance to get together again. I hope you're not leading up to the suggestion that the professor's mugging had some tie to his Castle House research."

"Probably not," Betz conceded. "But it was certainly a curious coincidence. Anyway, whether you or I agree, Jan believed he was onto something significant."

"What made you decide to bring me into it some two months after the fact?"

"Another curious circumstance." Betz swallowed the last of the sandwich and wiped his hands. "After Jan's death, I more or less put the whole business out of my mind. I was away most of the summer, working on my PhD. But then, in late August, I had a couple of days free before final dissertations, so I came back up to Widows Cape to attend a faculty meeting and to prepare my book list for the new semester. That's when Dr. Stevenson asked me to box up Jan's office files for shipment to his brother in Chicago. While I was doing that, I realized the files didn't contain any of his research on Castle House—just those couple of pages I found jammed into a desk drawer. So I checked with Dougherty, who was handling the same task at Jan's apartment. He claimed there weren't any such notes in Jan's home files, but I know he had to be lying. Jan was a meticulous researcher, Sheridan. There had to be notes somewhere."

"That doesn't mean Dougherty took them," I pointed out. "Maybe the notes were in the professor's office files and someone removed them before you got there."

"That's a possibility," Betz said. "But in either case, somebody has to have taken those notes. That was enough to convince me that Jan had been onto something big concerning Castle House, something someone else didn't want exposed. That's when I decided to send what little information I had to you. I know how much Jan respected your investigative skills."

"Why the Hardy Boys routine with the list of names? Why didn't you just write or call me and fill me in like you're doing now?"

"Because I'm not an investigative journalist and I wasn't sure if what I had was valid. I wanted to test the waters, see if the few fragments I had would be enough to convince a professional like yourself to drive up here and nose around. And it worked." He smiled. "You see, I made every effort to keep my own prejudices out of the process. I added the typed listing on Howard Johnson and the others mentioned in the notes so you'd have a reasonable place to start your own investigation."

I didn't say anything, just stared across the table. I suppose I hadn't expected to like Betz, let alone believe him. Instead, I found myself doing both. Maybe it was the earnest gaze behind those stolid wire rims, or perhaps just a reporter's instincts. Still, I wasn't yet ready to sign on for the duration.

"I'll give it a couple of days, shake a few trees and see what falls out," I said. "I may need some help."

Betz nodded eagerly. "Anything you need, provided I can squeeze it in between my duties at school. Which reminds me." He checked his watch, then fished out a pen and tiny pad from beneath the folds of his sweater. "I've gotta get back and finish those syllabi, but let me give you my home phone and address. If I'm not there, you can get me at the department offices most any time."

I assured Betz I'd be in touch, then watched him hurry off to his awaiting syllabi. Nothing particular was awaiting me that night, so I moved to a bar stool and ordered another bottle of ale. The three old gents had shuffled into the night a few minutes before, leaving only me, the bartender, and the dandy and his girl in the place. That number was reduced by two soon after the bartender set the fresh Molson's in front of me.

"Hey, what is this? I thought we had an understanding." The natty yachtsman was pushing off his stool, his windburned face turning several shades redder as he barked at the girl. "Goddamn mercenary's what you are, y'little bitch." He peeled off a couple of bills, tossed them down on the bar and made his way to the door, weaving unsteadily like a swabbie caught in a nor'easter.

The three of us watched him go, then the girl muttered, "Asshole," and took one of the bills off the bar. She winked at the bartender, hopped off her stool, and coolly strode out of the tavern, her narrow hips churning beneath the tight denim skirt.

"Lovers' spat?" I said to the bartender.

"Not hardly." He chuckled, the slash of mouth that peeked out from his heavy black beard stretching into a grin. The full beard and tiny diamond earring in his left lobe matched up well with Lord Jim's seafaring decor. Stick a parrot on his shoulder and he could play Robert Newton playing Long John Silver. "She's a working girl," he said.

"You're kidding. In this little town?"

"Hey, townies like sex too, y'know." He shook his head. "Seems like there's a new one every other year. College girls, mostly, lookin' to defray the high cost of tuition. This one here's real cute about it, got a business card and everything. Calls herself an escort service."

We were still schmoozing, the conversation having moved on to the pennant races, when the girl hurried back into the tavern. She glanced around the empty barroom, then slipped onto the stool next to me.

"Gimme a cooler," she said to the bartender. "And something for the gentleman."

"I'm all set," I said, hoisting the bottle of ale.

"What's your name?" she asked. She had a husky voice that contrasted sharply with her juvenile face and slender body. Her cornflower blue eyes seemed unfocused, anxious.

"Sheridan," I said after a moment's hesitation. "What's your name?"

The bartender brought over her bottle of wine cooler just then, giving her an excuse to ignore my query. "Do me a favor, huh? Act like I'm with you."

Before I had a chance to ask why, the door of the tavern swung open again and two men came in. Both were somewhere in their early thirties. One was medium height, slim, wearing a turtleneck sweater over gray cords. The other was short and stocky with close-cropped light brown hair. He wore jeans and a short-sleeved sweatshirt, the better to display his overdeveloped biceps. They crossed to the bar with the swagger of young men assured of their immortality. The taller of the pair ordered two Dewar's and water straight up, a French accent dripping like orange sauce from every word. His stocky compatriot leaned in next to the girl and appraised me with stone gray eyes.

"Had all your shots, have you, mate?" This one had an accent too, but it was more difficult to place. British Isles, certainly, with the harsh guttural inflections of the urban north. He laid his hand on the girl's shoulder. "Y'never know where this bit's been. Do we, now, Kara girl?"

"Be a good little mick, Des, and fuck off, huh?" The girl said. She winced as his hand began to squeeze her shoulder. I grabbed his wrist and yanked his arm away.

"Go play macho someplace else," I said.

"Cheeky bugger, you are," he said, grinning.

I was saved from having to respond by the Frenchman, who stepped in beside his stubby companion and, handing him a drink, said, "You are being unsocial again, mon ami. Let's take a table and leave pretty Kara to herself tonight, eh?"

The one called Des turned his dull stare to the girl and said, "Another time, girl." Then he followed the Frenchman to the same corner table Betz and I had used.

"You mind telling me what that was about?" I asked the girl. She was pale and I could still see the strain of fear in her eyes, but she was recovering fast. No more than twenty, I calculated, but already she'd developed the hard carapace of her trade. She smiled without emotion.

"Never sweat the small stuff, Sheridan," she said, pushing aside her untouched wine cooler. "How 'bout you do me another favor and walk me outa this dump."

"All right." I drank down the last of the Molson's and followed her out of the tavern, sneaking an admiring glance at the smooth tanned legs that seemed to extend forever below her abbreviated skirt. Out on the street, she swiveled abruptly, planted a platonic kiss on my cheek and muttered, "Thanks, I owe you one."

"You're welcome," I said, but I was talking to myself. The girl was already gone, clicking purposefully down the sidewalk on stiletto heels.

CHAPTER 10

THE sun and I rose at the same time the next morning, neither of us having any choice in the matter. The sun was a victim of the physical laws of the universe, while I was pulled from my bed by more elemental forces. In J-school they call them the Five W's; the who-what-when-where-why of a story. For anyone who'd cut his teeth in a newsroom, those few little words were as seductive as the call of the sirens who lured ancient mariners onto rocky shores.

An apt metaphor, I told myself as I stood in the feeble dawn light of the Clearview's parking lot and keyed open the Bronco's rear window. As I watched the window whir down, two men came out of the room next to mine, number nine, and stretched and yawned their way to a brown Dodge sedan parked in the next space. One was chunky and completely bald and wearing a sleepy grin. The other had coarse black hair barbered into a pageboy that had gone out of style back when the Beatles had grown moustaches. Curly and Moe go fishing, I told myself. Both men had on waterproof coveralls and pristine-looking Docksiders.

"Morning," I said.

Moe mumbled grumpily as he climbed into the pas-

71

senger seat of the Dodge. Curly turned up the wattage on the grin.

"Nothing like a little early troll upriver, huh?" he said amiably.

"Nothing like it," I agreed.

He got in behind the wheel and gunned the engine, spewing gravel as they drove out of the lot. Mustn't keep the fish waiting. I turned back to the Bronco and made a routine inspection of the fishing gear tucked away under an old olive drab army blanket—a rod and casting reel, tackle box, net, and stringer—and closed the window. Then I zipped my jacket high to ward off the early morning chill, hopped behind the wheel, and set off for River Street.

I had a lot on the agenda that day and probably not enough time to do it. Sometimes a story sees you coming and jumps all over you like a big sloppy Lab licking anyone who walks into the yard. But there weren't any public relations flacks salivating to hype Castle House or the Fellowship. That made this the second kind of assignment; the kind where you keep asking questions, any questions at all, until a few answers begin to coalesce into something resembling the truth.

So I would make the rounds and take notes and maybe upset an apple cart or two along the way. Then I'd make the rounds again. If Stefan Janezek had learned something worth knowing, I would find out what it was. But everything has a beginning, and this case began with a rich man's playhouse sitting on a chip of land surrounded by water.

Which is why I decided to start off an overcrowded day with a fishing trip.

"Forty for half a day, plus a two hundred dollar security deposit in cash or major plastic, refundable when you bring 'er back in one piece. Seventy for the whole day."

"I only need it for an hour or two."

"Half day's the minimum, no exceptions. If you don't have rules, you have anarchy."

The philosopher behind the rental counter only sounded like Descartes. What he looked like was a prosperous fiftyish store owner who'd made a quiet fortune selling lawn rakes to the locals and live bait to transients like me. He wore a navy cardigan over a starched flannel shirt and had whitewalls arcing over sunburned ears. I wondered fleetingly if he was related to Velda Fuller from the Clearview Motel or if they'd merely studied together at the Wharton School.

Seven-thirty was too early to haggle, even with the two cups of coffee and raspberry danish I'd stoked up on at the diner down the street. I surrendered my Visa card without a whimper. He read off the expiration date out loud, then checked the account number in a slim booklet he kept next to the cash register.

"Always best to err on the side of caution," he said when he finally got around to filling out the credit slip.

"Cogita ergo sum," I replied.

He was still mulling that over when I went out to the little quay that ran across the back of the store and connected up with the public dock. The boat in slip number seven was small and aluminum and had a nine-horse Evinrude troller clamped to its stern, nearly a twin of the one I had tied up outside my cottage. I loaded in my gear and got the motor running on the third pull, then cast off the bow and aft lines and nosed the boat around on a northwest heading.

Coffin Island was right where Howard Johnson had said it would be, the eastern tip lying about a half mile from the Widows Cape docks. According to the local lore I'd read up on at the library, the island was given its macabre name back in the earliest years of the original Cape Caledonia settlement. An influenza epidemic had swept through the town one winter, taking with it nearly a quarter of the population. Fearing further contamination, the survivors boxed up the bodies of the dead and hauled them across the ice to the nearest sizable island, figuring the river would act as a buffer. Coffin Island had earned its name.

A light fog was fast burning off the river as the sun rose higher. It would be one of those brilliant September days that sustained the people of the north country during the frozen Januaries to come. The small Evinrude purred confidently as I steered diagonally across the river's mild chop. The island loomed ahead like a cruising humpbacked whale, a pine-forested hillock at its center gradually tapering off to the east and west. As I closed within two hundred yards of the eastern end, I could make out the remains of the dairy farm Howard had mentioned—a once white frame house missing all its window glass and an imploded wreck of a barn surrounded by open meadow.

I maneuvered the boat to a spot about forty yards out from a small dilapidated dock and slipped the motor into neutral. Flipping open my tackle box, I took out a leather pouch and extracted from it a burnished brass spyglass. It was a handsome thing, handmade by my grandfather back in the twenties when he'd worked as a lens maker at Bausch and Lomb in Rochester. It had been a gift for my father, who later passed it on to me, a precious family heirloom from a lost time when skilled craftsmen took pride in making something that would last for generations.

I put the glass to my eye and scanned the abandoned farm. Wildflowers and weeds two feet high surrounded the house and barn. Rusted machinery dotted the meadow. On a slight rise just below the treeline at the edge of the farm proper, a small cemetery sat forgotten, its weathered headstones lying flat or canted at oblique angles as if trampled by Father Time.

I set aside the glass and took up my rod, baiting the hook with one of the minnows I'd ransomed back at the general store. I fed out some line off the back of the boat, then slipped the motor back in gear and slowly began trolling a parallel course west along the island's southern flank.

It took me half an hour to cover the three-quarter-mile trip. Part of the time was spent hauling in a middle-size bass. Another five minutes was lost when something large and predatory—most likely a northern or a walleye—

ripped off bait, hook, sinker, and leader with a single chomp. When I wasn't busy playing sportsman, I watched the island slip by. There wasn't much to see; just a narrow dirt road running along the lip of the pine forest before disappearing into a copse of maples.

I cut the motor and reached for the spyglass when I was about fifty yards out from the western terminus of the island. A few thousand years of erosion had carved a bite out of the shoreline, creating a partially sheltered cove that had been bolstered with a loose rock jetty that angled off from the southern point. A dock with half a dozen slips formed a T at the base of the cove. Some hundred yards beyond it, sitting on a slight rise and surrounded by a bowl of sugar maples, was the mansion: Castle House.

"Jesus, Mary, and Joseph," I mumbled, mentally calculating what it must've cost Maurice DuPree to reconstruct a layout like that.

The house was a sprawling two-and-a-half-story Tudor adaptation with wood-shingled walls soaring above the first floor's stuccoed exterior. Tall multipaned casement windows and a series of hipped-roof dormers helped to break up the mass of the place. A flagstone walkway curved gracefully from the main entrance down to a terrace overlooking the dock and the single boat that was tied up there. From where I sat, the whole grand pile looked as lifeless as the old graveyard at the other end of the island.

I shaded my eyes and searched up and down the river. There was a sailboat tacking across the main shipping channel some two hundred yards to my left and, beyond that, a pair of powerboats drifting lazily through the feeding beds along the southern flank of huge Wolfe Island. Nothing ventured, nothing gained, I told myself as I pulled in the dead minnow at the end of my line and restarted the motor.

I came in around the end of the jetty and berthed the rental boat catty-corner to the dock's only other occupant, a beautifully restored Dart inboard, its wooden hull gleaming with a dozen coats of varnish. I was still admiring the sleek launch as I tied off the skiff on a metal cleat and hoisted myself onto the dock. That explains why I didn't spot the dogs.

There were two of them, rangy Dobermans, grinning devilishly through pointy yellow teeth. They had arrived silently and stood poised on the weathered cedar decking about halfway between me and the foot of the dock.

"Good boys," I soothed, turning slowly. They didn't like that. The one on the left padded closer and growled, while the one on the right let out a shrill howl.

"Easy now. Nice doggies. No harm, no foul."

I continued mumbling gibberish for a century or two while the one mutt eyed my throat as if it was steak tartare and his twin kept up the staccato barking. My boat was tied up only a few feet behind me, but I didn't like my chances. Even if I somehow managed to jump into it, I'd never get the painter untied before Himmler and Göring chewed my face off. I was toying with the notion of diving to my left, hoping I could make it over the width of the Dart and into the water in one leap, when a man in an electric golf cart cruised down the stone pathway that led from the copse of maples. He hopped off the cart and came up onto the dock. It was the stubby hard case who had hassled the girl at Lord Jim's the night before, but I was too relieved to care.

"Cease, Arabelle!" He gave the order laconically, but the yapping dog shut up. "Peppy, hold! Arabelle, patrol!"

The one that had been measuring my jugular sat back on its haunches and stared at me, while the other one turned and trotted off toward the house. Their master—Kara had called him Des—ambled up the dock like a block of ice and peered over the edge at my rental boat.

"You're trespassin', boyo," he said in that hard accent. The girl had also called him a mick, but he didn't sound much like Barry Fitzgerald to me.

"My name's Sheridan. I'm a writer," I said. I began to turn, but Peppy the Wonderdog changed my mind for me with a low growl. "I just stopped by to see if I could get a look at the Castle House for a piece I'm working on—"

76

"This isn't bloody Disneyland and I'm no fuggin' tour guide." His voice was as flat and calm as the river.

"I just thought—"

"That's your problem, mister. You think too much. Like last night, with the girl. Thinkin' you can order people about." He bent over and untied the painter from the cleat and tossed it down into the skiff.

"Your boat's leavin' without you," he said.

"Look, Desmond. It is Desmond, isn't it?"

"If it was me, I'd be thinkin' about how fast I could move my arse off this dock." He forced a smile, exposing a ragged row of teeth that were only slightly dingier than the dog's.

I tried again. "Where's that legendary Irish hospitality my mother always told me about?"

He tucked the smile away. "You're wastin' my valuable time. Peppy! Cut!"

The Doberman and I moved at the same time, but I had fear on my side. I swear I could feel the dog's breath on the back of my neck as I cleared the end of the dock. I hit the water head first and came up shivering. The St. Lawrence has only two temperatures, cold and frozen. It took a moment to reorient myself. The rental boat was drifting a few yards to my right. Above me, staring down from the dock like a couple of malevolent gargoyles, were Desmond and Peppy.

"Don't be a stranger," Desmond called out cheerily, then began cackling.

I got myself turned around and set a plodding course for my boat. Doing a dog paddle, naturally.

CHAPTER 11

THE route inland from Widows Cape to Watertown is a dull twenty-mile mono-crome of gray secondary roads, stubbled fields, and the listing carcasses of old hay barns. The soil is mostly poor and thin and flinty, like the few dairy farmers who still try to scratch out a living on it. The landscape is as flat as a dead man's EKG.

The Bronco rolled over the narrow county roads effortlessly while I hummed along with the radio, determined to put Desmond and his friends out of mind. It wasn't easy. Just as I'd think I had myself focused on the task at hand, the anger would come back. I'd feel the frigid river soaking my pores and shiver. Then I'd picture Peppy's ugly snarl and I'd shiver again and I'd think about getting even. But then reason would seep back into my head and I'd realize I'd probably gotten off cheap considering. I had been trespassing, after all; the animals were only doing the job they'd been trained for—Desmond included. The question was, why would the Fellowship employ a cold-blooded lump like him in the first place?

I'd been mulling that one over since the sodden ride from the docks back to my motel room, but hadn't come up with an answer. By the time I'd taken a steaming hot shower to drive the chill out of my bones and changed into dry clothes, it was after ten, the morning half gone and a crowded schedule ahead. I had called Judge Dunleavy's secretary at the municipal building. The judge was out, but he had anticipated my call, instructing his secretary to schedule an interview over lunch at the St. Lawrence Club the next day.

After the call, I had driven over to the library to see Rita. She volunteered to phone a friend at the main library in Watertown to inquire if the materials I wanted were on hand. Then she agreed to have dinner with me that night. I figured I could take care of my business in Watertown and be back in Widows Cape by two, leaving me time to stop by the Riverside Nursing Home for a follow-up with Howard Johnson. Then maybe I'd contact Betz and see if I could pass along to him some of the legwork.

Busy, busy. But at least there was a light at the end of the tunnel. By seven-thirty that evening I'd be ensconced at a table for two with lovely Rita. I smiled at the thought as I negotiated the Bronco through a bend in the road.

Watertown's Flower Memorial Library was a handsome two-story marble affair with a domed roof and two carved lions guarding the entrance. According to the plaque on the door, it had been named after a nineteenth century politician with a decidedly Dickensian name: Roswell Pettibone Flower.

A puckish matron in a maroon dress met me at the front desk and, with a wink and a nod at mention of Rita Tonelli, led me to a quiet corner where a microfiche machine and several canistered spools of film were waiting. I laid out my notebook and pen and loaded a spool into the machine. It contained back issues of the *Watertown Times* from January through March of 1938. The story I was most interested in led off the January 2 edition. The banner headline screamed from the page like a carnival barker, proving that shock-and-shlock journalism hadn't been invented by Rupert Murdoch and the *New York Post*.

POSH PARTIERS PERISH IN ISLAND INFERNO

Lumberman Ernest Castle, 18 others murdered at New Year's Gala; Killers meet justice in watery grave; Robbery the motive, police say

Just below the lengthy subheads came the byline, shared by Harrison VanKuyper and Sanford Johnson. The reporters proved to be less hyperbolic than the copy editor who had written the headlines. The story was written in the standard inverted pyramid style employed in journalism since the Civil War; key facts bunched in the lead paragraphs, followed by a string of quotes from the chief investigator, Captain Lester Tinderlay of the state police, and continuing in descending order of importance to the last graph, where tentative funeral arrangements were noted.

The newspaper account backed up the story Howard Johnson had told me; the bodies of Ernest Castle, seventeen guests, and the caretaker Tommy Trevain found in the wine cellar, Trevain's body showing a bullet wound to the head. The name of the suspected killer, Jack Rose, scratched onto a foundation stone in the cellar. The hole out in the channel ice where, it was presumed by police, Rose and his "gang" had met their just desserts. About two-thirds of the way into the story, the reporters had included a one-graph bio on Rose, describing him as a local ne'er-do-well who once had served thirty months in Dannemora for stealing a truckload of antique furniture from a downstate dealer.

I read through the piece a second time, taking notes on a few points Howard hadn't covered. A list of the guests who had died in the fire, including the Spicer sisters, who received a paragraph of their own owing to their local connection. A reference to the valiant but unsuccessful efforts to put out the blaze by the Widows Cape volunteer firefighters and their chief, Manfred Porter. Special mention was given to four young men who had been first to arrive at the scene and had tried to enter the house to search for survivors, but had been driven back by the flames. The four were Marshall Stewart, Robert Burns Dunleavy, James C. Knox, Jr., and Angus MacKenzie.

I continued on, scanning the follow-up stories that dominated the newspaper's front pages for the first week of 1938. There wasn't much substance to the later stories, just more of the same, but I kept on reading. My instincts told me that something was missing, something to do with what Howard Johnson had said during our interview. Then I found it in a piece datelined January 5. A name: Emily Trevain, daughter of the caretaker. Howard had told me that both Trevains had been commandeered by Castle to work the party. And yet, the daughter hadn't been among those who had died. According to the short article, Emily Trevain had told police she had indeed been at the party earlier, preparing food and helping her father set up the bar. But she had been ill with a fever and Castle, not wishing to expose his guests, had sent her home to the farmhouse around ten o'clock. She claimed she was in her bed asleep from ten-thirty until about one o'clock in the morning, when police investigators arrived at the farm to question her.

The article went on to quote Captain Lester Tinderlay of the state police, who said Miss Trevain's questioning was routine and that she was not considered a suspect. Tinderlay added that a known associate of Jack Rose's, John Cawley of Alexandria Bay, had not been located despite an extensive manhunt by members of the New York State Police and the Royal Canadian Mounted Police. An unnamed police source said that Rose and Cawley are presumed to have drowned while attempting to flee to Canada from Coffin Island.

I quickly scanned the rest of the spool, finding nothing more of interest. Then I spent another hour going through the other spools of microfilm I'd requested, the dates ranging from the early thirties to the mid-sixties. The results were meager: a short article from 1933 detailing the arrest of Jack Rose for grand theft, followed a few weeks later by a still shorter piece covering his trial and sentencing. The only other useful clip was from thirty years later, August of 1963. A lightweight human interest piece on the discovery by two scuba divers of a body in a battered car submerged a few hundred feet off Birdsnest Island. The article said police were satisfied that the car had been used in the Castle House robbery and that the body was that of Big John Cawley, verifying Howard Johnson's account again.

Satisfied that I'd found all there was to find, I packed up the tools of my trade, returned the film canisters to the front desk, and asked for directions to the state police barracks.

"Excuse me," I said to the tall, gray-uniformed figure behind the reception counter. I don't know what the height requirement is for troopers, but I had yet to see one who was under six feet, including this one, who was female. "I'm interested in reviewing some old police reports."

The phone rang just then and she held up her hand. She put the phone to her ear with the other hand and said, "State police, may I help you?"

I glanced around the reception area while I waited. The building was a modernish, single-story structure of beige brick and smoked glass. From the outside, it resembled a small elementary school. The inside had the ambience and hush of a dentist's office.

"I'll have to check the duty roster, ma'am, hold on," the trooper told the caller, then she glanced up at me. "What was that you wanted, sir?" she asked as she began thumbing through a looseleaf binder.

"I'm interested in reviewing an old case file," I said again. "The investigator was a Captain Lester Tinderlay."

"Just a second, sir." She spoke into the phone. "Ma'am? Yes, he's due in at five. Yes. You're welcome." She recradled the phone. "Okay. Did you say Lester Tinderlay, sir?"

"Yes."

"Okay." She picked up the phone again, depressed a button, and punched in three numbers. "Les, someone to see you," she said. "He'll be right out," she said to me when she rang off.

I gawked at her. "He's still around?"

"Of course," she said, "Day shift doesn't go off duty until five o'clock."

I started to do some quick mental calculations. Let's see, if this guy was old enough to be a captain in the state police in 1937, then today he'd have to be, what? Eighty, ninety years old? Then a door behind the reception counter opened and a tall pudgy trooper strolled in, sipping from a Styrofoam cup. The black name tag on his left breast pocket read Sgt. L. Tinderlay. Only the tiny crowsfeet around the eyes suggested he was a day over thirty.

"Hi," the big man said amiably as he came around the counter. "You're looking for me?"

"Actually, I think I was looking for your grandfather. A Captain Lester Tinderlay, circa 1937?"

This Tinderlay had one of those open, friendly faces that you don't often see these days, particularly on lawmen. But the fleshy features took on new shadings at the mention of Tinderlay the Elder.

"Grampa? Geez, he's been gone for, what? Close to twenty years now. What's my—?" Sgt. Tinderlay looked over at the other trooper, who was scrutinizing her three-ring binder. "You wanna take five, Darla, grab a cup of coffee while I take care of this gentleman? I'll watch the desk."

Darla said, "Sure, Les, thanks," then hiked up her Sam Browne belt and disappeared into the back.

Tinderlay pivoted back to me. "This has something to do with that old Castle House case, doesn't it."

It wasn't really a question, but I nodded anyway. "My name's Sheridan. I'm a writer, researching a story on the case. I learned your grandfather was in charge of the investigation from some old marshal's files in Widows Cape. I was hoping to review the official files here—"

Tinderlay shook his head. "Grampa was always gabbing about that case. Y'know, you're the second guy I've had in here in the last few months asking about it."

"The other guy being Professor Stefan Janezek?"

"Yeah. Did you know the professor?"

"We were pen pals, you might say. He's the one who got me interested in the story."

"He was a nice guy," Tinderlay said solemnly. "I had him for a class once at the junior college while I was in the criminal justice program. He did some moonlighting over there during evening sessions. A shame what happened to him down in Washington."

I nodded in agreement. "I'm trying to follow up on some unfinished business the professor left behind. You think you can help me out with a look at your grandfather's old case files on Castle House?"

"I would if I could, Mr. Sheridan, but my hands are kinda tied." He heaved his broad, rounded shoulders. "It's like this. Those files only exist on computer down in Albany. Now, the way you have to do it is, you send a written request to state HQ down there, telling 'em what you're interested in, and you pay a small clerical fee and eventually they'll send you a hard copy of the file."

"How long will all that take?"

"Oh, probably six to ten weeks. I know it's a pain in the butt, but that's the procedure."

"Why do I have a nagging suspicion that you found a way around official procedures for the professor?"

Tinderlay reddened. "I guess that's why I haven't followed my grandfather into criminal investigation. My wife says I'm about as transparent as a pane of glass." He lowered his voice. "Look, I did Professor Jan a favor and accessed that old file for him, ran off a copy even. But the captain found out about it and read me the riot act. He's a by-the-book guy. If I pull another stunt like that, I'm looking at a suspension."

"I wouldn't want that," I said, thinking out my options. "Listen, you must've read the file when you printed it for Professor Janezek. Maybe you can hit up the highlights for me."

"Sorry, but I didn't pay much attention. Once I got it on line from Albany, I just let the printer spit it out and I tore it off page by page—about a dozen sheets—and gave it to the professor." He shrugged. "After hearing my grandfather go on about the case, I guess I just wasn't that curious anymore. Anyway, there wouldn't be much in the files that could throw any new light on the case. It wasn't any great mystery. Open and shut really. The killers, Rose and Cawley, met up with justice at the bottom of the river."

"When your grandfather used to talk about it, what did he say? Like, did he have any pet theories?"

"Well, he was satisfied that Jack Rose had pulled the job, probably with Big John Cawley. Then, back in the early sixties, when that old car was pulled out of the river—you know about that?" I indicated that I did and Tinderlay went on. "Well, that's when they found Cawley's remains, so that was pretty conclusive. Grampa was still alive then and I can remember him saying the new evidence fit with his original conclusions. There was one thing, though, that always nagged him about the case."

"What was that?"

"The caretaker's daughter, Emily Trevain. Grampa always maintained that her story didn't ring true. He half believed she was involved somehow. He picked up hearsay during the investigation, that the girl might've been seeing Jack Rose on the sly. Just gossip, though. He never was able to prove it and the department officially closed the investigation before he could go any farther with it."

"He was pressured to lay off Emily Trevain?"

"Oh, I don't think so, nothing like that. The pressure was just to close the case. Run with the obvious conclusion—that Rose and Cawley acted on their own—and get the thing off the books as solved."

"Is Emily Trevain still around, do you know?"

"No, she died back in the sixties, I think."

"Another dead end," I said, half to myself.

"Yeah, there aren't too many people around who'd still remember a case that old. Professor Janezek was having a hard time, too." Tinderlay's cherub face brightened. "There is one old-timer who might be a help to you, a guy named Johnson. I told the professor about him, but I don't know if he got around to talking with him."

"Howard Johnson? Yeah, I've seen him already."

"No, I mean Sonny Johnson. Actually, Sanford Johnson, but grampa always called him Sonny."

The name struck a chord. "I saw that name somewhere recently," I said.

"Probably in a byline in the old newspaper accounts," Tinderlay said. "Sanford Johnson was a stringer with the *Watertown Times* back in the old days. He was the first reporter on the story. Lives in a little house at Miller's Bay, a few miles west of Widows Cape."

CHAPTER 12

I WAS running behind schedule by the time I left the state police barracks and headed back to Widows Cape to see Howard Johnson. I didn't have a lot to show for my half-day sojourn to Watertown; a few bits and pieces from old news clips, a new name to follow up—Sanford Johnson—and a question mark penned in beside another name: Emily Trevain.

But, if nothing else, I had established one fact. Professor Janezek had received a twelve-page computer printout on the original Castle House investigation from Sgt. Lester Tinderlay, but the printout hadn't turned up in either the professor's office or home files. Which meant somebody had gotten to the files before Betz and Dougherty. Or, as Betz contended, Dougherty was lying when he claimed he hadn't found any research notes when he boxed up Janezek's papers. Of the two options, I was leaning heavily toward the latter, but the question was why? What did Liam Dougherty have to gain by stealing the file? Or what did he stand to lose if the file had been allowed to come to light?

I made it to the Riverside by two-thirty and parked beside a converted van with a hydraulic wheelchair lift adapted to its side door. The woman at the reception desk remembered me from my previous visit, which may explain why she wasn't smiling. When I asked to see Howard, she tut-tutted, said that wasn't possible and explained that "poor Mr. Johnson suffered a mild cardial episode this morning" and was confined to his bed. I asked for details, but she said Dr. Knox was the only one who could release medical information, so I asked to see him.

"Dr. Knox is somewhere on the grounds," she allowed. "I'd have to page him."

"That's fine with me."

"You're not a relative of Mr. Johnson's. The director may not be willing to discuss this with a nonrelation."

"I'll take the risk," I said.

We danced around for a couple more minutes until she grudgingly agreed to page his eminence while I waited in his office. I passed another five minutes perusing the Hudson River School prints in Knox's office before he showed up.

"Back again, Mr. Sheridan," he said evenly as he settled in behind his desk and picked up the phone. "Coffee, tea, soft drink?" When I shook my head no, he punched the phone's intercom button and said, "Pot of tea for one, Paula, thank you." Knox recradled the phone and waved me into an Eastlake side chair.

"Another hectic day in the health care profession," he said lightly. "Haven't had a minute to myself since ten A.M. rounds." It didn't show. He looked as fresh and sharp as the crease in his gray flannel slacks.

I said, "I hear Howard had a rough morning, too."

"Mm, more chest pains. A warning from Mother Nature, I'm afraid. Not uncommon with chronic pulmonary disease cases. The heart becomes overstressed over the years, working double duty to supply the damaged lungs."

"Can't you do something?"

Knox shook his head. "In his state, major surgery is a greater risk than simply controlling his disease with medication."

"How long does he have, doctor?"

88

"A day, a week, a year." He turned up his palms. "There's no way of knowing. To put it simply and crudely, Mr. Sheridan, Howard Johnson's body is worn out, like the old family station wagon."

"You can always do a valve job on the old family station wagon," I argued.

"Not if the pistons are shot and the engine mounts have corroded away." Knox smiled, not unkindly. "Look, Mr. Sheridan, we have a whole host of Howard Johnsons at this facility. They don't come here to get well, they come here to get by. As comfortably and with as much dignity as we can provide. And we're damned good providers, if I do say so myself. This is no underfunded state home. We're a fully staffed private care institution. My father set high standards for our clients when he founded this facility and I've tried to uphold those standards."

"I'd say you've upheld them quite well." Although I doubted the old man referred to his patients as clients. "It has to be expensive."

"Quality care doesn't come cheap," he said, sounding a shade defensive. "Obviously, the Riverside's clients and their families are willing to pay the price."

Willing and able, I thought to myself. Which begged another question, this one less obvious. "So how does an old merchant marine get into a place like this with only Medicare and a forty-year-old disability pension to cover him?"

The good doctor blanched. "Howard has some additional financial support beyond his pension," he said after a pause.

"Family?"

Knox shook that off. "He has no living relatives."

"Then what 'additional financial support' are you referring to, doctor?"

"That's privileged information. It wouldn't be ethical for me to discuss a client's financial affairs."

"I can ask Howard. I don't think he's into ethics."

"That wouldn't be very kind of you," Knox said acidly, then exhaled. "Look, Mr. Johnson's fees here are supplemented by a local charity. When he first applied for admission some years ago, it was obvious he couldn't afford the Riverside on his own. But he had this strong desire to come back to his hometown for the remaining years of his life and the letters he kept sending moved my father. He decided to help him, one hometown boy to another, so he arranged to have the Stewart Fund underwrite Howard's expenses. I'm not even sure Howard knows the details, which is why I say it would be cruel of you to bring it up."

"Understood," I said. I took out my notepad and flipped through a few pages. "The Stewart Fund, you said. Would that have any connection to a Marshall Stewart?"

"Well . . . yes, actually. It's named after him."

I looked up from my notes. "Is this the same Marshall Stewart that was first on the scene at the Castle House fire, along with your father, Robert Dunleavy, and Angus MacKenzie?"

"Yes, it is. He—" Knox was interrupted by the arrival of his receptionist with a pot of tea. She poured for him, then examined me critically before speaking.

"We may have a slight problem developing on B wing, Dr. Knox," she said, frowning. "Howard Johnson heard through the jungle telegraph that Mr. Sheridan was here to see him. I suspect Mrs. Grassly passed the word. She was idling near the reception area when Mr. Sheridan came in."

"Damn," Knox muttered, then sipped carefully from the steaming teacup. "I suppose he's making a fuss now."

"To put it mildly," the receptionist said. "He's demanding that Mr. Sheridan be sent along to his room. I just thought you should know."

"Yes, thank you, Paula. You'd better go tell him Mr. Sheridan will be along to see him presently." Knox watched her leave, then zeroed in on me with a look that was finally beginning to show the ravages of a hectic day.

"I wasn't planning on letting you see Howard at all today, considering his condition," he said. "But I find myself having to choose between a short visitation or an extended temper tantrum. A short visitation appears to hold the lesser health risk. But I emphasize the word short."

"I'll keep it low-key, doctor," I assured him. "I only have a few questions. Shouldn't take more than fifteen minutes."

"Ten. Please."

"All right." I started up from the chair, then sat back. "One more thing. This Stewart Fund."

"What about it?"

"It sounds admirable. What other sorts of good works does it do, besides underwriting an old sea dog's nursing home expenses?"

"Well, really, there's a host of things. The fund pays the utility bills for a few of our older citizens living on fixed incomes. It provides an annual scholarship to Clampett College for one of our deserving high school seniors. Last year it made a sizable donation to the fire department's fund drive for a new ambulance."

"Where does the fund get its funds?"

"Many of the town's more affluent citizens contribute to it. But the core financial support comes from a trust set up many years ago by Marshall Stewart's parents and the Dunleavy family. The Stewarts and the Dunleavys were close. The aristocracy of Widows Cape, you might say. Unfortunately, Marshall was the last of the Stewarts and he died very young."

"How did he die?" I asked.

Knox didn't answer right away. Instead, he made a production out of pouring himself more tea.

"Why so curious about Marshall Stewart, Mr. Sheridan?" he said after a moment.

I shrugged. "I'm interested in all the people who were on the scene the night of the Castle House tragedy. You never know what bits of information will turn out to be useful when you're trying to piece together an article."

"I suppose," Knox conceded skeptically. "Well, to answer your question, Marshall Stewart died in a hunting accident. He was out alone. Tripped and fell on his shotgun, which went off. That's all I know. It happened several years before I was born. Spring, 1938, I think."

"Just a few months after the Castle House fire?"

"Mm, yes. I guess it would've been."

CHAPTER 13

HOWARD'S room resembled single occupancy at a Holiday Inn. Everything was done in earth-tones of burnt orange and umber with dashes of forest green and yellow. The entrance door was flanked by a small bathroom on the right and a large walk-in closet on the left. A couple of vinyl barrel chairs surrounded a stubby round table and a lowslung dresser hugged one of the walls. A Zenith television was perched on a tripod stand in the corner. Just about what a road-weary salesman would expect to find, with the exception of the bed. It was one of those motorized, adjustable behemoths that people like Monty Hall pitch on late-night TV.

Howard didn't look that much worse for wear, but it wasn't easy to tell with someone who had started out in such bad shape. Spotting new lines of deterioration on that wasted face was like trying to pick out fresh graffiti on a New York subway car. The only giveaways were the thin plastic tubes that ran from his nose to a portable oxygen unit beside the bed, and a harsh blueness in his lips.

"It's about goddamn time they let you in," he croaked at me. "Thought I's gonna have to raise holy hell."

The mattress had him propped up at a forty-five-degree angle, a copy of the *Thousand Islander* and a couple of news magazines splayed across his lap. I parked myself gingerly on the edge of the bed and tried to smile away my concern.

"You look pretty good, considering," I said. "How do you feel?"

"Like somethin' you'd step in at a dog show." His breathing was heavy and moist and seemed to pound at his chest like rolling surf.

"I can come back tomorrow."

He snickered, a humorless glint in his eye. "Better stow that notion, Sheridan. Tomorrows ain't a sure thing with me and I got things need to be said."

"Okay," I said, shifting around on the slippery sheet. "But we'll take it slow and easy."

"Like I got a choice? Shit." He inhaled another wave of oxygen and started in.

"It's got to do with Jack Rose and the Castle House heist. Somethin' I never told no one, not even Janezek. I woulda probably told him, but then he got himself killed. I'm tellin' it to you because I think I can trust you, boy. Don't have enough time left not to trust you. But first we gotta have an understanding."

"I'm listening."

"I got a notion that all the loot took off Castle and his fancy friends didn't end up in the St. Lawrence with Jack and Big John Cawley." He read the skepticism in my face and held up a knobby paw. "I got some strong facts to back me up and I'll give 'em to you. But first you gotta give me your word. That any treasure you come up with, I get a fair split. You gimme your word on that?"

"I do," I said solemnly. I figured Howard's fixation on treasure was pointless, but also harmless—an old pirate fantasizing about the what-might've-beens.

"One more thing," he said, dropping the raised hand back down to the sheet. "In case I kick off before you find the loot."

I thought about laying on the usual well-intended bull, telling him he was a tough old coot who'd most likely outlive us all. But then I glanced down at the hand and saw more of the blue discoloration around the fingernails. Cyanosis. I remembered first hearing the term from a pathologist, who said it occurred when the blood suffered from chronic oxygen deprivation. Howard Johnson would be lucky to outlive his next chest cold, and we both knew it.

"Anything I can do," I said.

"It's like this. I got a plot out to the town cemetery bought and paid for. Had Doc Knox pick me out a little spot on a hilltop. What I need is for someone to see I get done up proper by the undertaker. And then there's this here." He leaned to his left and pulled a glossy four-color brochure from under a stack of old newspapers on the bedstand.

"Take a look," he said, handing me the brochure. "The one I want is marked."

I spread open the fan-folds and skimmed over the slick photos. Caskets. Every manner and form of casket, from a basic pine economy model to a child-size aluminum and steel number to the top of the line, a carved mahogany jewel box with brass corner braces, felt stays, and satin lining. It was called the Monticello, and it had been circled with a red marking pen. The price listed below the photo was more than I had paid for my first two cars.

"It's impressive, Howard," I said.

"You think I'm nuts, right? Too damn much money for a thing that's gonna end up buried in the ground, am I right?"

"Well—"

"You remember me tellin' you about bein' torpedoed into the Atlantic back in the war?"

I nodded.

"Well, I'm still livin' that day, Sheridan, right here." He tapped the side of his head. "Still smell the diesel fuel and the blood floatin' on the water, still feel the hot metal burnin' into my legs. Phantom pain, the quacks all tell me, but it's real enough to me. But you know what I remember most of all?"

94

I waited through another long, ragged intake of breath. "It's the god-awful cold," he continued. "That icy green sea creepin' into my bones happened over forty years ago, but I'm still shiverin'. And I made myself a vow. No damn burial at sea for me, and no chintzy pauper's grave, either. I'm figurin' to spend eternity high and dry, all cozied up in the best coffin money can buy." He paused, the gaunt face coloring slightly. "Anyway, that's how I always figured I'd do it, if I could come up with the cash. That's how come I'm tellin' you about the Castle House loot."

"What about the Castle House loot, Howard?"

He appraised me with that milky blue orb. "What I'm gonna tell you, you can write it up any way you want after I'm gone. But in the meantime, I don't want you usin' my name in any stories, like they do in the papers. This is off the record."

"Not for attribution," I said, nodding my agreement.

"Right." Howard nestled down into a more agreeable position and started his tale off with the punchline. "I got reason to believe Jack Rose left his share of the haul with Emily Trevain the night of the robbery. And I don't think Emily ever did nothin' with it, 'cept probably stash it out at that old farm somewhere."

"What makes you think—"

"Let me tell it!" he snapped at me. "First off, most people never knew about Jack and Emily, but I was one of the few that did." His voice softened. "They were sweethearts."

I kept my mouth shut and listened, my notepad propped on my knee, as Howard slowly related the story of Jack and Emily. She was a quiet young woman that most men would've called plain. A wallflower whose father had taken her out of school in the eighth grade so that she could take care of him and the farmhouse on Coffin Island. Her few contacts with the mainland were mostly limited to the twice-weekly trips over to buy groceries and to sell her homebaked berry pies to the tourist homes. Oftentimes, she was accompanied by her taciturn father, Tommy, but occasionally she made the trip on her own. That was how she met and fell in love with a local outlaw named Jack Rose.

Howard didn't know the particulars of how they had first met. Down at the public docks, maybe. Emily struggling to unload a stack of pies from her little boat, Jack Rose happening along to lend a hand. However it had started they began meeting secretly whenever the opportunity presented itself. Afternoon trysts at Jack's shack whenever Emily came to town alone. Moonlit assignations in the maple grove out on the island. According to Howard, only a few close friends of Jack's were ever let in on the affair. Tommy Trevain was a selfish man who wanted to keep his daughter chained to her chores, cooking and cleaning for him out at the little island farm. And, even if Tommy hadn't been so petty, Jack Rose, with his muddied reputation, was the last man Trevain would let court his daughter.

"Anyway, that's how old Jack got the idea about Castle's New Year's Eve party," Howard rasped. He was breathing easier now despite the effort of telling his story, the memories seeming to calm him. "Emily give him all the skinny on the shindig. I imagine he wheedled it outa her, tellin' her how this was their chance to make a big score, get her away from her old man once and for all."

"Excuse me, Howard," I interrupted. "But just how do you know all this?"

"Jack told me himself, that's how." The old pirate smirked. "Jack come to me first, y'see, askin' did I want in on the heist. Hell, I wasn't no angel, Sheridan. I done my share of bootleggin', even boasted a few boats with Jack now and again. You gotta understand, times were tough in those days. But, still, I had to draw the line at armed robbery and I told Jack so. That's how he ended up with that murderin' moron, Big John Cawley, backin' him up."

It took me a moment to absorb the implications of what Howard was telling me, and the cavalier manner in which he told it. Nineteen people had died as a result of a robbery that Howard might've prevented had he blown the whistle on Rose's scheme. Still, I suppose it was a little like expecting an Indian to feel bad about Little Big Horn.

"Anyhow," Howard went on enthusiastically, "Jack laid out the whole plan for me when he tried to sell me on it. Emily—Emmy, he called her—she was supposed to make up an excuse to leave the party and then let us in through the kitchen on her way out, timed so everybody'd be out to the dining room for the big buffet at ten o'clock. We take all the jewelry and loose cash, lock everybody in the cellar, and hightail for Canada. But here's the interestin' part." He gave me that solo squint of his, just to make sure I was paying attention.

"Jack didn't want no one tumblin' to the fact that Emmy was in on the job. He wanted to protect her, see, if anything went wrong. But he had another reason for keepin' her out of it. As Jack told it, he was plannin' to drop off the take with Emmy—all but the cash—before headin' across to Canada."

"Why would he do that?"

Howard tapped a finger against the side of his head. "He was always thinkin', that Jack. He figured the valuables were better off stayin' right there on the island while he was off givin' the Canadian Mounties and the troopers and everybody a merry chase. Anyway, he didn't have no place to fence the stuff in Canada. Then there was the girl. Jack really did care for Emmy. I guess maybe he wanted to prove to her he'd really come back for her after the heat was off, like he said he would."

I started kicking it over, deciding that perhaps the old pirate wasn't as senile as I'd first thought, when a caution light blinked on in my brain.

"What about the wreck they found in the river back in the sixties?" I said. "Some of the stolen items were found in the car."

Howard dismissed that with a wave. "I figured that one out a long time ago. Cawley was stupid and greedy. Chances are, Big John didn't trust Jack, wouldn't leave his split with the girl, so Jack lets him take his share with them."

"That brings us back to the girl," I said. "If your version of events is true, then Emily Trevain was left sitting with a load of stolen jewelry, waiting for her lover to come get her. Only Rose wasn't going to come back and she had to know it. And her father was dead, too. The logical thing for her to have done would've been to sit tight for a while, then take off for parts unknown, using the valuables Jack left behind to start a new life somewhere."

Howard shook his head. "You'd think so. That's what you and me would do, sure. But we're talkin' about a backward sort of a girl here. No tellin' how her mind was workin', but the fact is, Emily Trevain never moved off that island." He sighed, his lungs bubbling ominously, and dropped his voice to a whisper. "Poor little Emmy froze to death in her bed at the farmhouse in the winter of '67. The way I heard it, she come down sick with pneumonia, didn't have nobody to take care of her. By the time anybody in town got to missin' her and went out to the island to check up on her, she was long gone."

CHAPTER 14

SERENITY is a small college campus a week before the fall semester begins.

The parking lots and bike racks were all but empty, the looming oaks that lined the streets hinted at the brilliant palette of color that would come in the next month, and the clusters of brick buildings sat silently on the lawns like so many merchant ships becalmed on a still, green sea.

I parked near the library and followed a winding sidewalk across a broad commons, pausing in front of a bronze statue of Josiah Elwood Clampett, the school's founder. He looked forlorn standing there on his granite perch, but then years of oxidation and pigeon droppings have a way of trivializing immortality.

It was late afternoon by the time I'd left the Riverside. Knox had sent a nurse along to flush me out before I had a chance to ask Howard the thousand follow-up questions that had sprung to mind during his discourse on Emily Trevain and the Castle House take. I didn't give the nurse much of an argument, though. As it was I had used up twice the ten minutes Knox had allotted me, and besides, Howard had given me more than enough to think about for the time being. Not that I had much faith in Howard's hidden treasure theory. When it came right down to it, the cynic in me was convinced that Howard Johnson would go to his final rest in a simple, one-size-fits-all casket.

But the journalist in me knew the makings of a good story and, if even half of what Howard had told me about Jack and Emily was true, the Castle House story was good enough to write itself. The end of an era in a swank mansion on a lonely island in the middle of a frozen river. A pair of secret lovers plotting to finance their future by robbing the robber barons. Then the terrible irony of it all: the girl's father shot dead by her lover, the innocent guests murdered in a panic, the killer meeting fate under the ice. And the poor girl, left to live out her life alone and forgotten on that empty island. It was the sort of romantic tragedy that spiced up the glossy pages of women's magazines or ended up as a TV movie under the cautious heading, Based on a True Story.

But still, I felt hectored by a pair of persistent questions. What did Professor Janezek know about the Castle House tragedy that I didn't know? And what did it have to do with the Fellowship?

I found Alan Betz in a small conference room just down the hall from the history department offices. He was bent over a long trestle table, precariously balancing a heavy stoneware mug in his left hand while dividing a stack of paper into four neat piles with his right. The room was painted institutional beige and smelled of herbal tea and fresh ink.

I said, "So this is what it means to be untenured."

Betz looked up from his mimeos, focused in on me through the wire-rimmed spectacles, and smiled ruefully. "Hi, Sheridan. If you think this is meager, you should see my paycheck." He set the mug down and absently wiped his hands down the sides of his baggy brown cords. "What brings you to our hallowed halls this afternoon?"

"You still willing to help with my investigation?"

"Of course." He swept his hand over the piles of paper. "I'm just finishing up with my reading lists and I still need to organize some of my lecture notes, but that won't take long. I should have plenty of free time between now and the start of classes next week. How can I help?"

"Research," I said. "And maybe a little creative snooping." I filled him in on what Sgt. Tinderlay had told me about the Castle House case file.

"Well, that proves it! I knew Jan had to have had a substantial collection of material somewhere. Obviously, Liam Dougherty found a file at Jan's apartment and stole it."

"Or more likely destroyed it," I said. "I'd like to find out one way or the other. That's where the snooping comes in. Is Dougherty on campus now, do you know?"

"Yes, I just saw him in the faculty lounge."

"Good. Can you get away for an hour or so?"

His eyes shone like a pair of new pennies. "You want me to search Dougherty's apartment, is that it?"

"I want you to get me into the building so I can check out Professor Janezek's apartment to see if he might've hidden the file someplace. We'll check Dougherty's place, too, if we can get in. Later I'll want you to search Dougherty's office. It's a long shot, but I'd like to know if he held onto the professor's file. What do you say?"

Betz stared down at the table for a moment and I was sure I saw trepidation pulsing away at his temples. But then he looked up at me and grinned and I knew I'd misread him. He was as eager as a Boy Scout on his first overnighter.

"Why the hell not?" he said. "I'm sure I can handle Mrs. Lansdowne. She's the landlady. She's a bit dotty, but that should work in our favor. Let's go give it a shot."

It was a short ride from the campus to the apartment house, just long enough for me to brief Betz on the other assignment I had for him. I needed background on the Fellowship; the nature of the symposia and lectures it held, a calendar of past events, what sort of reports it had published, and where it had published them. Betz took a few notes as he rode along in the Bronco's passenger seat.

"No problem," he said. "Dr. Stevenson archives all Fellowship publications and documents in the faculty research room." He glanced up from his jottings. "Anything else?"

"Yes, if you have the time, I'd like you to see if you can put together an abstract on Coffin Island. Particularly on the years between Ernest Castle's death in 1937 and Maurice DuPree's purchase of the island in the seventies."

Betz frowned. "I'll look into it, but I thought the island just sat there unused for all those years, after the state took it for taxes."

"Not quite," I said. "From what I hear, Emily Trevain stayed on out there for another thirty years after the murders. I'd like to find out how she managed that."

The apartment house was a large and immaculately maintained Queen Anne, gray with white and teal trim, that had undoubtedly started out as a single family home back when live-in maids and heating oil came cheap. It was the kind of place that conjured images of kids in knickerbockers playing croquet on the lawn, supervised by a proud father who looked like Clifton Webb.

I parked at the curb and we made our way up a brick walk and onto the broad front porch. Double oak doors with elliptical beveled glass in the upper panes opened into a roomy vestibule. There were four narrow mailboxes mounted on the side wall, each with a door buzzer installed above it. Betz pushed the one marked 'G.C. Lansdowne'.

"This may take a minute," he remarked. "Mrs. Lansdowne is hard of hearing." He laid into the buzzer again. Half a minute later, the interior door was swung open by a wizened old woman wearing a shocking pink jogging suit and Reebok hightops. A silvery Harpo Marx perm all but hid the hearing aids that were tucked in behind each of her ears.

"Alan! I haven't seen you in a coon's age!" Her voice was as harsh as day-old whiskey. "Who's your friend? I hope you're not here about Professor Jan's old rooms. I told that fool down at the newspaper to stop that ad. I already found a tenant, supposed to move in this weekend."

"Actually, we are here to have a look into Jan's apartment," Betz told her, speaking loudly. "This is Mr. Sheridan, a friend of Jan's. We're trying to locate some papers we think he might've kept here."

"Papers, you said?" She turned and led us into a large foyer paneled in moody dark oak. "I think Professor Dougherty did that already, but you're welcome to look. Did I tell you I rented the rooms?" She grimaced. "A couple of college girls. I broke my own rule, renting to students, but the apartment's been empty almost two months now. It's just terrible trying to find a painter around here during the summer months. The college kids are all gone and the locals are busy with the tourists." She stopped to scratch at her curls. "Did I give you the keys, Alan?"

"No, you didn't, Mrs. Lansdowne."

"I'll get them, although I don't think the apartment's locked. The painters have been in and out all week." She pivoted and went through an open door to the right of the foyer. A few seconds later, she returned with a big key ring. "It's on here some place. I'll let you figure it out." She handed the keys to Betz. "Is it five o'clock yet? I think I'm missing Oprah."

After assuring her that she still had plenty of time to warm up the Motorola, Betz and I climbed the stairs to the second floor. There we found two doors facing each other across a narrow corridor.

"This is Jan's old place," Betz said, indicating the door on our left. A brass B was centered in the upper panel. Betz turned the knob. "It isn't locked."

The smell of a recent paint job was faint in the air as we stepped into the apartment. The walls declared their neutrality with an off-white eggshell finish. The natural wood trim and hardwood floor gave the place character, but hominess would have to wait until the next tenant trucked in the potted plants and framed art posters. Someone had done a good job of converting what had once been three

103

roomy bedrooms into one bedroom, a living room, a galley kitchen, and an efficient bath. The apartment was airy and clean, and as empty as a politician's promise.

"I guess the painters moved everything to the basement or someplace," Betz said as he went to check the bedroom.

"We'll have to ask Mrs. Lansdowne on the way out," I called back to him as I browsed through the kitchen cabinets. "Maybe we'll find the file taped to the bottom of a dresser drawer, I should be so lucky."

Betz came into the kitchen. "Nothing in the bedroom or john. You find anything?"

"Zip," I said. "Well, it was a long shot. Let's go next door and see how the other half lives."

We walked across the hall to the door adorned with a big brass C. Betz glanced up at me as he tried a series of keys in the lock.

"I'm kind of sorry she gave us these," he said. "I was looking forward to seeing you open the door with a credit card, like they do in the movies."

"Yeah," I said. I didn't bother to tell him that the only way I could get into a room with a credit card was by handing it to a hotel clerk and signing the register.

"Ah, here we are." He turned the lock and let us in. Dougherty's apartment looked like a head-on collision between a Salvation Army truck and a books-on-wheels van. Any way you turned, there was worn, mismatched furniture covered with stacks of magazines and dogeared paperbacks. An old Royal manual typewriter squatted on a wooden desk amidst leaning towers of loose-leaf notebooks and hardbound reference books. A gunmetal gray two-drawer file doubled as an end table beside a tired sofa.

I rummaged through one of the piles of detritus on the desk, uncovering some blank sheets of Fellowship letterhead and some published reports by groups like the Heritage Foundation and the Brookings Institution. Apparently Dougherty and his friends weren't particular about who did their research for them. "Why don't you take the file cabinet, I'll give the desk the once-over."

We spent ten minutes searching in the obvious places and turned up nothing on the Castle House investigation. That was a long trespass for a couple of basically honest citizens and, as the minutes ticked by, I could feel the tension bunching up in my shoulders. Betz was at least as relieved as I was when, finally, I suggested we head back downstairs to quiz Mrs. Lansdowne on the whereabouts of Professor Janezek's old furnishings.

We found the landlady nestled in by the television, munching a Granola bar while listening to Oprah interviewing transvestite couples who wanted to adopt. Without taking her eyes from the screen, Mrs. Lansdowne impatiently informed us that, yes, Professor Jan's furniture was being stored in the basement and why didn't we just help ourselves.

The basement was as dank and shadowy as a cave. A monster of an old converted coal furnace dominated the main floor area, its round heating ducts running off in all directions like tentacles from a mechanical octopus. The furniture was crowded into a small partitioned bay that probably once served as a coal bin. Betz and I waded into the pile, judiciously inspecting table bottoms and empty dresser drawers and overstuffed chair cushions, finding nothing. We were on our way out of the basement, dusty and discouraged, when I stopped and stared at the brick vent stack beside the old furnace. A metal door was embedded in the stack about two feet off the floor.

"Is that an incinerator?" I asked Betz.

"I guess so. Most of these old places have them. Of course, there's an ordinance against using them these days, but some people still—" He paused, eyebrows rising speculatively. "Some people still use them to burn old newspapers and things."

I yanked down hard on the heavy cast-iron locking lever and swung open the door, its hinges screeching. The paltry light from the basement's ceiling fixture did nothing to cut the yawning blackness inside the incinerator cavity. I took off my jacket, handed it to Betz, and rolled up my shirt sleeve. Lowering myself onto one knee, I carefully inserted my arm through the opening and began feeling around. My hand met up with a pile of loose ash. I sifted through the ashes, hoping no one had been careless enough to toss any broken glass in there, until my fingers stumbled over something substantial. I got a grip on the object and extracted it, shaking the loose ash onto the floor. It was the metal spine from a three-ring notebook, with a triangular portion of the notebook's lower left corner still intact, although badly charred. Whatever materials had been contained in the notebook had burned away.

"Look familiar?" I asked Betz.

He studied the metal binder closely. "It's the same type we're issued through the college supply office, I'm sure of that." He shrugged helplessly. "Every faculty member on campus uses them."

"Well, let's take it with us anyway. I saw a bundle of grocery bags by the stairs."

I took one of the bags and slipped in the charred binder, then headed back up the stairs, Betz following behind with my jacket. Just as we stepped out into the relative brightness of the foyer, the vestibule door swung open and in came Liam Dougherty. He was talking animatedly over his shoulder, but the chatter stopped abruptly when he saw us.

"Sheridan. Betz. What are you doing here?" His face registered only mild suspicion until he noticed my bare arm, blackened with soot, and the paper bag I was holding. Then suspicion moved over to make room for something closer to fear. "What are you doing here," he repeated anxiously.

"We're doing some moonlighting for the gas company," I said. "Inspecting furnaces for the heating season."

Dougherty took a step forward, allowing his two companions to crowd in from the vestibule: Jamie, the kid I'd seen at Dougherty's office, and the slim Frenchman who had been at Lord Jim's with good old Desmond the night before. The kid was wearing a sneer that would do Bruce Dern proud. The Frenchman was too sophisticated to do anything more than arch one brow. Dougherty hadn't taken his eyes off the grocery bag.

"It's amazing how inefficient some of these old burners are," I said.

Betz moved around beside me and stared hard at Dougherty. I took turns looking from Jamie to the impassive Frenchman, while Dougherty continued to stare at the bag. Everybody was doing his best to look macho, as if a scene from *West Side Story* was about to break out. Then Frenchy shattered the mood with a quiet laugh and a familiar quote that sounded a lot like a threat.

"Ashes to ashes, eh, mon ami?"

Before I could think up a snappy retort, the Frenchman took Dougherty by the elbow and urged him up the staircase, Jamie falling in behind. Betz and I watched their feet disappear beyond the landing, then let out a collective sigh. We were just about to exit the foyer when Mrs. Lansdowne pulled open her door and peered out at us.

"Alan!" she said after a moment. "I haven't seen you in a coon's age."

CHAPTER 15

RITA Tonelli should've been a pleasant diversion after a long day of Q&A. She was, after all, intelligent and educated. She had interesting work, libraries being as important to a writer as lumber to a carpenter. And she was undeniably attractive, particularly so in the pleated salmon jumpsuit and matching heels she was wearing.

So why wasn't I enjoying myself?

To be fair, a large portion of my evening of discontent had to be attributed to my morning confrontation with Desmond and his canine buddies, followed by Betz's and my chance encounter with Liam Dougherty and company. I couldn't shake the feeling that something cruel and calculated motivated them, particularly Desmond and the Frenchman. Every time I thought of those two, a chill ran through me. Was it a reporter's intuition or, as my sainted grandmother would've insisted, had someone just walked across my grave?

But there was more to my mood than that and it had to do with Rita herself. Everything was fine at first. I had picked her up at seven-thirty at her tidy townhouse condo on the southern edge of the village and we had kibitzed like old friends during the ten-mile ride to the Garson

House, a comfortable colonial-style inn with a view of the soaring Thousand Island suspension bridge to Canada. But then, about halfway through our dinners and a bottle of a fine Finger Lakes Chardonnay, Rita had turned the conversation to the institution of marriage. Maybe it was because she was twenty-nine and could hear the first few ticks of the biological clock, or maybe she was unnecessarily worried about continuing as what previous generations had called an old maid. Whatever the motivator, she had started in on her past and future romantic prospects, which eventually brought us to my own checkered love life. Before I knew it, she had me talking about my marriage and divorce.

"I don't mean to pry," she said while daintily trimming away at the edges of her veal. "It's just that I have these, mm, theories on what makes for a good, lasting relationship and I like to test them against someone whose marriage, well . . . didn't work out."

I refilled our wine glasses. "Free-lancing is an iffy line of work," I said after a moment. "There are no set hours, which means you end up working all hours. And there are no guarantees; no weekly paychecks to depend on, no company pensions to look forward to. The life-style didn't suit Janet. She's a nine-to-fiver. The uncertainties—living in Manhattan on a prayer and a promise—wore her down. We gradually lost the spark." I turned up my hands. "She found somebody else and that was that. When the initial hurt stopped, I realized it was for the best."

"But you've done well as a writer," Rita protested, then blushed. "After you came by the other day, I located your book in our stacks and took it home. The one on that murder case down near Geneva. I was impressed."

"Thanks, but all that came about after our breakup, hand in hand with the inheritance from my uncle." I pushed away the plate and my remaining dinner. "I guess Janet's leaving me had as much to do with the book as anything. If we had stayed together, I probably wouldn't have moved to Mohaca Springs and gotten myself involved in the investigation of Uncle Charlie's murder. Anyway, it worked out okay."

"No regrets?" she asked cautiously.

"There are always regrets. I was raised to believe marriage was a life-long commitment."

"Me, too. Maybe that's why I'm still single." A tiny smile played at the edges of her mouth, then slipped away, replaced by a frown of equal proportions. "I believe very strongly in compatibility. It seems to me that if two people share the same interests, have similar habits and routines, you have the basis for a lasting marriage."

She paused, expecting a response from me. When I didn't give her one, she went on.

"Then there's compatibility of intellect and professional goals. Two people should know where they're going and what each is willing to do to get there." She paused again, this time tilting her brunette bob just enough to let me know an acknowledgment was required.

"Janet married me because I made her laugh," I said.

Rita smiled politely and sipped her wine. "I hope I don't sound too, mm, clinical about this. It's just, I think there are several important factors that should be present before two people even consider marrying."

"I hope one of those factors is love."

"Well, of course. It goes without saying that there has to be love. And romance. Being courted, flowers and candy, candlelight and music. But you can't allow yourself to be dazzled by that sort of thing, with no thought to the more practical considerations, that's all I'm saying."

"Speaking of music," I said as the waiter brought the check. "I understand there's entertainment in the lounge. Why don't we stop in for drinks?"

A piano player sat at a baby grand in a spotlighted corner of the darkened bar, breezily chatting up the thin crowd while noodling away at the keyboard. As Rita and I settled at a back table, he started doing an Anthony Newley vocal to a Billy Joel tune. "Just the Way You Are" came out sounding like "What Kind of Fool Am I."

110

"Maybe this wasn't such a good idea," I said to Rita after the waitress had taken our drink orders.

"Nonsense. We'll just pretend this is a comedy club."

"All right, but if he degenerates into an Elvis impersonation and sings "Viva Las Vegas," I'm outa here."

We listened to the piano man do his number for a few minutes, each of us smiling at our private joke. When the waitress brought our drinks—a Cognac for Rita, scotch rocks for me—Rita grabbed the opportunity to pick up on her favorite topic.

"I hope you don't think I was putting you through some kind of test," she said. "With my gabbing on about marriage and compatibility and all that. I mean, I'm not measuring you for a tux or anything. It's just a good opportunity to get a man's point of view from a disinterested party."

"I don't mind," I said, telling a polite lie.

"It's just that this is such a small town. A woman's prospects are limited. I suppose that makes me sound a little more desperate than I really am."

"What about Ellis Turnbull?"

She ran a painted fingernail around the rim of her glass. "I don't know. Ellis is a good man. I do care about him, more than he knows, but . . . he's limited himself so much. To his job, this town. I guess the problem is I see Widows Cape as a good place to start a career and he sees it as a good place to spend the rest of his life."

"There's a lot to be said for small-town life."

"I agree," she said, nodding emphatically. "But there's small and then there's really small. Besides, Widows Cape is so insular. You're not considered a native unless your grandparents were born here, and outsiders are always under the microscope. Believe me, I know. I have no doubt I'd be let go or demoted in a flash if one of the locals came along clutching a master's in library science. And it's even iffier for Ellis. His contract would be canceled in a New York minute if he stepped on the wrong toes. The town council would see to that."

"And Mayor MacKenzie pulls the council's strings?"

"He's the head puppeteer," Rita agreed. "He and Judge Dunleavy both. The mayor heads up the council, of course, and the judge, while he doesn't actually sit on the council, has a lot to say about who does."

"Where do the voters come into it? Don't the council members have to stand for election?"

"Oh, sure. But the election's merely a formality." She took a sip of Cognac before continuing. "Widows Cape has been Republican since Lincoln. If you want to sit on the council you have to go to the party leaders—that's Mayor MacKenzie and Judge Dunleavy and one or two others. If you can convince them to nominate you as one of the five Republican candidates for one of the five town council seats, you're as good as elected."

"Something like the Soviet Politburo, huh?"

"Now, now, Sheridan." Rita wagged a finger at me. "Don't you go making up quotes for me. I did not—repeat, did not—compare the Widows Cape town council to a Russian oligarchy."

"Certainly not," I said. "MacKenzie and Dunleavy are just a couple of benevolent despots, is what you mean."

She smiled. "All right, I'll settle for benevolent despots. Particularly the judge. He wields a lot of power in the town, but the worst you can say about him is that he's paternalistic. Mayor MacKenzie, on the other hand, can be, mm, authoritarian, I guess is the word." She finished her drink and sighed. "Which is why I worry about Ellis and his future. And our future, if we have one together. There isn't a lot of job security in being chief constable."

I downed the last of my scotch. The piano player was attempting a Bobby Short treatment of "Stairway to Heaven." It seemed like a good time to leave. On the other hand, it also seemed like a good time to segue into one last question.

"What about Liam Dougherty?" I asked. "I assume he's tenured at the college, so he has job security. And there must be a certain amount of intellectual and professional compatibility between you. To borrow a phrase, do you know where he's going and what he's willing to do to get there?"

"Goodness, I'm beginning to regret having opened this Pandora's box," she said, shaking her head. "Leave it to a journalist to throw a person's words right back at her."

"Can I quote you on that?"

"Nobody likes a wise guy, Sheridan," she said playfully. Then, "Liam is . . . not what he seems."

"What does that mean?"

"His personality is complex. When you first get to know him, he comes off like this very open, garrulous man. Into all the right causes—which is to say all the left causes. The stereotypical well-adjusted college professor." She shook her head from side to side. "But there's something else going on there; something deadly serious and so deep down inside that it can't be touched by anyone else. He reminds me of a line from Hoffer's *The True Believer*. A mortal enemy of things-as-they-are." She tossed her shoulders dismissively. "At any rate, something burns at his core, and it isn't the desire for a wife and a family."

My room was looking pretty good by ten that evening, which only goes to show how a long day and a tired brain can distort one's senses. Rita and I had exchanged harmless pecks on the cheek at her condo door a few minutes earlier. She had invited me in for the traditional nightcap, but had followed up the invitation with a joke about this being "a school night." I took the hint and declined the drink offer.

I wasn't the only one who'd made an early night of it. Half a dozen cars were spread out across the Clearview's parking lot, including the sedan belonging to my neighbors in room nine, Curly and Moe. I bought a can of cola from the vending machine outside the motel office and carried it back to the room and placed it on the nightstand next to a Bill Pronzini mystery I'd brought from home. Then I turned the television on to a Canadian station out of Kingston and let an exhibition hockey match keep me company while I reviewed my day's notes sprawled across the bed's mushy mattress. Every page I turned raised new questions, and I wasn't in the mood. I let my attention shift to the TV. The hockey match was between periods and someone was interviewing a retired hockey great, asking if the players were tougher in his day. The old pro spoke with a typical French-Canadian accent, the THs sounding like Ds, the Rs coming out as hard as the granite bedrock that dominated the Quebec countryside.

I was about to change the channel when a knock on the door intruded.

"Hi, sailor," she said when I swung open the door. "You look like you could use some company."

CHAPTER 16

SHE was wearing a different outfit this time; a pair of silky green jogging shorts that exaggerated her long legs, a tight yellow polo shirt that made the most of her small breasts, a bulky black leather purse slung from her left shoulder. The blonde from Lord Jim's who called herself an escort service.

"Kara, isn't it?" I asked.

"Yeah. So, you gonna let me in or what?" She swept past me confidently, like a warm breeze, leaving a faint smell of lilacs in her wake. Strange men and motel rooms were part of the job description.

I glanced outside before closing the door. The parking spaces to either side of the Bronco were vacant.

"Hockey, yuck." She switched off the TV set, then switched on a taunting smile with equal agility. "The only thing I like on ice is bourbon," she said, sounding very Lauren Bacall.

I watched her drop her purse onto the dresser and move over to the bed. She settled onto the edge of the mattress and crossed her legs and started swaying slightly from side to side, hearing an inner rhythm, waiting for me to catch up with the program.

"This a new marketing approach in your business?" I asked. "Direct door-to-door selling?"

"This isn't business," she said, putting on a pout. Emotions were something to be applied for effect, like lipstick or mascara, and just as easily wiped away. "I figured I owed you something for last night. For the way you helped me out with those two goobers."

"You're welcome."

"So you gonna just stand there by the door or what?"

"I'm thinking," I said.

"About what?" She stopped swaying back and forth and began gently bobbing her right leg.

"About the letters section in *Playboy*, where this sort of thing happens monthly. And about how I always figured the letters were phony."

"God, try and be nice to some people and what do you get?" She tisk-tisked. "I was just a little lonely tonight, so I figured I'd drop by and see if you wanted to party."

"How'd you know where to find me?"

"Hmm?" She picked an imaginary loose thread off her shorts. "I just called around to the local motels, asked if they had a guy named Sheridan registered. You think you journalists are the only ones who can track somebody down?"

"How'd you know I was a journalist?"

She went after another invisible thread. "Pat told me, I guess. The bartender at Lord Jim's."

"He must be clairvoyant, because I never mentioned it." I moved over beside the dresser. "You're not very good at this, are you?"

"At what?"

"Lying."

"Well, fuck you, too." She uncrossed her legs and stood, hands on her hips. "Listen, I thought we could have some fun, that's all. If you're not interested—"

"I didn't say I wasn't interested."

"Well, all right then." She turned the smile back on and stepped over beside me. Our knees bumped together as she worked her hands down my sides and slowly began tugging at my belt. Her breath smelled of mint and the pink, moist

116

tip of her tongue eased out across her lower lip as she leaned in to kiss me.

"It's just that I'm shy," I said, brushing her hands away from my belt. "Why don't you go first?"

She stepped back. "You like to watch, huh, baby?"

"Yeah."

"That's cool." She started with the polo shirt, pulling it up over her head, then tossing it onto the dresser and shaking her blond hair back into shape. Her breasts were small and firm, and she cupped her hands around them and squeezed gently. The hands slid down her flat belly to her narrow hips. The jogging shorts and panties shimmied down her legs and gathered at her ankles. She stepped out of them and kicked them aside. The wedge-heeled sandals came last.

"Your turn," she said. Her gaze held a challenge, and something else. Contempt.

"Get in the bed first."

She smirked, then casually bent down to turn back the covers. Her taut thighs spread slightly as she moved, revealing a delta of golden hair.

"You just wanted me to warm the sheets first," she said coquettishly as she wiggled down under the covers.

"Something like that," I said as I began gathering up her clothes. I tucked them under my arm and lifted her purse off the dresser.

"Hey! What the hell—"

"Make yourself at home," I said as I went out the door.

Out in the parking area, I quickly tossed the clothes into the Bronco and relocked it. As I was sifting through the purse, the motel room door eased open six inches and Kara's face peered out at me.

"What is this, you son of a bitch!"

I dug out her wallet and found a Clampett College student ID card. Karen Majeski, age twenty. I shoved the wallet back in and rummaged through a hodgepodge of makeup vials, chewing gum, a Trojan three-pack, and a spray tube of Mace, until I came up with a small black

117

address book. The girl abruptly pulled her face back from the cracked door and slammed it shut. A few moments later, just as I was working my way from the Cs to the Ds, she came flying out of the room in one of my shirts and tried to knock me into the St. Lawrence with a roundhouse swing that only worked in bad Westerns. I stepped inside the punch, wrapped an arm around her waist, and hauled her back into the room.

"Take it easy," I said, tossing her onto the bed.

She came up swinging and swearing. I sidestepped a knee aimed at my crotch and managed to grab her wrist. I pulled the arm up behind her back and forced her face-first down onto the bed and straddled her.

"Relax, Karen," I said soothingly.

"It's Kara, you asshole! And if you don't let—"

"According to your ID, it's Karen Majeski."

"Ma-YEW-ski. And I don't give a shit what it says, my name is Kara and if you don't get the fuck off me I'm gonna call the cops, I swear I will!"

"Be my guest." I climbed off the wriggling girl and pointed to the phone on the bedstand. She sat up tentatively and blinked, like a wild animal who'd just realized the cage door was open. She looked at me, then stared at the phone for a few seconds, deciding it wasn't a viable option.

"You can't keep me here against my will."

"You're free to go right now," I said. "But I keep your little black book."

She stared at me, quietly seething. "Shit!" she said finally, her eyes misting with frustration. "I knew this was a stupid idea."

"Who put you up to it?" I began thumbing through the address book again, trying to keep it casual, one eye on the girl in case she began to revert.

"Forget it." She crossed her arms. "This whole goddamn deal sucks, that's all I know."

"What're you studying at Clampett, public speaking?" I asked as I made my way up to the Ms. Most of the entries

118

were merely initials followed by phone numbers or, in a few cases, what appeared to be room numbers from local motels. But some of the entries included the notation, "For Mack," and the name Mack, followed by two phone numbers, had been listed prominently at the beginning of the Ms.

"Who's Mack?" I asked.

She didn't answer the question, so I rephrased it. "Is Mack your pimp?"

"My pimp?" She laughed, short and harsh, then as quickly frowned. "Look, I run an escort service, okay? I'm just a student trying to make a few bucks to pay my tuition." Then, in an aside to herself, she mumbled, "Damn! Never go with a guy under forty. Everytime I break my own rule, I end up in the shit."

"Like with Desmond and Frenchy?"

Her head snapped up at me. "That was . . . nothing. I overreacted, okay?"

"They scared the hell out of you."

"They're a couple of animals!" she said heatedly. Calming herself, she added, "I got into a bad scene with them. Broke my own goddamn rule again."

"For Mack?"

She retreated into a stony silence. I pulled open a drawer and took out the crumpled grocery bag containing the burnt remnant of a loose-leaf binder. Her eyes went to the bag like a moth to lamplight.

"Is this what they sent you for?" I asked. "Get me into bed, then later, after I nod off, search my room for this and whatever tidbits you could turn up in my notes?"

I was hoping she'd do a Perry Mason and lay out a tearful confession, but we weren't on the same script. Still, there was just enough animation in the eyes to tell me I was on the right track. My next gambit didn't take a great leap of imagination, just a little applied logic. How might a part-time hooker keep herself in business in a town as small as Widows Cape? Maybe by lucking into a protector with a weakness for young flesh, someone with enough juice to keep the local law from revoking her work permit.

"Mack is your sugar daddy," I said. "In return for your services, he watchdogs you. Sometimes he sets you up with other guys. That's how you got stuck with Desmond and Frenchy. And me." I waited a beat. "Mack is Mayor Rodney MacKenzie."

"Whoa!" She stood up and glanced at the door. "Look, this was a mistake, okay? No more questions. I'm leaving."

"If you do, I'll have to take my questions to the mayor. I'd rather not do that, Kara."

She began muttering and pacing in quick, short strides. Then she studied me a moment, muttered some more, and sat back on the bed. "Christ, I warned him this was a bad idea, so it's not my fault."

I put the paper sack on the bureau and sat on the edge of the bed. "No, it's not."

"I'm just trying to get by, like everybody else. I mean, if I'm gonna be used by somebody, I like it to be my own idea, you know?" She paused. "But sometimes we don't get to make our own choices. I'm not sure I can explain it."

"You can try," I said.

"If I do, it's just between you and me, right?"

"Your name won't come into it," I assured her. "Just fill me in on your connection with MacKenzie and why he sent you here. When you leave I'll give you a story to feed him. Deal?"

She considered it for a moment, then shrugged, resigned. "Why not? It's none of my business anyway. Screw Mac-Kenzie. But . . . it's kinda complicated. I gotta tell it from the beginning, okay?"

She wasn't kidding. For the next ten minutes I heard all about a girl named Karen Majeski, an army brat whose staff sergeant father moved Karen and her mother all over the world in two-year intervals. By the time her father had received his posting to Fort Drum, just outside Watertown, the mother was dead of cancer and sixteen-year-old Karen was left to make new friends again in another strange school and to fend off a father who was drinking heavily and eyeing his budding teen-age daughter with something less than paternal affection on his mind.

It all came to a head one night in Karen's senior year of high school. The old man came home stewed and climbed into her bed. She fought him off with knees and elbows and left him retching his guts out on the bedroom floor. She moved in with a girlfriend's family and finished up the school year. The father—Sarge, she called him—never attempted to contact her or make amends. That summer, he took his twenty and retired to half-ownership in a Georgia filling station. She recited it all casually, as if she were telling me the story line from her favorite afternoon soap opera, and maybe she was. But I believed her.

When she stopped talking, there was an awkward silence. I reached across the bedspread and gently uncurled the slender fingers that had shut themselves into a fist and I took her hand in mine.

"I'm sorry," I said.

"Hey, don't go feeling sorry for me, Sheridan," she said, a touch of her earlier brashness returning. "I've done all right and I'm gonna do even better. I'm a computer science major at Clampett. In two more years, I'll be able to get a good job as a programmer. Laugh if you want, but I'm good."

I didn't laugh. "So why the 'escort service?'"

She withdrew her hand from mine and shook her head. "God, you're one of those guys who likes to brag how he never had to buy it, aren't you?"

"No." I'd left a few crumpled bills on a stranger's nightstand more than once. At seventeen, on a bet, in a tiny bedroom tucked away over a sleazy topless bar in Rochester. I remembered being scared and eager with a hardtiming woman who hid behind laminations of mascara and rouge, the upclose smell of stale bedsheets and the roar of a train outside the window. Then at twenty, drunk and fatalistic in a nameless Saigon alley. Sloe-eyed girls who called you Joe and flashed their wares from darkened doorways. "I sowed a few wild oats when I was a kid," I said.

"But now you won't even take a freebie, huh?"

"Not without a blood test and a body condom."

"Christ, tell me about it. Why d'ya think I only go with middle-aged married guys?"

"Why do you go at all?"

"Look, I'm on a measly partial scholarship and I need to pay the bills. I tried waitressing but I've got flat feet, okay?"

"So tell me how MacKenzie figures in."

"Easy. I hit on him in a bar a year ago last summer. I didn't know he was the mayor. He took me outa there like he was gonna give me a lecture. Instead, we go to this apartment over a bakery on Second Street and he had me do this high school cheerleader bit for him." She was trying to brass it out, but there was a slightly manic quality to her voice. "Next thing you know, we had a regular thing going. I live in the apartment now. Mack owns the building. A simple business arrangement."

"When did Desmond and Frenchy come into the picture?"

"Claude Beauchamp. That's the French-Canadian. The mick is Desmond Day." She shivered and hugged herself. "A couple months back. Mack sent me out to that Castle House place. He goes, 'I just need you to do a favor for a friend who's been cooped up out on the island.' Only he doesn't tell me there's two of them and they're both into leather and all that shit. I told Mack that was the last time with those two. I go, 'I don't mind when you set me up with some old dork who wants me to pee on his chest, but I draw the line with psychos.' Mack gets really humble and apologizes and says it won't happen again."

She ran her hands down the sleeves of the oxford shirt she'd thrown on earlier. "Anyway, he kept his promise until today, when I tried to beg off coming over here. Then he like threatens me with it. He goes, 'Don't force me to have Des and Claude come by to discuss this with you.'"

"What was it, exactly, that MacKenzie wanted from you?"

"Like you figured. Come onto you like I was saying thanks for your help and get it on with you." She grinned impishly. "And on and on, until you're wrung out like a dishrag. Then, while you're off in dreamland, I was supposed to go through your stuff, see if you had any notes or papers or anything that mentioned Mack or this club he belongs to. The Fellowship, it's called. He was especially interested in some partly burnt notebook." She glanced over at the top of the bureau. "He said it might be stashed in a grocery bag."

"Did he say anything more specific, like what he thought was in the charred notebook itself?"

She shook her head. "Not really. He just acted sorta paranoid. He said something about politicians always having enemies, people who want to smear them by spreading lies."

I asked a few more questions, about the Fellowship and MacKenzie's and Liam Dougherty's connections with it, but I was pumping a dry well. Kara had a class with Dougherty once, but didn't know anything about him except that "he seemed to know his stuff when it came to dead writers." I also asked her about Jamie, the surly undergraduate I'd seen with Dougherty a couple of times.

"Jamie Velez," she said. "We've had a few classes together. He hit on me once, but I chilled him. He's like a student rad, like from the old days in the sixties, y'know? Protesting Nicaragua and stuff. I hear he's at Clampett on a scholarship. He's Professor Dougherty's student assistant, I know that much."

I shook my head and sighed, trying to fit everything Kara had told me into neat little mental compartments. Later, when I had more to go on, I'd pull the pieces back out one at a time and reexamine them and, I hoped, find some common thread that would tie the whole story together. But for the moment, my brain was as overloaded as a traveling salesman's valise and I was too tired even to think about unpacking it.

"Listen, Sheridan," Kara said when my brooding had gone on long enough. "What I said about wanting to thank you? For standing up to Desmond like you did? That wasn't all just a come-on. I mean—" She frowned, her cheeks coloring. "I owe you one, that's all. Maybe that's the real reason I let Mack push me into coming here."

I smiled and patted her hand. "If you owed me anything, we're even now, Kara." I stood and went back to the dresser, picking up the grocery bag. "Okay, here's what we're going to do. I'm going to get your clothes and drive you home. When you see MacKenzie, tell him you snuck a peek in this bag while I was taking a shower, right?"

"Uh-huh. Then what?"

"You tell him it was burned pretty badly, but that you could make out Professor Stefan Janezek's name on the inside flap. Tell him there weren't any papers left inside the binder, but you couldn't tell if they'd burned up or been removed or what. Will you do that?"

"Sure," she shrugged. "Is that all?"

"That's all. Don't ask MacKenzie any questions, don't show any curiosity, just let the matter drop."

"Okay." She played with the buttons on the oxford shirt and smiled coyly. "So what do I say if he wants to know how you were in bed?"

"Keep it simple. Tell him I was godlike."

CHAPTER 17

MILLER'S Bay was a comfortable little hamlet tucked away below the main highway about three miles west of Widows Cape. Its single street was home to a Methodist church, a marina and baitshop, a ramshackle tavern, and a post office not much bigger than one of those photo-developing kiosks that spring up in suburban parking lots. The "bay" that gave the community its name was no more than a cattail-rimmed cove that had been dredged here and there to accommodate the marina and numerous private docks.

I cruised down the street, following its horseshoe bend past the tavern and along the riverfront. A scattering of cottages and mobile homes seemed to hug the shoreline tentatively, like a row of early-summer Cape Cod bathers with one toe in the water. Most of the properties had kitschy wooden signs posted near the aprons of their gravel driveways bearing the street numbers and fanciful names for the family retreat—The Do-Drop-Inn, Haydn Place.

I found number 37, christened SonnyShore, at the second bend in the horseshoe. The driveway entrance was flanked with tall, heavily bowed fir trees, just as it had been described to me by its owner, Sanford "Sonny" Johnson. I had found Johnson in the phone book and called him first thing that morning to introduce myself and ask for an interview. The request had been granted enthusiastically and a breakfast invitation had been extended.

I drove the Bronco through the gap in the trees, up a modest incline, and parked on a concrete pad in front of a two-car garage. A large dish antenna was partially visible behind the garage, its metal snout aimed toward the southwest. The house, a ranch-style prefab, was connected to the garage by an open cedar deck. As I stepped out of the Bronco, a short, stocky man who had to be past eighty came out onto the deck.

"Mr. Sheridan? I'm Sanford Johnson, everybody just calls me Sonny, ridiculous as that sounds at my age." He was bald but for a garland of close-cropped white hair. Large, soft brown eyes peered intelligently from a tanned, fissured face that reminded me of the famous Karsh photo of Picasso.

"Everybody calls me Sheridan," I said, shaking hands.

"Well, come on in. I'm doing up the homefries."

I followed him into a small foyer. Straight ahead, across a surprisingly large living room, patio doors looked out on another cedar deck and, beyond it, a fine view of the river. An efficient modern fireplace dominated one end of the living room and a large television and a stereo outfit filled an armoire along the opposite wall. Big band music was playing softly from a pair of Klipsch speakers.

"That piece you're hearing is a CD of Benny Goodman's Carnegie Hall concert in 1936. Never sounded better," Sonny said. "Scrambled eggs okay by you?"

"Perfect."

"Good. Why don't you help yourself to a look around while I get things ready. I think it's warm enough for breakfast al fresco," he added, heading for the kitchen.

I went into the living room. Floor-to-ceiling bookshelves covered the wall separating it from the kitchen. The shelves were packed with books and magazines. Novels by Twain, Huxley, Steinbeck, Vidal; nonfiction by Carl Sagan and Daniel Boorstin; stacks of periodicals ranging from *The*

126

New York Times Book Review to *Popular Mechanics* and *Better Homes and Gardens*. I moved over to the stereo outfit and was perusing the labels on a stack of CDs when my host came in carrying a plate of English muffins and a carafe of coffee.

"This oughta get you started, young man," he said, motioning me to follow him through the patio doors to the deck. Two places had been set at a glass-topped table. "Bernie—that's my wife, Bernice—would've liked to join us, but she's out on a blood drive with the Red Cross this morning. Her loss, hmm?"

"I want to thank you, Sonny, for agreeing to see me about—" I began, but the old man cut me off.

"My pleasure, Sheridan. I enjoy talking about my early days as a newspaperman. But first we eat, a civilized breakfast, a little friendly chatter. Then we get down to business. That sound all right?"

We spent half an hour out on the deck, dispatching heaping platefuls of eggs and homefries, muffins and coffee and juice. Watching the gulls swoop down onto the river, listening to the music filtering out through the patio doors, and exchanging resumés. As it turned out, newspaper work was only one stop along the road for Sonny Johnson. He'd been a student, forced to drop out of college by the Great Depression, and after that an insurance salesman, again forced to make a career change due to the hard times.

"Nobody had money for life insurance in those days, so I had to get into another line. I began free-lancing a few pieces for the local papers, then got hired as a stringer for the *Watertown Times*, all the while doubling as a clerk in a store over in Cape Vincent."

At the outbreak of the Second World War, Sonny moved down to Syracuse to take a better-paying job doing defense work at the General Electric plant. There, he met and married Bernice. After the war, he continued on at G.E. for a few more years while Bernice pursued her teaching degree.

"We came back home here in '51," he said between bites. "Bernie got a job teaching in Cape Vincent and I went into a p.r. job for the county tourism office. Bought a little farm here at Miller's Bay with the savings from G.E. Everybody thought we were nuts, paying what we did, but it turned out to be the best move we ever made. We started selling off lots for summer homes, saving the best one for ourselves. Made out like a couple of bandits. We put plenty aside for our old age and even managed to put our son Randall through medical school in the bargain. He's down in Atlanta."

"Speaking of bandits," I said, pushing away my plate.

"Oh, yes. That is what brought you here, isn't it? The Castle House robbery." Sonny poured the last of the coffee into our mugs. "Well, like young Tinderlay told you, I covered the story for the *Times*. Had to share the byline with one of the regular staff writers, old Harry VanKuyper, but it was my story all the way."

I nodded. "I picked up a lot of good information on the incident by reading the clips of your stories, combined with some local interviews." I mentioned Howard Johnson's contribution, wondering if he and Sonny were related.

"Howard Johnson? Retired merchant marine, you say." Sonny shook his head. "The only Howard Johnsons I'm familiar with are the restaurant and that kid who plays third base for the Mets. Of course, he could be from farther down river. One of the Alex Bay Johnsons maybe."

"What about Professor Janezek, Sonny? You said he did contact you about Castle House?"

"Yes, some months back. Not long before he went off to Washington, poor fellow."

"Can you tell me what he asked you? I'm trying to pick up the story from where the professor left off," I explained. "But I'm not clear on exactly how far he'd gotten."

"Well, he already knew the basics when he interviewed me. He was more interested in sorting out a few of the personalities he'd come across."

"Which personalities?"

"The Spicer girls, mostly. Alice and Victoria." The rich

brown eyes sparkled. "Now, there were two beauties. Daughters of William Spicer, the foreman out to the Dunleavy Saltworks Mine, south of Widows Cape."

"As in Judge Dunleavy?" I asked.

"Yep. His family started it up way back in the last century. Robbie Dunleavy sold it off back in the sixties, when he quit his law practice to join the county bench."

"I thought Dunleavy was just the town justice."

"Oh, he is now. He retired from county court about ten years ago. Took the J.P. appointment to keep his finger in local politics, I suppose."

"Back to the Spicer sisters," I prompted.

"Right. Your Professor Janezek heard about the girls being engaged to a couple of the local boys. He was trying to establish what they were doing out at that ill-fated New Year's Eve party with a randy old bachelor like Ernest Castle." He sipped from his mug and smacked his lips. "Well, as I put it together when I was doing the story, the girls took the invitation after a tiff with their boyfriends. Seems they wanted to make them jealous."

"And the boyfriends were?"

"Robbie Dunleavy, for one. He was semiengaged to Victoria Spicer. Her sister Alice was officially engaged to Marshall Stewart. Ironically, Stewart and Dunleavy, along with a couple of friends, were about the first ones to spot the fire on the island and to rush out to try and save the Castle House. They damn near got themselves cooked trying to get into the place. By the time I got out there, Manfred Porter, the fire chief back then, had the boys restrained and had poured about a fifth of brandy into them to sedate them." Sonny shook his head sadly. "They took it hard. Robbie Dunleavy has remained a lifelong bachelor. And poor Marshall, well, that's another story."

"He died a few months later in a hunting accident," I said evenly. "Isn't that the official line?"

The old man stared at me a moment, then exhaled. "That's the way it went into the books. I should know, since I covered it for the *Times*. The truth, of course, is

129

that Marshall Stewart took his own life one cool spring morning in 1938. Took his Remington out to the woods and ended it. The police knew it, I knew it. But his family had pull, and there really wasn't any point in writing it up as suicide."

Sonny took advantage of the ensuing silence to stare pensively off toward the river. I used the pause to fish out my notepad and take a few notes. The difference was that, for me, it was simply another piece to a complex puzzle. For the old man, it was a living memory. When he finally brought himself back to the present, the distance between us was far wider than a glass-topped patio table.

"At any rate," he said quietly. "That was the crux of what the professor asked me. The Spicer girls."

"Did he ask you anything else?"

"A couple things. First, he wanted to know what I could tell him about Emily Trevain. I couldn't help him there. I never met her before the Castle House tragedy and she refused all interviews with the press thereafter. She died an enigma out there on Coffin Island."

"And the second thing?"

"He asked me a hypothetical question. Very odd."

"What was it?"

"Well, we were talking about the history of the river, particularly the days when smuggling was a growth industry. Not just Prohibition, with the rumrunners bringing the booze in from Canada—the St. Lawrence run, they called it. But earlier, all the way back to the Revolutionary War when the English would sneak guns across to the Indians. So, your professor friend asked me, 'What would anyone want to smuggle across the river today?'"

"Did you have a theory for him?"

"Oh, I speculated a bit on the usual stuff—drugs or arms." Sonny said. "But later, as I got to thinking it over, I came up with another notion."

"What's that?"

"Well, I was remembering a little more history. The Underground Railroad, for example. How, back in the years before the Civil War, the abolitionists used to sneak runaway slaves across to Canada and freedom. And more recently, Vietnam." He squinted at me. "Your war, am I right?"

I nodded.

"Draft dodgers, war resisters, whatever your politics tells you they were. This jumble of islands was an easy place for someone to head north to avoid the draft. Or to sneak south again without going through Customs whenever the urge to visit old friends and family got too strong. Anyway, I thought to myself, 'So what would anyone want to smuggle across the river today?' And the answer I came up with is people."

CHAPTER 18

PEOPLE.

I was still turning that one over as I jogged up the steps of the Widows Cape library and into a mild contretemps involving my favorite librarian and a chief constable I could do without entirely.

"For God's sake, Ellis, you could have someone else fill in for one night." This from Rita, standing at the corner of the L-shaped checkout counter and looking very Anne Klein in a fitted charcoal business suit.

"The roster is set, Rita. Besides, I can't always be sticking the other men with Friday rounds. I'm sorry." Turnbull was looking decidedly earth-tone, from his brown Dexter walkers to the tan double knits to the orange red flush on his cheeks. Then he spotted me and his face took on a deeper shade. "Why don't you go with him? Again."

Rita did a quarter turn. "Oh! Hi, Sheridan."

"Morning," I said. "If I'm interrupting—"

"No, no. Ellis and I were just . . . having an argument, actually."

"Who's winning?"

The chief hit me with a blank stare. "I think you are," he said evenly. Then he nodded to Rita, mumbled, "Talk to you later," and headed for the door.

After he'd gone, I said to Rita, "Sorry about that. It's just that his hostility bit wears a little thin."

"Yes, it does. Anyway, don't worry about it, it wasn't your fault." She shook her head. "First Ellis was upset that I'd gone to dinner with you last night, then I got upset when he said he couldn't make the reception tomorrow night."

"Reception?"

"Dr. Stevenson, the college president, is having a cocktail party at his home for the new man, Professor Janezek's replacement. All the local bigwigs will be there. I heard Maurice DuPree was even coming down."

"Now, there's a guy I'd like to meet," I said. "Liam Dougherty made it sound as if DuPree was always locked away in some ivory tower in Montreal. He forgot to mention he was coming to town on Friday."

Rita frowned. "That's odd. After all, Liam's the one who told me DuPree was expected to attend."

"Yeah, well, there are a lot of people in this town who don't seem to appreciate my poking into Castle House. I have the feeling everyone would be happy if I'd write a nice, sunny piece about the bass fishing and go home."

"I did warn you how insular this town is, Sheridan. Xenophobia seems to be our most popular neurosis." She smiled. "At any rate, since I need an escort tomorrow night and you need an excuse to corner Mr. DuPree, how about it?"

"Sure." I hesitated. "But, if you don't mind my asking, why aren't you going with Dougherty?"

She shrugged. "Simple enough. He didn't ask me. I guess he's finally getting the message that I'm interested in him as a friend, but that's as far as I want to go."

"Well, his loss is my gain. I'd be very pleased to escort you to the reception. For Professor Janezek's replacement, you said?"

"Yes, a man named Alston. I understand they lured him away from a teaching position at Boston College."

133

"That sounds like a questionable career move," I said. "Leaving a big school like B.C. for tiny Clampett College."

"It wouldn't be the sort of move I'd make," Rita agreed. "On the other hand, it isn't every day that a person is offered a department chairmanship. Maybe this Professor Alston subscribes to the big fish, small pond theory."

"Maybe so," I shrugged. "Anyway, it's too bad the reception isn't being held out at the Castle House. I'd love to get a look at that place. You ever been in it?"

"A couple of times, as Liam's guest. Both times were for public receptions to kick off special Fellowship events," she said. "It's quite an impressive place. Too bad it isn't used more often, but then, it is a little inconvenient when you have to ferry a large number of guests back and forth. Its main use is as a retreat for Fellowship members and official guests, which means it only gets used when a symposium or lecture series is scheduled."

"How often is that?" I asked.

"Oh, only four or five times a year, I'd say. The last function was held during the July Fourth weekend. A symposium on the new U.S.–Canadian trade agreement, I think." She wrinkled her nose. "I was just as happy not to be invited out for that one."

"Can't say I blame you," I mumbled, then added, "Oh, before I forget. The reason I came by was to see if there was a pay phone on campus. Touchtone. I need to make a long-distance call."

"There's one next door in the Student Union."

After promising to pick up Rita at seven-thirty the next night, I followed her directions across the quad to a squat, modernish building of red brick and tinted glass. The phone was tucked away in a corner of the atrium, next to a door leading to the men's room. I knew it was the men's room because of the simple male stick figure that was stenciled on to the door's upper panel. It was comforting to see that even institutions of higher learning were doing their bit to promote illiteracy.

"J.D. Staub," said the voice on the other end of the line after I'd punched up nearly two dozen numbers.

"Shouldn't you say 'Sheriff Staub speaking?'" I said.

"Sheridan?" J.D. chuckled softly. "Yeah, I guess I should, only I'm still not used to it. Too many years as second banana, I suppose."

"Old habits and all that," I said. Staub had been under-sheriff of Quincy County for twenty years before winning election to sheriff the previous autumn. He and my Uncle Charlie had been friends, a relationship I had stepped into by proxy after moving to Mohaca Springs. Our collaboration on finding my uncle's killer had cemented our friendship.

"You calling from the cottage?" he asked.

"No, I'm up at Widows Cape at the Thousand Islands." I explained briefly the series of events that had drawn me north, including the death of Professor Janezek at the CHANA convention and the ensuing research material sent to me by Alan Betz. I also mentioned the stone wall I was up against in trying to figure out what it was that had piqued the professor's interest in the original Castle House case and the Fellowship.

"It sounds curious, all right," J.D. said. "Assuming this Janezek was as straight as you seem to think he was. Which reminds me . . . hold on a second, Sheridan." I could hear him muttering and shuffling through papers. After ten seconds or so, he said, "Here we go. On this Janezek deal? I got a call two days ago from a D.C. homicide detective. A Lieutenant Bliss. The one who had you in for questioning at the time of the Janezek mugging."

"That's right," I said. "What'd he want?"

"Well, it was all pretty vague. Bliss said he'd tried to reach you at home, but that all he got was your machine. So, he called me to try and locate you. He had my name and number from before, during the initial investigation, when one of his detectives called up here to run a background check on you."

"You never told me about that."

"It was just routine. I vouched for your character, such as it is."

"You're a prince among men."

"I know. Anyway, Bliss said he was just calling to see if you had remembered anything more about Janezek and this reference to Castle House. I couldn't tell him anything, except what little you said to me about the whole deal when you got back from Washington."

"That's because I didn't know anything about Castle House at the time. Bliss already knew that."

"Well, like I said, Sheridan, the lieutenant was pretty vague. He did say if I heard from you, I should have you call him. That's the other curious thing. He left his home number, told me to have you call him there. Got a pen?"

I took out my notepad and pen and jotted down the number. "This thing is starting to turn very weird."

"I'd say so, kid. You better start curbing your enthusiasm a little. Remember, a crime story is a crime first and a story second."

I laughed. "What in hell does that mean?"

"It means if something bad's going down, you turn it over to the authorities to handle and worry about your story later. None of this New Journalism horseshit." J.D. was quiet for a moment, letting the message sink in. "Okay, the lecture's over, Sheridan. Now, if there's anything I can do from this end to help—"

"I thought you'd never ask. You didn't think this was a social call, did you, J.D.?"

"Give me the wish list," he sighed. "Slowly. I don't take shorthand."

"Well, first, there's this old state police file on the Castle House case," I began. I still wanted to look at the files from the original investigation and I reasoned that J.D. could use his influence to expedite matters. Then I told him about my contact with Howard Johnson and the background he'd given me on Jack Rose, leaving out, as I'd promised Howard, any mention of Howard's theory about the missing valuables. I asked J.D. to run Rose's name through the usual police databanks, including any old records that might tell me more about his prison stretch at Dannemora.

"Anything else?"

"I don't want to inconvenience you."

"You won't be inconveniencing me," J.D. said. "I plan to dump all this on Tony's desk. Delegating, we call it." Tony was Tony Areno, J.D.'s undersheriff and former chief of detectives.

"Well, in that case, you might run a couple of names by the people in Albany who keep tabs on nonprofit groups operating within New York State. That would be somebody with the Department of State, I think."

"What names?"

"The Midstream Fellowship, for one. And something called the Marshall Stewart Memorial Fund."

"And what do you want to know?"

"I don't know. Anything they can tell you, I guess."

"Sheridan, did I ever tell you the story about the little boy who pissed into the wind?"

"Is this worth listening to long-distance?"

"Not really."

"I didn't think so. Listen, J.D., I appreciate this."

"I owe you one. I'll try to get this done by tomorrow afternoon, but you better give me until Saturday noon to be on the safe side, okay? Call me here."

"Will do."

"And Sheridan?"

"Yeah?"

"You watch your step, kid, hear me?"

I made two more calls before heading out to the library parking lot to fetch my wheels. The first was to my answering machine back at the cottage in Mohaca Springs. It was one of those computerized whizbangs, crammed with more chips than a tollhouse cookie. I waited for my voice to come on the line to tell me I wasn't home, then I tapped out a three-digit code that told the machine to play back any messages. There were several, including one from J.D. and one from a woman in Geneva I'd been dating off and on. It seemed she wanted it to be on again. Nothing I could do about that now. The message I was interested in was from Lt. LaVerne Bliss, but it didn't tell me anything I hadn't already heard from J.D. Whatever Bliss was up to, he was playing it close to the vest. My second call was placed to his home phone number. As could be expected in the middle of a working day, there was no answer.

I was unlocking the Bronco's door when the sibilant sizzle of shoes on gravel caused me to turn around. Ellis Turnbull was standing there, hands tucked into his pockets.

"I'd like a friendly word with you," he said in that hushed baritone of his.

"I'm all ears, but the friendly part is up to you."

"I'm going to suggest you leave town."

"That's a little Dodge Cityish, isn't it?"

"Shut up and listen." The voice didn't vary a decibel. "This doesn't have anything to do with Rita, Sheridan. Certain people think you're screwing around in things that are none of your business. You keep doing it, they're gonna want something done about you. I don't want that to happen and, believe me, you don't, either. But you keep pushing and I'll have your butt in a cell. We'll start with a charge of soliciting a sex act with a known prostitute and then we'll come up with a few other things." He raised one arm slowly and pointed a finger at my face. "You reading me, friend? Go home now and save us both the aggravation."

"You done, Turnbull? Is it my turn?" I was battling to stay as cool as he was, but I was losing. Granny would say he'd gotten my Irish up.

"First," I said, "you can put that finger back up your ass where it belongs." He bristled, but dropped the arm back to his side. We glared at each other just long enough to establish how tough we were, then I hopped into the Bronco and fired up the engine. Before backing out of the space, I rolled down the window and tossed in another two cents.

"And second, if you want to try and frame me with the girl, you better make sure it's a tight fit, because I'll sue you for defamation of character, false arrest, and harassment. You reading me, friend?"

CHAPTER 19

LUNCH at the St. Lawrence
Club was probably a big deal forty years ago when the
membership consisted of local aristocrats and the occasional millionaire yachtsman. But when a resort begins to
lose its luster, exclusivity is usually the first casualty.
These days anyone with money in his pocket and shoes
and socks on his feet was welcome to feed there. Since I
had all three going for me, I walked into the place without
a second thought about my wrinkled slacks and rumpled
corduroy jacket.

An attractive middle-aged hostess escorted me across a
large, rococo dining room to a table with a river view. Dunleavy was seated with two other men. One was a florid,
husky guy I didn't know. The other was Rodney MacKenzie. The truculent little mayor was the last person I
wanted to see just then, but I didn't want to blow the interview with the judge, either. So I decided to grin and bear it.

"Glad you could make it, Mr. Sheridan," the judge said,
rising from his seat. "I believe you know our mayor. And
this is Fred Porter. Fred is on the town council, too, when
he isn't too busy running his business to attend meetings."
Dunleavy followed up the verbal jab with a light punch to
Porter's arm.

"Don't you believe it, Mr. Sheridan," Porter said, shaking hands. "The council couldn't function without me. I'm chairman of the refreshment committee."

"Ah, speaking of which," the judge said, motioning for the waitress. We all placed our drink orders—martinis for Dunleavy and MacKenzie, beer for Porter and me.

"What business are you in, Mr. Porter?" I asked.

"Real estate. North Jefferson Properties, Inc., that's us. Residential and commercial properties all over the north half of the county. If we don't list it, you don't want it." Porter chuckled. "That's been our informal motto for fifty years, ever since my dad and Rodney's father, Angus, put the agency together."

"Actually, it was my father who already had an established agency," MacKenzie interjected imperiously. "He took Manfred on because he needed a good talker to handle sales." He looked at me and feigned a friendly grin. "Manfred Sr. had the gift of gab, which, as you can see, he passed along to his son."

Porter laughed uncomfortably. "Well, technically that's true. But my dad brought in a lot of good will and new business thanks to that gift. He was a farm implements salesman at the time and the local fire chief, so he had a lot of contacts. Anyway, he worked his way into a full partnership eventually. And today," he glanced at MacKenzie, paying him back with a grin of his own, "I own the agency."

I said, "Now I know where I heard the name Manfred Porter. Your father was fire chief back when the Castle House burnt down."

"That's right. He led the effort to try and save the place. In vain, as I'm sure you know, Mr. Sheridan."

"I'd like to interview him, if I could."

"I'm afraid Dad passed on three years back."

"I'm sorry," I said, then turned to MacKenzie. "Is your father still living, mayor?"

"After a fashion. He's an invalid."

"Angus has had a series of strokes, Mr. Sheridan," the

140

judge said. "He lives with Rodney and Estelle—that's Rodney's wife. She spends most of her day seeing to Angus."

"Would it be possible for me to visit him?"

"No, it wouldn't," MacKenzie shook his head curtly. "Father is senile. Visitations are limited to family and old friends like the judge." His cool blue eyes studied me. "What interests you in my father, Sheridan?"

"The Castle House case," I said, returning his stare. "There were four young men already at the scene when Mr. Porter's father and the fire company arrived. The judge here," I nodded toward Dunleavy, "Angus MacKenzie, James C. Knox, and Marshall Stewart. I know that Dr. Knox's father, James, is dead. And, of course, we all know about poor Marshall Stewart." I paused to let that last statement sink in. None of the men reacted overtly, but the judge's shoulders seemed to sag. I went on, "I'd like to get as many firsthand accounts as possible. That puts your father and the judge here at the top of my list."

"You can scratch my father's name off your list," Mac-Kenzie said. "Frankly, if it were up to me, you wouldn't even be sitting here with the judge. I find the sort of muckraking you do distasteful."

I wanted to tell him what I found distasteful. Pimping for a co-ed hooker, for example. It would've been fun to see the self-righteous frown run off his face, but that wouldn't have done Kara any good. So I said, "I think we have widely differing views on what is and isn't distasteful, Mr. Mayor."

The waitress arrived with the drinks just then and remained nearby, idling in anticipation of our lunch orders. Judge Dunleavy announced cheerily that he was picking up the tab and encouraged everyone to order big, but no one did. I was still full from the breakfast Sonny Johnson had laid on and restricted myself to a bowl of clam chowder. The others each had the soup du jour—minestrone—and club sandwiches. By the time the food and a second round of drinks arrived, the conversation around the table had settled into the usual banter of business lunches everywhere. Golf was a popular topic, along with the Lions Club agenda, the price of gold, the Montreal Expos' fading pennant hopes, and the new line of Caddies. Congress came in for a pasting, of course, and it was decided that interest rates were choking the small business man. Ronald Reagan was declared this century's greatest president and FDR its worst. I brought up Warren G. Harding, but all that got me was cool stares. By the time our plates were empty, I was almost convinced I should get my hair styled and join the Junior Chamber of Commerce.

"Now, about your particular area of expertise, Mr. Sheridan," the judge said. "I believe Fred wanted to speak to you concerning a possible free-lance assignment."

The realtor leaned toward me and patted my arm. "As it happens, the regional tourism council, of which I'm a member, is planning a new directory on area hotels, motels, bed and breakfast places, et cetera. We're looking for a professional writer to do an introductory piece on the recreational pluses here in the Thousand Islands, along with a brief synopsis on each of the establishments on the list. Now, we don't have unlimited funds for this project, but businesses will be buying ad space in the directory and we think that will cover production costs, including the fee for your services."

"Thanks for thinking of me, Fred," I said. "But that isn't the sort of work I do. Besides, as I said earlier, I'm already on a kind of busman's holiday, looking to land a few lunkers while seeing if I can come up with a marketable story angle on the Castle House."

"I see," Porter said, his jowls drooping. "We just thought, on the off chance that this other thing didn't pan out for you—"

"Thanks anyway."

"Well, then." Porter glanced at the judge and the stoic mayor. He pushed his bulky body back from the table and got to his feet, offering me his hand and a small smile. "I guess it's no sale. Nice to have met you, Sheridan. I have to run along. I'm showing a cottage to a nice young couple from downstate this afternoon."

MacKenzie shot an I-told-you-so look at Dunleavy and tossed his napkin onto the table. "I have an appointment, too. Thanks for the lunch, judge. The next one's on me. Sheridan." He nodded curtly and stood.

The judge and I said our good-byes to the two men and watched them navigate across the dining room.

"Well, Mr. Sheridan," Dunleavy said. "You've been very patient, but I suspect you're eager to ask your questions. What do you say we do this over coffee on the veranda?"

"Tell me about that night, judge," I said. We were seated in matching green Adirondack chairs, coffee cups resting on the chairs' broad wooden arms. Dunleavy had fired up a cigar and was watching a sailboat tack its way upriver.

"It was a horrible night," he said softly. "I hardly know where to begin."

"How is it that you and the others spotted the fire and got out to the island first?"

The judge exhaled a plume of smoke. "It was New Year's Eve, 1937. I was home from Dartmouth for the holiday break. Some friends and I—you know the names—had been down in Watertown, drinking and carousing, as you'd expect. Around ten or so, we drove back up to Widows Cape. We were bored—Watertown isn't exactly festive, Mr. Sheridan, even on New Year's Eve—and so we decided to go back to Glenaire and play billiards."

"Glenaire?"

"Glenaire is my family home, out on Point Breeze Drive," the judge said archly. It was as if I'd displayed igno-rance on some immutable fact of nature, like the speed of light or the innate superiority of the Ivy League. "My grandfather commissioned it in 1877. I've lived there all my life, except for my years at college and law school."

"I see," I said. I'd had a fairly typical Irish Catholic up-bringing where the kids were named after saints and the house had no name at all. What would you call a suburban

143

split-level anyway? Since Tara and Xanadu were already taken, I mean.

"As I was saying," the judge continued, "the boys and I thought we'd ring in the new year over champagne in the billiard room, since mother and father were away at a party in Alexandria Bay. We were pulling up to the drive when Angus MacKenzie spotted the fire on Coffin Island. Glenaire is located out on the point, Mr. Sheridan, almost directly south of the island's western half." He took a long drag on the cigar. "Well, we just stood there for a moment, mesmerized by the sight. Obviously, the Castle House was on fire, it couldn't have been anything else. We heard the village fire bell go off just then and it woke us from our stupor. I drove the Packard down the ramp on our boat launch and out onto the ice. It only took a few minutes to cross and, as it turns out, we were first on the scene. We tried to get into the house but it was engulfed, an incredible inferno. There was nothing we could do."

He stopped to drink from his cup. He kept his face impassive, but the eyes wouldn't let him bring it off. They exposed a fathomless sorrow that not even half a century of distance had been able to eradicate.

"We circled the house like madmen, searching for the guests, waiting interminably for the fire crew to arrive. I suppose it was only a few minutes before Chief Porter and his men did show up, but it seemed like forever. Of course, it didn't matter." He sighed. "It was around two in the morning, I think, before the fire was brought under sufficient control for anyone to get inside. A couple of the firefighters came back up from the basement with the news all of us had been dreading. Castle and . . . the others had all been found in the wine cellar. It was determined later that everyone—except Tommy Trevain, of course—had suffocated before the flames actually made it into the cellar." He looked over at me. "Ironically, the dead all had to be cremated later, such was the poor condition of the bodies.

"As you no doubt have learned, the name of Jack Rose, a local thief and troublemaker, was found scratched onto one

144

of the foundation stones in the wine cellar. He and his accomplice drowned while attempting to drive across the ice to Canada. And that's about as much as I can tell you about the terrible Castle House tragedy, Mr. Sheridan." He checked his thin Swiss wristwatch. "And now, young man, I have fifteen minutes to get to an appointment of my own. So, if you have no other questions—"

"I have a great many questions, judge."

Dunleavy checked his watch again. "I can give you five more minutes, Mr. Sheridan."

"All right." I was caught off guard for a moment, unsure where to start. But then I remembered a lesson I'd learned as a cub reporter, faced with my first real story and a half hour until deadline. Type out the first fact that comes into your head, then keep on typing until a frantic assistant editor comes along and rips the copy out of your machine. And pray you've got it right.

"Alice and Victoria Spicer," I said. "I understand you and Marshall Stewart were very close to the two of them."

Dunleavy glanced away. "Actually, Marshall was, more so than myself. He was engaged to Alice. His parents didn't approve—they felt he would be marrying below his station, so to speak. The girls' father was just a foreman at my family's mining operation. But Marsh was adamant and his parents had eventually given their reluctant blessing."

"I heard you were unofficially engaged to Victoria."

"Where did you hear that?" He scowled. "Never mind. I recognize that, after so many years, there are plenty of unfounded rumors associated with the notorious Castle House case." He flicked the ash off his cigar and gathered himself in the chair. "I had known both girls since childhood. Victoria and I dated a few times, on the sly. My parents had the same outdated notions as the Stewarts, however, and I wasn't as, mm, headstrong as Marsh. I had no plans to go against their wishes."

I reasoned that it was possible that Sonny Johnson had overstated when he'd told me Dunleavy had been "semiengaged" to Victoria Spicer. As the judge pointed out, the rumor mill had had half a century to grind out the gossip. There was one fact, however, that I was certain an old newshound like Sonny wouldn't have gotten wrong.

"Your friend Marshall," I said, pacing the words with care. "His suicide must've come—"

"Marshall Stewart died in a hunting accident, Mr. Sheridan." It was a flat, cold statement, leaving no room for debate. I pursued it anyway.

"A despondent young man goes into the woods and accidentally trips over his shotgun?" I asked. "That was a fabrication to protect his family, judge. You know that."

"I know what the official death record states and that's all I—or anyone else—need know." He glared at me down his long, patrician nose. "And I don't know where you think you're going with this line of questioning, but I assure you I don't intend to go along. Your five minutes are now up, young man." He pushed himself up from the chair.

"I was leading up to a question about the Stewart Fund, sir," I said, as I stood.

"Yes, well, what about it? It's a local charity, set up by Marshall's and my families to do good works in his memory. Anything wrong with that, Mr. Sheridan?"

"No, sir. I was just wondering what an old seaman like Howard Johnson had done to deserve the fund's support. I'm assuming you know Howard."

"I know him, yes." Dunleavy tossed his dead cigar into a nearby bucket of sand. "He used to do odd jobs around town back in the old days, before he joined the merchant marines. Why shouldn't the fund give him a helping hand?"

"It just seems like an odd pairing. The Stewart Fund underwriting an old cohort of the infamous Jack Rose. You did know he was a friend of Rose's?"

"I knew he associated with some of the local riffraff back then, including Rose," the judge said stiffly. "But being charitable, Mr. Sheridan, includes having the capacity to forgive. We've all made our share of youthful mistakes."

CHAPTER 20

BY late afternoon the sky had clouded ominously and the river had turned sullen, its surface jagged with white caps. A chilling breeze coursed across the water like a shiver up the spine.

I lifted my left hand away from the shaft of the casting rod and flipped up my jacket collar. With my right hand I made a languid sidearm cast, jerking the wrist hard at the end like Tom Seaver snapping off a curve. The red wriggler rode the ten-pound test line out some forty feet and hit the water with a tiny splash. I let it settle, then slowly began reeling in. I had the concrete pier to myself except for an older couple who sat huddled together at the far end; a man and woman, both gray-haired, both wearing thin nylon jackets and sitting in lawn chairs. They stared out at the river with sober resignation, watching the last days of summer die. Maybe they would head south soon, like the chevron of geese that was making its way overhead, following their instincts to a winter retreat alongside some central Florida canal.

There's a lot to be said for instincts. Mine had led me there, to the end of the Widows Cape public pier. Sometimes a story can come along too fast, the various facts and conjectures of the investigation blurring, running together

147

like the colors in a cheap shirt at the first washing. Sometimes it's better to stop a moment, take the time to separate the items; whites in one pile, colors in another, an especially handy exercise when sorting through other people's dirty laundry.

After leaving the St. Lawrence Club, I had driven back over to the college to make a couple more calls from the pay phone in the student union and to see if Alan Betz had made any progress on the tasks I'd given him. It proved to be a wasted trip. Lt. Bliss still wasn't answering his phone and my second call, to Professor Janezek's brother in Chicago, had turned up nothing useful. I had spoken with the brother's wife, who had sounded harried and distracted and too busy taking care of three young children to worry about her late brother-in-law's old papers. The box containing the professor's files had been packed away in the attic with the Christmas decorations and the rest of the family junk and, as far as she was concerned, there was where it would stay. As for Betz, he was out of the office when I arrived, but he had left a message for me with Miss Witherspoon, asking me to stop by his apartment anytime after six that evening.

I'd found myself behind the wheel of the Bronco, listening to an old Doors tape while cruising aimlessly around town, waiting for inspiration to jackrabbit across the road so I could run it down. My wanderlust led me to Point Breeze Drive. I followed its meandering course along the river, past a row of handsome old homes on large lawns, until I came to the last and the largest. It was a white Georgian revival surrounded by a stone wall. A brass plate at the entrance to the long driveway read Glenaire. It was a far cry from the SonnyShores and Do-Drop-Ins of Miller's Bay. To my right, far out on the river, Coffin Island sat placidly under a cloudy sky, the Castle House hidden behind its curtain of maples and firs. I pulled the Bronco to the side of the road and stared at Glenaire for a few minutes but, like its owner, it refused to tell me any of its secrets.

My luncheon interview with the judge had left me with an unsettled feeling at the pit of my stomach, and it had nothing to do with the clam chowder. Rita had called him paternalistic. The town patriarch, protecting his people against the outside world, with or without their knowledge or approval. Maybe that explained why he had downplayed his relationship with Victoria Spicer and the circumstances surrounding Marshall Stewart's "hunting accident." Maybe.

Jim Morrison was singing "Riders on the Storm" on the tape deck just then and my mind called up a line I'd read who knows where. "When the doors of perception are cleansed, man will see things as they truly are; infinite." It had been written by the poet William Blake. Aldous Huxley had paid tribute to the line by naming his book on psychedelic drugs *The Doors of Perception*. Morrison had truncated the phrase even further to come up with a name for his band.

That's when I decided to try hosing off my own personal door of perception. To quit pushing, find a quiet place to kick back and wet a line. Let the thoughts flow naturally.

I turned around and drove back downtown and up River Street toward the pier. As I passed the constabulary, I noticed my two neighbors from the Clearview, Curly and Moe, coming out. I watched them walk off in the other direction until they faded away in my rearview mirror. I asked myself what business a couple of visiting anglers could have with Ellis Turnbull, but I couldn't come up with an answer.

I ran the lure up near the tip of the rod, adjusted the reel's bale and made another cast. When the line had settled, I eased myself down onto the edge of the pier, dangled my desert boots over the side, and began reeling in again. Fishing is largely an exercise in patience and persistence. You find a likely spot, toss out a line, and take your chances. If you've found the right stretch of water and chosen the proper bait, you've done all you can. I watched the gray green water roil around the pier's moldy pilings, the turbulence reflecting my state of mind. Somewhere amidst the flotsam of the Castle House story was a connecting link.

Somewhere.

Start with the basics.

Item. Professor Janezek apparently suspected there was a direct tie-in between the half-century-old Castle House case and the present-day existence of the Fellowship. But the professor had been conveniently killed while attending a convention in Washington and his research file had subsequently been destroyed by Liam Dougherty, who just happened to belong to the Fellowship.

Item. Mayor MacKenzie, who belonged to the Fellowship as well and had a tenuous connection to the old Castle House case through his father, had sent Kara to my room to find out what was in the paper bag I'd brought up from the basement of Dougherty's apartment house. Then the good mayor had instructed his chief constable to warn me off.

Item. Maurice DuPree had obviously spent a huge pile of cash to rebuild the Castle House estate and establish a think tank of sorts. But DuPree, through his minions Dougherty and MacKenzie, also seemed to be making every effort to keep the Fellowship an obscure, arcane little organization, even going so far as to employ trained attack dogs and a couple of sadistic caretakers to keep the public at bay.

Item. The men who were first at the scene of the Castle House fire were Robert Burns Dunleavy, Marshall Stewart, Angus MacKenzie, James C. Knox II, and, subsequently, Fire Chief Manfred Porter. Dunleavy had granted me an interview, only to gloss over the truth about his relationship with Victoria Spicer and Marshall Stewart's suicide. Angus MacKenzie's son had refused to let me interview his father and had made a point of discouraging my research into the tragedy from the outset. Dr. Knox, the son of James Knox II, had attempted to discredit Howard

Johnson's competence in order to dissuade me from interviewing Howard further. And the old fire chief's son, Fred Porter, had tried to buy me off the case by offering me a freelance assignment.

Preliminary conclusions?

First, Dunleavy and his friends—and now their sons—had spent half a century guarding some secret about the Castle House tragedy. But was it something they had seen, or something they had done? Or didn't do? And who were they protecting: themselves, the reputation of their town, or someone else?

Second, the Fellowship had some hidden agenda that had nothing to do with its stated purpose as an academic association dedicated to promoting scholarship at Clampett College and researching global sociopolitical trends. But what common goal would bring together such a disparate group as a French-Canadian multimillionaire, a Socialist college professor, a humorless small-town mayor, and a pair of hired thugs?

Of all the principal players, the one with the strongest connections to both groups was Rodney MacKenzie. As the son of Angus MacKenzie, he was privy to whatever secret the town fathers knew about the Castle House incident. And as Maurice DuPree's attorney and confidant, he also had to know the true purpose behind the Fellowship.

I could go straight at MacKenzie, using what I knew about his relationship with the girl to squeeze him. But MacKenzie was tough, he knew the law, and he had a lot of local pull. He'd likely dig in his heels and brazen out any pressure I tried to apply, and besides, that approach would make the girl vulnerable. I had to make an end run to get at MacKenzie. From the Castle House side of the ledger, I figured the mayor's father Angus was my best shot. As for the Fellowship half of the equation, Liam Dougherty was as good a place to start as any. If only I could push Dougherty into—

"Hi, Sheridan."

I turned my head and glanced up. Kara. She was wearing

151

jeans and running shoes and an oversized sweatshirt imprinted with the Clampett College emblem. The co-ed look. It may have been as calculated as the previous night's spike heels and short shorts, but I liked it. She sat down Indian fashion and watched my hands as I worked the reel.

Eventually, she said, "I saw Mack last night, after I left your place. Fed him the bull about the notebook."

"Thanks," I said. "How'd he react?"

She shrugged. "He was really bugged when I said I couldn't tell if the papers all burned up or what. He starts mumbling about what a fuckup Dougherty is, like under his breath, right? And then he gets out of the bed—" She paused, the flush in her face quickly passing from embarrassment to anger. "It's what I do, remember?"

"I remember." My lure broke the water. I reeled it up and made a short cast. "What else did he tell you?"

"He didn't tell me anything. I mean, at first he was just talking to himself, like I wasn't there, you know? Then he tells me we better keep away from each other for a few days, which was cool with me. Then he gets up and goes out to use the kitchen phone, even though I've got one sitting right there on the nightstand." She laughed contemptuously. "It's an answering machine with a speaker phone. The little prick forgot about that."

"You listened in?"

"Yeah. He phoned some guy named Maurice."

"Yeah?" I stopped reeling for a moment and looked at her. "This guy Maurice have anything interesting to say?"

She studied me for a few seconds, then looked out at the river and frowned. "What's going on, Sheridan? I mean, what's this story you're supposed to be investigating? And why's Mack so uptight about it?"

"Last night you said it was none of your business, Kara. You were right. You're better off not knowing."

"Bullshit! It's too late for that. Anyway, if you want to know what I know, you gotta clue me in."

I turned it over for a few moments, looking at both sides and not particularly liking either one. If she was stringing me along, she'd be able to go to MacKenzie with everything I knew. And if she was playing straight with me, telling her what I knew could endanger her. On the other hand, if I held back, she wouldn't tell me about the phone conversation. In the end, I rationalized it by telling myself she had a right to know the kind of people she was running with. Then I told her everything I knew. When I finished, she had only one question.

"So, if the Fellowship turns out to be some kind of illegal deal, Desmond and Claude could be in big trouble, right?"

"And MacKenzie, too," I reminded her.

"That doesn't exactly break my heart, either."

She started in, relating what she could recall of the phone conversation between MacKenzie and Maurice. The Widows Cape mayor had spoken of the notebook, while the other man listened, grunting occasionally. Dougherty had blown it. Dougherty was panicky. This writer who was snooping around had to be dealt with somehow, MacKenzie had said. No, the other man had countered. There was no reason to think the reporter had found anything useful left in the notebook. The weak link was Dougherty. He could be handled.

"That was all?" I asked when Kara paused.

"Yeah. Except this Maurice guy goes, 'We can finish this discussion on Friday' and Mack goes, 'Beauchamp will meet you with the launch, as planned.' That was it."

"DuPree, arriving for the reception," I said, half to myself. Then, "Thanks for coming to me, Kara. I—"

Before I could finish the thought, a powerful jolt surged through the rod and the slack in the line quickly played out. I scrambled to my feet, letting the fish run, feeling the ten-pound filament stiffening as it spun out across my index finger. Suddenly the line slackened as the fish changed course. I reeled in the slack and firmly jerked the rod. The bass jumped once, its scales flashing, then tried to head for deep water. I stayed with it, reeling in, keeping the line taut, until I could feel its strength ebb. It made one last, weary attempt to jump as I brought it close to the pier, then gave in to its exhaustion as I pulled it from the water. I held it up for Kara's inspection, smiling broadly, primeval man triumphing over nature.

She gave the bass a cursory glance, made a face, and said, "Yuck."

CHAPTER 21

ALAN Betz lived in a small, one-size-fits-all apartment building just north of the campus. The building was beige stucco, four stories, with a postage-stamp parking area crammed in on the left and a permanent sign out front hawking one-bedroom units for rent. The monthly rate posted on the sign was about what a Manhattanite would pay to berth a car.

I slipped the Bronco into a spot at the back of the lot and headed for the lighted portico at the main entrance to the building. I was alone, but it wasn't Kara's idea.

I had bought her dinner at the Glass Gazebo as a payback for the information she'd brought me, but it didn't satisfy her appetite. She was hungering for excitement. At least, that was the reason she gave for wanting in on the investigation. But there was more to it than that. It had something to do with a tough little girl's skewed sense of friendship. It didn't seem to matter that I had more or less blackmailed her into allying herself with me against MacKenzie. I had sat on a bed with her and held her hand and listened to her life story. I hadn't talked down to her or treated her like a cheap bimbo and, better still, I had offered her a means to pay back those who had. To her, all that somehow made us fast friends. And, oddly enough, I felt the same way.

She had pestered me all the way through the salad bar and the sandwich plates. She told me about the time Mac-Kenzie had sent her out to the Castle House to "service" Desmond and Claude. How she'd had a glimpse inside a librarylike office at the mansion—an IBM PC and modem on the desk—and reminded me what a whiz she was at computers. She could use her connections with MacKenzie, she had said. Get back into the place, find an opportunity to hack through the computer's files, maybe find out what the Fellowship was really up to out there.

I had to give her credit, she knew my weak spot. My story was sitting out there on that island and, eventually, I was going to have to find a way to go out there and get it. But I wouldn't use Kara to pay my fare, not as long as Desmond and Claude were the ticket-takers.

We'd argued about it on the drive back to her place. She kept insisting she knew how to handle a couple of sickos like Day and Beauchamp. I kept insisting she wasn't going to have the opportunity to find out. When I dropped her off, she was still pouting but she agreed to leave it alone. I promised I'd keep her posted, let her know if I needed anything, and she seemed to accept that.

I let myself into the vestibule of Betz's building. Set into the side wall were a dozen locking mailboxes. Above each box was a door buzzer and a name card. Betz had apartment 3-C. A folded piece of paper was wedged in his mail slot. I pulled it out and spread it open.

"Sheridan—Got a call to meet L. D. at his place at seven. Sounded nervous, said he wanted to talk things over. Wait here or meet me there, whatever—Alan."

I checked my watch. 7:45. Betz could come home any time now, but waiting wasn't something I did when given a choice. I tucked the note into my coat pocket and headed back out to the parking lot. Dougherty's place was only three blocks away. That was one of the handy things about small-town life, I remember thinking as I pulled up in front of Mrs. Landsdowne's neat Victorian. Everything was within a few blocks of everything else.

The porch was well lit by a pair of milk glass globes mounted to either side of the double doors. I entered the vestibule and pressed the buzzer for Dougherty's apartment, waited ten seconds, and pressed it again. Nothing. I was about to buzz Mrs. Landsdowne when I noticed that the interior door was ajar. I let myself into the foyer and took the stairs to the second floor two at a time, pushed on by a growing sense of urgency I didn't fully understand. When I reached Dougherty's door, it too was cracked open.

"Professor Dougherty? Alan?" No response.

I stepped to one side of the door jam, mimicking every TV cop I'd ever seen, and pushed the door inward. I waited for a spray of hot lead that didn't come, then peered around the jam tentatively.

"Dougherty?"

Nobody invited me, but I went in anyway, treading softer than a sinner in a cathedral. The apartment looked the same as it had during my last visit: cramped, cluttered and empty. I crossed over toward the desk, then stopped short. Dougherty was lying on his side near the doorway to the kitchen, his head resting in a pool of blood, a red rivulet running down his face from a small hole just above the right temple.

"Oh, Christ." I felt the bile begin to churn in my stomach and my last meal start to retrace a path up my esophagus. I closed my eyes and breathed deeply. After a moment, I forced my eyes open and stared down at the body.

Dougherty's right arm was slung out awkwardly, the hand resting palm up, fingers half clenched. Lying next to the hand, partially concealed by the overhang of an end table, was a pistol. It had polished wood stocks and a five-inch barrel and a gun oil sheen that made it sparkle under the lamplight. I started to reach down for it, then pulled my hand back as if it had been slapped.

I coaxed my legs into moving, back out into the hallway, down the stairs to the landing, the shock beginning to wear off, my breathing cycling down closer to normal. I would rouse Mrs. Landsdowne, use her phone.

"Hold it, Sheridan!"

I stopped dead on the landing. Below me, standing in the foyer, a shotgun cradled in his arms, was Ellis Turnbull.

"So if Dougherty was already dead, how'd you get in?"

"I already told you. The front door was ajar. So was the apartment door."

"And you waltzed right in and found the body."

"That's right."

"Didn't touch anything. Just took a look, then headed downstairs to the landlady's to call it in. That right?"

"That's what I was intending to do, until I ran into Turnbull in the foyer."

"Say again why it was you went over there?"

I sighed. "To find Alan Betz. I showed you the note he left for me."

"Which you picked up at his place about a quarter to eight? Then you went right over to Dougherty's?"

"Yes."

"Right. Sit tight."

The speaker was a tall, rangy state police investigator named Craven. He pushed himself up from the desk and motioned Turnbull to follow him into Turnbull's office. I glanced up at my keeper, Smiley Chase, who was leaning against the front door of the constabulary, digging a finger into his ear and grinning.

"Hell of a night," I said.

"And still early," Smiley replied.

I took a look at the wall clock. Almost ten. I'd been at the constabulary for some two hours, the first of which I'd spent waiting with Chase while Turnbull and the state boys handled the grisly details out at Dougherty's apartment. When Turnbull and Craven had come back to the office, Craven had Mirandized me—"Just a formality, you're not being charged with anything"—and started in with the questions. What was I doing at Dougherty's place?

How long had I known him? What did the deceased have to do with the story I was supposedly researching? What was the dead man's mental state the last time I'd spoken with him? Did I have any reason to think Dougherty was distraught, possibly contemplating suicide? How did Alan Betz link up with Dougherty? Did I have anyone who could verify my bona fides? On and on.

I had held back most of what I'd learned about Castle House and the Fellowship, not wanting to open up in front of Turnbull. I'd brought Alan Betz's name up reluctantly, not that I had much choice under the circumstances. Anyway, the cops were approaching Dougherty's death as a suicide and, for the moment, that was fine with me. Early on in the questioning, Craven had asked for a character reference. I'd given him J.D. Staub's name and a call was placed to the Quincy County Sheriff. J.D. had assured Craven that I was who I claimed to be and, for good measure, explained that I made a habit of turning up in the middle of messy police investigations. After the testimonial, with Craven and Turnbull eyeing me, I spoke to J.D. long enough to assure him that everything was okay and that I'd call him back as soon as I was free to talk.

At that point, I had hung up the phone and Craven, a touch more tactful, had gone back to grilling me on Dougherty. Now he emerged from Turnbull's office with the chief constable in his wake, both men looking grim.

Craven plunked himself down on the corner of the desk where I was sitting and studied me carefully.

"I just got off the phone with the head of our forensics team," he said. "Guess what, Sheridan?"

"What?"

"The deceased has just been upgraded from probable suicide to suspicious death." Craven waited for a response, but I couldn't think of one fast enough, so he went on, "Silver nitrate tests indicate the deceased hadn't fired a weapon. 'Course, silver nitrate tests aren't all that reliable. But then there's this other thing." He canted his head to one side. "A man shoots himself, he's apt to leave his prints on the weapon, wouldn't you say?"

"And Dougherty's fingerprints weren't?"

"Dougherty's or anybody else's." Craven pushed off the desk and stood with his hands on his hips. "Some moron wiped the pistol clean, then dropped it next to the body, hoping we'd get sloppy and buy suicide. Lucky for you, the same witness who called Chief Turnbull here to report a gunshot also says he saw you show up at the house after the shot was fired. Now, assuming for the moment that you really didn't touch the murder weapon, that only leaves us with your buddy Betz. And a whole bunch of questions."

"You're forgetting, Betz left me a note telling me where he was," I said. "Why would he do that if he was planning to kill Dougherty?"

"I didn't forget," Craven shook his head. "I never said the killing was premeditated."

I conceded him that point and tried another angle. "Betz's note said he went to see Dougherty at seven. He could've taken care of his business and been out of there in fifteen, twenty minutes, leaving plenty of time for someone else to show up and kill Dougherty before I arrived." It sounded pretty lame, I'll admit, but then Craven didn't know about the phone call MacKenzie had made to DuPree. The one where DuPree had said he'd take care of Dougherty. And I wasn't about to enlighten Craven, not with Turnbull sitting there giving me the evil eye.

"If Betz is so clean on this, Sheridan, why hasn't he shown up back at his place?" Craven asked, frowning. "I got men over there, over to the college, combing the village. Nothing." He shook his head slowly from side to side and turned to Turnbull. "I'll tell you something, Ellis, this whole deal is screwy. College professors knocking each other off—Christ. And how do you figure an amateur like this Betz coming up with an expensive Swiss automatic. SIGs don't exactly qualify as your ordinary Saturday night special."

Turnbull mumbled a response, but it didn't register. My brain was too busy catching up to Craven's last comment. A Swiss-made SIG pistol; where had I heard that before? The same place I last saw a corpse with a neat little bullet hole just above the right temple.

"What caliber was the gun?" I asked.

Craven pivoted back to me. "A 7.65 millimeter. Why?"

"Because two months ago in Washington, someone used the same kind of gun to murder Professor Stefan Janezek."

CHAPTER 22

IT took another twenty min-
utes for Smiley Chase to get Lt. LaVerne Bliss of the D.C.
police on the phone. I filled the time by answering a new
barrage of questions from Craven and Turnbull, telling
them what I knew about the Janezek murder. They listened calmly, considering each piece of information carefully, skeptically, as good cops should.

"It could be just coincidence," Turnbull said. "Same
type of gun, but different killers."

"The lieutenant told me the cartridges found at the
scene were Italian, not commonly found in the States." I
looked to Craven. He shook his head.

"Our ballistics people haven't got that far yet. All I know
is it was 7.65 millimeter. I'll tell you, though, Ellis—assuming this Lieutenant Bliss verifies Sheridan's story, I'm
not about to chalk this up to coincidence. I mean, I'm a
collector, I know guns, and there just aren't that many SIG
P-201 pistols out there. Not at sixteen hundred bucks
apiece."

Smiley finally was able to convince a bureaucrat in the
D.C. police to forward his call to the lieutenant's home
phone. I could've saved him some time by looking the
number up in my notepad, but that would've meant ex-

plaining how I happened to have Bliss's unlisted private number handy. I wasn't in the mood to discuss it just then, particularly since I still didn't know myself why Bliss had wanted me to get in touch with him.

Craven got on the horn with Bliss and, after identifying himself, gave a terse rundown of the evening's events. My name was mentioned several times. Craven cited the make and caliber of the gun that had killed Liam Dougherty, then lapsed into a concentrated thirty seconds of silence marred only by an occasional grunt.

"Can you fax me a copy of the ballistics report, along with the FBI lab report?" he said eventually. "Uh-huh. Yeah, but it's hard to say. I'll light a fire under them, lieutenant, get back to you with our results ASAP." Pause. "Sure thing. I'll put him on. Just a second."

Craven looked to Turnbull. "Ellis, would you mind having your man get on the radio, see if any of the patrols have come up with anything on Betz's whereabouts? And you might start calling around for some background on Betz, see if we can scare up a motive. How many phone lines you got?"

"Three," Turnbull said. "I'll use my office phone."

"Good. Meanwhile, I gotta get ahold of the lab." Craven swung around to me and held out the handset. "Lieutenant Bliss wants a word with you, Sheridan."

I took the phone and watched Craven move over to a corner desk. "Hello?"

"Sheridan? Bliss. I've been trying to reach you for three days."

"So J.D. Staub told me. What's going on?"

"That's what you're supposed to tell me," Bliss said angrily. "All I know is that a simple murder-robbery case from July suddenly seems to be everybody's favorite item. First you call me out of the blue a week ago looking for an update. Next thing I know, I've got federal heat breathing down my neck. Now I'm getting rousted outa bed by the goddamn New York State Police, asking me for information on this same simple-looking mugging."

"Wait a minute," I said. "What do you mean, federal heat?"

"Never mind that for now," Bliss barked at me. "Let's get back to you and the dead professor and all this Castle House crap. Investigator Craven says you've got another professor blown away with a 7.65 millimeter SIG auto. I want to know what you know about all this."

I clued him in on the key details, starting with the sample of the professor's research notes that Alan Betz had sent me and blitzing right on through to the sudden and unexpected departure from this world of Liam Dougherty. For my finale, I identified the cast of characters as if I were reading it from a playbill; Judge Dunleavy, Mayor MacKenzie, Maurice DuPree, et cetera. The whole recitation was done sotto voce, with one eye on Craven, sitting at a corner desk with a phone to his ear, and the other eye on Turnbull's office door. I expected Bliss to comment on my paranoia, but as it turns out, he was too busy cultivating his own.

"You think you got problems?" he grumbled. "I've got the federales flagging my case files down here, fucking with our computers, maybe even tapping my phones, all because some tourist got himself dusted by a junkie. Or so I thought."

"I don't follow you, lieutenant."

"The Janezek case," he said. "It looks open and shut, right? The guy gets mugged. No witnesses, no leads, no nothing. We investigate, but when nothing turns up, we move on to the next pointless homicide. I mark the investigation down as open but inactive and send it down to Records, so they can log it into the computer. This was about a month ago. Two weeks later, I get an official request, supposedly from INS, for a hard copy of the complete file."

I cut him off. "Why would Immigration pick up on the Janezek case?"

"I have no idea what they'd want with it. But then, I don't think it was INS that made the request."

164

"Who—?"

"Let's put it this way. There are certain government agencies that like to operate in the dark. Sometimes these agencies use other agencies as a front, so as not to tip off anybody that they're interested. You follow me?"

"Yeah, but I'm getting dizzy."

"Hold on to your hat," Bliss laughed mirthlessly. "Sometimes these sub-rosa agencies get cute and put electronic moles into other folks' databanks. The mole is supposed to look for any references to a particular subject, say like 'strawberry shortcake.' Everytime this mole runs across 'strawberry shortcake' in some agency's computer files, a red flag goes up."

"You think one of the intelligence agencies had a mole in the D.C. police databank," I said. "The mole found something in the Janezek file that matched with the search order it had been given. This other agency uses the INS as a front to get you to send along everything you've got on the case."

"You got it so far," the lieutenant said.

"I wonder what the mole found in the Janezek file that caused it to send up a flag?" I said, half to myself.

"I got no idea," Bliss said. "But there's more. I didn't get too worked up about it at the time. Frankly, we're used to this kinda shit. Cops are second class citizens as far as the federales are concerned. They don't tell us squat. So I forgot all about it. But then, a couple days ago, I get a visit from a couple of Feebies."

"FBI?"

"Right on. They wanted a copy of the Janezek file, too. And they also had some questions, like did I have any information on this Midstream Fellowship you've just been telling me about. I couldn't tell them anything, and they wouldn't tell me anything. Which leaves me standing on the proverbial slippery slope. I got this unsolved murder sitting in my files and all these federal hard-ons poking around, and I gotta wonder, is my ass covered here? Or is this harmless little case gonna come back to screw me and my pension? You getting the picture, Sheridan?"

"I am," I said. "But right now, lieutenant, all I've got are questions of my own."

"Yeah, well you better start coming up with a few answers," Bliss said gruffly. "And when you do, I'd better be the first to know. And if I find out you've been holding back anything that'd help me clear the Janezek case, I'm going to land on you with both feet."

"Understood," I said evenly. "But—"

The phone clunked in my ear, followed by a dial tone. The lieutenant wasn't one for long good-byes. I didn't take it personally. I was too busy staring at the wall opposite the desk, trying to sort through this new flood of information before it could inundate my brain cells and short out my reasoning powers. I was still bailing when Turnbull appeared in front of the desk.

"I just got off the phone with Dr. Stevenson from over at Clampett," he said. "He had quite a lot to say about your friend Alan Betz."

Craven and Smiley Chase had joined the congregation around the desk by that time. I sat back in my chair, waiting for Turnbull to continue.

"It seems Betz had a grudge against Professor Dougherty," he said in that maddeningly quiet way of his. "According to Dr. Stevenson, Betz believed he was being persecuted by Dougherty. Kept off some faculty search committee, shut out of involvement in the Fellowship. The way Stevenson paints it, Betz is an ambitious young man who just might've convinced himself that Dougherty represented some sort of professional roadblock."

"So he maybe decided to remove that roadblock?" the state police investigator offered, chewing it over. "Took all the crap he felt he could take, then just snapped, hmm?"

"Don't surprise me any," Smiley tossed in his two cents. "Most of them people are half nuts to begin with."

"The thing that bugs me is the note," Craven admitted. "That pretty much rules out premeditation, like I said. But if it wasn't premeditated, why would he bring the pistol?"

"Exactly," I said. "And, speaking of the gun, what about the Janezek murder? If it's the same gun—"

"It still points to Betz," Turnbull cut me off. "Professor Janezek was an even bigger roadblock to Betz's professional goals than Dougherty was. Janezek was the chairman of the history department. No doubt Betz wanted the job."

"You're reaching now, Turnbull," I said. "Betz doesn't even have his doctorate yet. And he certainly wouldn't expect to get a department chairmanship without it."

The chief scowled at me. "Stevenson says Betz was close to finishing up on his Ph.D. Maybe he figured he'd be named interim department chair. And one more thing. Betz spent the summer in graduate school at the University of Virginia in Charlottesville." He allowed himself a small, congratulatory grin. "If I remember my geography, Charlottesville is an easy two, two and a half hour drive from D.C."

"I'm liking it better all the time," Craven said, as he began to pace the small constabulary. "We got possible motive, we got opportunity for both cases, probably a common weapon. And the suspect appears to be on the run."

"Patrols ain't seen any sign of him," Smiley agreed.

Craven said, "We'd better get out and join 'em, Ellis. I think we might as well let Sheridan here go home, unless you've got anything else for him."

Turnbull eyed me speculatively, but then shook his head. "No more questions, for now."

"I've got one for you, though, chief," I said, standing. "This guy who reported hearing a gunshot at Dougherty's apartment house, and who later verified that I arrived after the shot was fired. Who was he?"

Turnbull's grin expanded, spreading tiny laugh lines across his thin, chiseled face. "That's privileged information, Sheridan. And you aren't among the privileged."

No one was among the privileged at Floyd's, the roadside diner just down the highway from my motel. I pulled in for a cup of decaf, parking the Bronco in a shadowy corner, far removed from the semis and pickups that were nosed up around the neon-lit diner like pigs at a trough.

The place was about a quarter full, the clientele mostly male. Half were wearing jeans and light rain jackets and caps with the names of auto parts companies and breweries on the crowns. The rest sported the usual fishing attire, including a few in waterproof camouflage suits, the better to sneak up on unsuspecting walleye. Randy Travis sang a country lament on the jukebox, his vocal chords trapped somewhere in his sinus passages.

I took a stool at the end of the lunch counter and ordered a wedge of blueberry pie with my coffee on the theory that fueling the body might fire the brain. It didn't work. No matter which way I studied the events over at Dougherty's apartment, I could construct only two scenarios, and each one put Alan Betz right in the middle of a murder. First there was Craven and Turnbull's version. That a young associate professor had been driven over the brink by his own ambitions, coolly murdering his boss so he'd have a clear shot at becoming department chairman, then, in a rage, killing the man who had blocked him from getting the job. I suppose you could make it fit, particularly if you were a police investigator looking for quick solutions. But Craven hadn't spent the previous days picking through the whole Castle House riddle, examining the Byzantine connections between the Fellowship clique and the town fathers of Widows Cape.

No. I couldn't see Betz as the killer. But the second scenario wasn't any better. Betz turning up at the apartment just as one of DuPree's hired hands was about to send Dougherty on a permanent sabbatical. That would explain why the killer, surprised at the intrusion, had done a hasty job of arranging Dougherty's death to look like a suicide. It also explained why Betz had disappeared. The killer, most likely Desmond Day or Claude Beauchamp or both, wouldn't leave any witnesses. Which meant poor Alan Betz was probably lying at the bottom of the river by now.

"Can I warm that up for you?"

I came out of my funk abruptly. The waitress was standing there with a pot of Sanka, staring at me. I glanced to my right and noted that my nearest neighbor, two stools down, was stealing a glance in my direction. I realized I'd been mumbling to myself. No one would've paid any attention in the city, where everyone ends up talking to himself sooner or later. But this wasn't the city.

I smiled as sanely as I could. "No, thanks."

I paid the check and headed out to the parking lot. The moon was hidden behind a cloud bank. The night grew blacker with each step I took away from the garish neon of the diner. The only sounds were my feet scuffling through the gravel and the high hum of tires as the odd car whizzed by out on the highway.

I was standing beside the Bronco, trying to see through the ink to unlock the door, when I heard to my left the hiss of a shoe dragging the gravel and, simultaneously, felt a hand grip my arm. Impelled by fear and adrenaline, I shot my elbow up and felt it connect solidly with bone. There was a cry of pain as a shadowy form slumped against the Bronco's fender and slid to the ground. I leaned down, my right arm cocked and ready, and peered at my "attacker." He was wet and trembling, a nasty bruise marring his forehead, his eyes closed up tighter than the post office at five o'clock.

The late Alan Betz, risen again.

CHAPTER 23

IT was a fair morning for a stakeout. The previous evening's heavy cloud cover had given way to a lapis lazuli sky, studded here and there with cumulus cotton balls. The sun had crept a few inches above the eastern horizon, promising a comfortable autumn day, and the condensation on the Bronco's windshield had evaporated.

I had lucked onto a perfect vantage point at a rest stop along Route 12E just west of the village. It sat atop a hill with a view to the treelined St. Lawrence a quarter mile to the north and, more to the point, offered an unobstructed sightline to a house on a private side road that meandered down toward the river from the main highway.

Cool jazz blew through the speakers mounted in the door panels and the brass spyglass lay ready on the dashboard. I drank coffee from a Styrofoam cup and kept my eyes on the house, while my mind played back last night's comedy of errors.

Alan Betz couldn't have weighed more than a hundred and forty pounds soaking wet, which, in fact, he was. And out cold to boot, which made hoisting him into the Bronco's back seat a frustrating exercise akin to pushing a sack of jello up a playground slide.

I got him inside and checked him over. Besides the ugly bump on his forehead, he had a trickle of blood running from the corner of his mouth, thanks to my elbow, and the wire-rim glasses were missing. His pulse was regular and he seemed to be breathing okay. I yanked the wool army blanket up from behind the seat and covered him. Then I climbed around to the driver's seat and gunned the engine to life.

I drove west, away from Widows Cape, with no destination or purpose other than to put some distance between myself and the police dragnet that was out looking for my passenger. By the time I'd covered the few miles to the next town, Cape Vincent, the Bronco's heater had filled the compartment with stale warmth and Betz had begun to come around.

I glanced back over the seat. He glared at me accusingly. "You hit me!"

"Yeah, I'm sorry," I said, turning back to watch the road. "But you shouldn't grab onto people in the dark looking like the Creature from the Black Lagoon."

"I . . . I, uh." He tried sitting up, then fell back, gingerly laying a hand across his forehead. "Oh, God. Somebody else hit me, too. Back at Liam Dougherty's place. He's . . . he's dead, Sheridan!"

"I know."

We were through Cape Vincent's four-block main drag in two blinks. The shops were all closed for the night and the town's single stoplight had switched to flashing yellow for the duration. I steered the Bronco through a sharp turn in the road and spied a roadside hamburger stand just ahead.

"Stay down under the blanket," I told Betz. "I'm going to get you something hot to drink, then we're going to talk."

It was the kind of place that used to exist all over the country twenty years ago. Now you only find them in towns too small and isolated to support a McDonald's or a Burger King. A squat, white cinderblock bunker with faded signs in the front windows advertising chili dogs, hot fudge sundaes, and Perry's ice cream by the scoop. No dining room or counter service, just a walk-up window with a sliding screen over it under a flat roof overhang embedded with bare fluorescent lighting and dead moths.

I parked well away from the lot's only other car—a rusted twelve-year-old Monte Carlo jammed with teenagers—and walked up under the glare of lights to the window. The kid behind the screen had bad skin and a matching attitude. When I ordered a large black coffee, he smirked and said the coffee machine was "down." When I asked about tea, he rolled his eyes and informed me that nobody drinks tea. I asked if anybody drinks hot chocolate. He frowned and admitted that they did. I ordered a large, hold the marshmallow, and the kid grudgingly went to work. Eventually he shuffled back to the window, slid open the screen, took my dollar, rang up seventy-seven cents on the cash register, and slid the cup of hot chocolate and thirty-three cents toward me. Johnny can't read, and he can't make change, either. I left the coins on the counter and returned to the Bronco.

I pulled back onto the highway, heading southwest. Once we were clear of the town's lights, Betz sat up a bit and I passed him the cup of hot chocolate. He sipped from it reverently, as if it were a Communion chalice.

"Where are we going?" he asked after a moment.

"Someplace we can talk. The cops are looking for you back in Widows Cape. Turnbull and a state police investigator named Craven have already decided what went down at Dougherty's," I said. "Now I want to hear your version."

I kept my attention on the dark, winding road while Betz haltingly told his story. It began with a phone call from Dougherty, asking Betz to stop by his place to talk. It was about the Fellowship, Dougherty had said, and he sounded anxious. Betz left his apartment around seven, leaving me a note, but then he remembered that he'd left some papers he wanted me to see in his office, so he went over to the college to get them before continuing on to Dougherty's apartment house. It was closer to seven-thirty by the time he arrived, and he bumped into Mrs. Landsdowne letting

172

the cat out. She let him in and he went straight up to Dougherty's rooms without first buzzing him from the vestibule. When he knocked on the door, he heard Dougherty call out, so he let himself in. Dougherty was standing over near his desk, a terrified look on his face. Before Betz could ask what was wrong, he caught a movement from the corner of his eye. Then the lights went out.

"I must've been out for about five minutes," he said. "When I came to, I was holding a gun in my hand. I crawled over toward the desk and . . . Dougherty was lying there, dead." I made eye contact in the rearview mirror. He pulled the blanket higher on his shoulders and continued.

"I guess I panicked, Sheridan," he said quietly. "I used my handkerchief to wipe my fingerprints off the gun and then I dropped it next to the body and got out of there. My head was throbbing. I . . . couldn't think straight. I wandered awhile, heading out of town, away from . . . all that. I guess I lost my glasses somewhere, I don't remember. Then I was out along the highway, keeping down in the ditches—that's how I got soaked—and I decided to go to your motel to look for you. Only you weren't there. A police car came along and cruised through the lot, so I hid in the shadows and began to backtrack. I was coming along up the ditch near Floyd's when I saw you coming out to your car. You know the rest."

By this time, I'd driven as far southwest as Sackett's Harbor on Lake Ontario. I pulled into a darkened tourist lot beside the remains of an old stone fort that had been built back during the War of 1812, and cut the engine.

"We've got a real problem here, my friend," I said. I told him about the weapon, how it connected up with the Janezek murder in D.C. Then I related the scenario Craven and Turnbull had concocted. "The key question right now," I concluded, "is, can you prove you weren't in Washington on the morning of July fourth?"

Betz mumbled to himself, then looked up, his eyes straining without the glasses. "I was at U.Va. There was a big Fourth party, but it didn't start until afternoon." He sighed. "I spent the morning studying in my room. But I can't prove it."

"Mm." I stared out at the gloom while Betz finished the hot chocolate. "I think your best shot right now is to turn yourself in at the state police barracks in Watertown. Give me a chance to—"

"I can't do that! I'd be charged with murder! Even if I get off, my career at Clampett will be ruined. Any sort of felony arrest is grounds for dismissal. Look, Sheridan, you've got to help me, hide me somewhere." He reached over the seat and gripped my shoulder. "Please. It'll buy us some time, give the police a chance to investigate further and find out what really happened."

"But where—" I began to say, then stopped. Inspiration had made a call. I nodded at Betz. "I know a place."

The MacKenzie house was a sprawling single-story ranch that had been tarted up to look French Provincial with a steep hipped roof, stucco wall cladding and phony half-timbers poking out below the flared eaves. Probably had a Louis XIV Barcalounger in the den, I thought absently as I studied the place through the spyglass.

It was already after eight o'clock and, so far, not a creature was stirring. I placed the glass back on the dash and began rereading the papers Alan Betz had given me the night before, the ones he'd stopped to pick up at his office before going to Dougherty's. They were the notes on the two subjects I'd asked him to research for me: the Fellowship's publication credits, and an abstract on the Coffin Island property since 1938. They were crinkled and damp from his ordeal, but handprinted in neat characters that were easy to decipher.

The information on the Fellowship didn't tell me anything I hadn't already suspected. The organization had published about a dozen reports over the few years of its existence, the subject matter including third world debt management, the destruction of tropical rain forests, economic development between eastern and western Europe,

174

and so on. Each of the papers was derivative, unimaginative, and politically safe, a scattershot approach to world affairs that Betz summed up as "nothing a good student couldn't glean from reading *The New York Times* or watching C-SPAN."

The Coffin Island stuff, on the other hand, was anything but dull. Betz had been able to find most of the information at the town assessor's office. A couple of phone calls to the county offices in Watertown had provided the rest. According to the records, the State of New York had taken proprietorship of the island in 1938 to settle a tax lien against the Castle estate. The state, in turn, had signed an open-ended lease with the town of Widows Cape for the use of twenty-two acres and all existing structures located at the eastern end of the island. Even more interesting, the town had then sublet the property to the Stewart Fund, which had paid all fees and taxes until March of 1967. At that time, the town terminated its lease agreement with the state. From there, Betz leaped forward to 1979, when the state sold the whole island to Maurice DuPree. The agent for the sale had been Manfred Porter, Jr. of North Jefferson Properties, Inc. The attorney who handled the closing was Rodney MacKenzie.

In a nutshell, the Dunleavys and Stewarts and others, through the Stewart Fund, had acquired legal use of the old caretaker's farm so that Emily Trevain could continue to live on the island. The fund had paid all the bills for twenty-nine years, until poor Emily's death in 1967, after which it allowed the lease to be canceled.

Question: What had motivated the Dunleavys and the rest of the Widows Cape elite to choose Emily Trevain as the first recipient of the Stewart Fund's largesse?

Answer: Simple human compassion. After all, she had just lost her father tragically, she was a young woman alone with no place to go. Why not help Emily Trevain?

Fine. Maybe that's all it was; a charitable act for someone in need. But that begged the second question. Why the complicated maneuvering to ensure that Emily Trevain would live out her days on an isolated island farm? Why didn't the fund simply rent her a little place in town? Was it because Emily didn't want to leave the island? Or was it because someone else didn't want her to leave?

I was still mulling over the possibilities when movement down at the MacKenzie manse jerked me back to Eastern Daylight Time. The center door on the attached three-car garage swung up and a shiny brown Cadillac backed out into the turnaround. I grabbed the spyglass in time to glimpse the mayor's sour visage behind the wheel before the big car lumbered out into the street. I followed its progress as it drove toward the main highway, then I started the Bronco and cruised out of the rest area.

From close up, MacKenzie's chateau smelled like money. The emerald front lawn looked as if it had been laid by carpet installers, and the winding brick walkway that led to the front entry was flanked by boxwood that had been trained and trimmed into topiary perfection. MacKenzie was doing all right for a small-town lawyer, but then he was a politician, too, and politicians often seem to find ways to get rich.

I left the Bronco in the turnaround and made my way to the front door. I tapped a heavy brass knocker three times and waited, taking out my notepad as I thought out my approach. The art of the bluff, an old newshand had called it back when I was a young reporter getting my feet wet at my first daily. Smile and act like you belong. The door swung in and a vaguely attractive middle-aged woman in a flowing red housecoat stepped into the morning light. I smiled.

"You must be the mayor's wife," I said, glancing at a page in the pad. "Estelle MacKenzie?"

"Yes," she said hesitantly.

"I'm Sheridan."

"Yes?" There was wariness in the way she stared at me, but not a glimmer of recognition. I had counted on that. Married men who cheat fall into a habit of leaving their wives in the dark about other things as well.

"T.S.W. Sheridan, a free-lance writer," I said, holding up the notepad as if it provided my bona fides. "I spoke to your husband and Judge Dunleavy over lunch at the St. Lawrence Club yesterday. About interviewing the mayor's father for an oral history I'm working on."

"Oh!" She covered her embarrassment with a wistful smile. "Rodney is so . . . busy all the time. He often forgets to tell me things. I should be used to it by now. Today of all days!" She checked her wristwatch. "I was just preparing to go out, Mr. Sheridan. I have a hair appointment and a thousand other things to do today. We have a function to attend tonight, you see, and I—"

"At Dr. Stevenson's," I interjected. "I'll be there, too, as a matter of fact."

"Oh!" That seemed to ease her mind. I'd taken a couple of giant steps up the social ladder and no longer could be kept waiting on the stoop. It just wasn't done. She stepped back from the door. "Please, come in, Mr. Sheridan. Forgive me for being so dense, it's just one of those days. You wanted to talk to Father MacKenzie?"

"Yes, for this oral history I'm working on."

"You do know father isn't, mm, very lucid these days."

"Your husband told me about his condition," I said. "But I thought I'd try a few questions anyway. Shouldn't take more than ten minutes."

"Well, I'm sure he'd appreciate the company," Mrs. MacKenzie said. "I'll just introduce you and then I'm afraid I'll have to finish dressing."

Angus MacKenzie was seated in a rocking chair in a sun-washed enclosed porch that his daughter-in-law called the solarium. She leaned over him and, speaking loudly and slowly, explained the reason for my visit. Then she excused herself and went off to put on her face.

I sat in a wicker chair and returned the old man's stare. The left side of his face was slack, the corner of his mouth turned down. There seemed to be an intelligence at work somewhere behind the faded blue eyes, but it came and went sporadically, like a flicker of sparks from the wind-blown embers of a dying campfire.

"Rodney?" The name slipped from the side of his mouth, garbled and confused.

"No, my name is Sheridan, Mr. MacKenzie. I'm here to ask you about the Castle House tragedy."

"The fire? I've told you—" His words trailed off and he paused for a moment. "We kept trying to go back in, you know. It singed my eyebrows; Marsh had burns on his hands." He slowly turned his head away from me and looked out at the yard. "Did Estelle let the dog back in?"

I moved my chair closer and gently gripped the old man's thin wrist. "The Castle House fire, Angus," I said, spacing the words. "You were telling me about the Castle House fire."

But he kept staring out the window, the dull eyes focused on infinity. For lack of a better idea, I began reciting the names, softly, steadily—Ernest Castle, Jack Rose, Robbie Dunleavy and Marshall Stewart, the Spicer sisters, Emily Trevain—hoping to nudge his fragmented thought processes back on track.

Nothing.

I sat back and exhaled, frustrated that I had wasted my time and already considering my next move. Just then, the old man began to mumble to himself, the residue of memory beginning to leak out like droplets from a leaky faucet, but I couldn't make out the words. He turned back to me.

"Maybe you're right, Rodney," Angus said, his voice suddenly stronger. "But we weren't hard men; not like you. We couldn't just . . . get rid of the girl."

"What girl, Angus?" I urged him.

"Wasn't the girl's fault was it? That she . . . that we didn't . . . I've told you, it wasn't anyone's fault!" He cried out, a child's petulant pout rearranging the slackened features of his face.

I tried one more time, quietly pleading. "The girl, was it Emily Trevain? Tell me about Emily, Angus."

But the flicker had died. The old man turned back to the window and began rocking slowly. After a moment, he said, "I don't think Estelle let that poor dog back in."

CHAPTER 24

ONCE upon a time, I was the world's worst Boy Scout. I spent my entire two-year enlistment as a lowly tenderfoot, in which time I managed to memorize the oath and earn exactly one merit badge for mastering the Gordian complexities of the half-hitch and the square knot. But I came away from the experience with at least one lesson well learned.

Be prepared.

After leaving the MacKenzie place, I drove down to River Street and rerented the skiff from the cracker barrel philosopher at the general store. We haggled a few minutes, finally agreeing on a rate for the whole weekend. Things were moving fast and I knew that, sooner or later, I was going to have to make another attempt to visit the Castle House. I blew the rest of the morning taking the little boat on a shakedown cruise that included a complete circle around Coffin Island. This trip, the old Dart inboard tied up at the T-shaped dock had company, a sleek fiberglass launch. A westerly breeze had made the river rough and the powerful boat bucked in its mooring like a two-year-old thoroughbred eager to bust through the starting gate at Saratoga.

My circumnavigation of the island didn't provoke any

revelations, but it did give me an idea on how I might sneak onto the estate, if and when the time came. On the way back to the docks in town, I cruised past half a dozen fishing outfits—open-bow bass boats mostly—taking advantage of the clear, dry morning. At one point, in the inner channel between Coffin Island and the mainland, I spotted the shaved dome of Curly, one of my motel neighbors. He was alone in an aluminum skiff not much larger than mine, his eyes shielded behind a pair of Wayfarers, his line dangling straight as a plumb bob over the side of the boat. I passed within fifty yards, but he didn't seem to notice me. I wondered fleetingly where his buddy Moe was, but dropped the thought as I turned my attention back to steering the skiff diagonally across the swift current.

After tying the boat off at its slip, I retrieved the Bronco and drove over to the library. Rita Tonelli pounced on me the moment she spotted me crossing the rotunda, her green eyes wide with concern as she pumped me about Liam Dougherty's demise. The day's most popular rumor was a variation on the scenario that Craven and Turnbull had jerry-built the night before.

"I can't believe Alan Betz would murder anyone," Rita was saying.

"You're right," I said.

"Not that I know him all that well, but he seems so scholarly and . . . What do you mean, I'm right?" She peered up at me. "You know something, don't you, Sheridan?"

"Yeah," I nodded. "Look, let's grab a couple of chairs and I'll explain it from the beginning."

We moved to a small reading room off the rotunda and sat side by side on a green vinyl couch. I started slowly, explaining the deeper motives for my coming to Widows Cape. When I was finished, Rita scowled as if she'd just caught me marking up a library book with a highlight pen.

"You used me," she said, biting off the words.

"No—" I said, but she shook her head adamantly.

"And now you're telling me that everybody who is any-

180

body in this town is involved in some kind of conspiracy. And a double murder. The mayor, the town justice, Ellis. Let's see, who else? Oh, yes, Fred Porter, who sold me my condo and whose wife bakes pies every year for the library's bake sale. And Dr. Knox, right? This unscrupulous nursing home operator who spends his free time playing the organ at the Lutheran church and umpiring Little League games. These are your crazy conspirators, Sheridan?"

I held up my hand like a traffic cop. "I admit the story has a lot of holes, Rita. All I'm trying to do is fill them in. And remember, I'm not the one who first suggested there was something odd going on in Widows Cape. This whole thing was started by Stefan Janezek, a man whose judgment and intellect you respected."

"Yes, I respected Professor Jan," she sniffed. "At least he didn't go around deceiving people about his work. He was forthright and—"

"And now he's dead," I said flatly. "Probably because someone decided he knew too much." I took Rita's hand. "I came up here cold. True, at the time, I figured the professor's death was what it appeared to be: a mugging, unconnected to Widows Cape. But I still had a story to dig out, a mystery to unravel. I had to play it carefully, ask my questions, get a feel for the situation before I could begin to sort out the good guys from the bad guys."

"And you thought I might be one of the bad guys?"

"No, but I did have to consider your relationship with Ellis Turnbull."

She pulled her hand back and crossed her arms under her ample chest. "I still don't believe for a minute that Ellis is involved in anything shady."

"He's MacKenzie's man, Rita. You as much as told me that yourself. And he did try to scare me out of town."

She started a retort, then closed her eyes and sighed heavily. After a moment, she looked at me, her voice controlled, and said, "I can't be that wrong about Ellis, Sheridan. I know him. He can't be a part of this, whatever this is." I started to interrupt, but she shook her head vigorously. "Let's leave Ellis out of it for the moment. I have to admit, what you've told me is very disturbing. Something odd is going on and I suppose you have to pursue it. But promise me you'll be thorough and fair and make sure you've got your facts straight before you even think of writing a story."

"I always do," I said. "But in order to do that, I need more information on DuPree and some others. Which is the reason I came by. That reception at Dr. Stevenson's tonight, the one for Professor Janezek's replacement—"

"Terrance Alston," she supplied.

"Right. Is that still on?"

"Yes. I received a call from Dr. Stevenson's administrative assistant this morning. Apparently Mr. DuPree insisted on continuing the reception as planned. The only change is that there will be a short ceremony for Liam at the campus Interfaith Chapel at seven, prior to the reception."

"Then I'll pick you up at your place at a quarter to."

The pay phone in the student union atrium was being used by a gangly teenager sporting an oily pompadour, a pair of baggy pleated slacks, and a polka dot bow tie. Back in my school days, he would've been president of the A/V Club, the one who set up the projector for the science teacher. But the nerd look was in these days, and I suppose that had its up side. Now everyone could score a date for the prom.

The kid finished assuring his mother that he'd arrived for freshmen orientation intact and hung up the phone. I took his place, referring to a credit card as I punched in a long sequence of numbers. The sheriff's secretary picked up on the third ring and put me through to the man.

"Okay, Sheridan," J.D. said as soon as he picked up the phone. "What the hell you got yourself into up there?"

"A riddle wrapped in a mystery inside an enigma, or however that line goes."

"If I want to hear Churchill quoted, I'll tune in 'Masterpiece Theater.' What I wanna know is, where does that homicide investigation stand and are you lining up as part of the problem or part of the solution?"

There was just a hint of Staub's official voice in the remark, enough to remind me that, no matter how friendly we were, he was a duly elected county sheriff. The job came with a badge, an oath, and a firm set of ethics that didn't include muddying up the waters in someone else's murder case. Conveniently, the ethics of my profession are somewhat less cut-and-dried. I didn't tell him about my backroads cruise with Alan Betz the night before, or that I had Betz stashed away in a safe place. I did tell him the rest of it, however, starting with the fact that both Dougherty and Janezek had been shot with SIG P-201s and ending with what I'd learned in my conversation with Lt. Bliss.

"FBI, huh?" J.D. said. "And that ruse involving Immigration, that sounds like the CIA. No wonder Bliss wanted you to call him at home. He's afraid they've tapped into his office phones."

"What I'd like to know is what this computer mole found in the Janezek case file that triggered the interest of the spooks in the first place."

"It must have something to do with this Midstream Fellowship. Some foreign connection that the CIA traced to them."

"But there wasn't any mention of the Fellowship or Maurice DuPree in the original case file," I said.

"Hmm." I could hear J.D. tapping a pen on his desk. After a short silence, he said, "Well, something triggered the spooks and it's got to tie in somehow. Give me some more to work with, Sheridan. What sorts of things have you run across up there that stand out?"

"All kinds of things, some of them to do with the old Castle House tragedy and others involving the Fellowship."

"Stick with the Fellowship stuff for now."

"Okay." I paused a few seconds. "To begin with, the organization doesn't seem to have a legitimate purpose.

None of its published reports have anything new to say, and there's no point of view. Is it a conservative think tank, or liberal, or what? And the location, out there on Coffin Island, isolated and ignored. It's like the whole idea is to make the place as bland and boring as possible, so that nobody will take any interest. Another anomaly is those two caretakers or security men or whatever that I told you about, Day and Beauchamp. A couple of real cold customers, particularly the Irishman.

"Then there's Liam Dougherty to consider. Dougherty apparently was the key liaison man between the college and the Fellowship and its founder, Maurice DuPree—who happens to be a major contributor to the school's endowment fund. Dougherty was known for his leftist political views, which would seem to make him odd company for a major capitalist like DuPree. So what's the attraction?"

. "Good question," J.D. said. "And what about this mayor you mentioned? What was his name?"

"Rodney MacKenzie," I said. "In the same way that Dougherty was the Fellowship's liaison with the college, MacKenzie is the group's point man with the town. He's also an attorney in private practice and his biggest client is Maurice DuPree."

"Your point being?"

"That it's more than coincidence that Maurice DuPree chose Coffin Island for the site of the Fellowship. Look, let's assume that the Fellowship was created as a front for some other, illegitimate activity. Say DuPree—for whatever reasons—is smuggling something back and forth from the U.S. and Canada. Guns, dope, computer chips, even people—"

"People?" Staub interjected.

"Yeah, people. I'll come back to that in a minute," I said. "So, whatever he's up to, it's illegal and it involves moving something across the border undetected. To do this, he needs a convenient, yet out-of-the-way location. Coffin Island. It can be reached from either side of the river without having to go through customs. All you need is a boat.

Okay, next he needs an excuse for buying the island and making busy out there. The Midstream Fellowship. A nice, dull collegial club for second-rate scholars. He legitimizes the place by dropping a huge donation on Clampett College for its sponsorship of the Fellowship and he recruits Dougherty to maintain appearances."

J.D. said, "And in addition to Dougherty, he's got this Mayor MacKenzie in his pocket, too. That gives him someone to run interference with the town council."

"Exactly. And the icing on the cake is the old Castle House tragedy. Through MacKenzie, DuPree knows that Judge Dunleavy and the other local shakers and movers have a natural aversion to the place. It represents something out of the town's past that they'd as soon forget. So DuPree rebuilds the Castle House as his headquarters for the Fellowship, insuring that Dunleavy and the others will avoid the place like the plague."

Staub thought it over for a moment, then said, "I like it. As a working theory, anyway. But you'll need a lot more before a D.A. or federal prosecutor will give you the time of day. Some evidence of what it is DuPree is smuggling, for starters. You mentioned people as a possibility."

"I got that notion from an old newspaperman named Sonny Johnson. He explained to me how smugglers have been running contraband across the St. Lawrence since Revolutionary War days. One of the most popular commodities has always been people, from runaway slaves to draft dodgers."

"People move freely across that border every day," J.D. objected. "All they have to do is answer a couple of questions at a customs station and they're in."

"If they're legitimate, sure," I said. "But what if they're not? What if it's someone who needs to get in or out of the U.S. without being noticed by the authorities? It's a hell of a lot easier to get into Canada than into the U.S. And a lot easier to get back out of the U.S. by slipping into Canada when your business is done, instead of undergoing a passport check at Kennedy International."

"I guess that could have some merit, if it was undocumented workers they were bringing in," J.D. conceded. "But myself, I wouldn't discount some kind of contraband, like computer tech stuff. The government's got a mile-long list of electronics that can't be sold to or shipped into any of the Iron Curtain countries. What with the FBI and maybe the CIA lurking in the background, I'd say . . . hold on a sec, Sheridan. Tony just came in with something."

I leaned against the brick wall of the student union and waited while J.D. held a distant, muffled conversation with his second-in-command, Tony Areno. After half a minute, J.D. came back on the line.

"I don't know if this will help you any, Sheridan, but Tony just passed along some of the information you wanted on the Fellowship and this Stewart Fund."

"Great. What'd he come up with?"

"Don't get antsy," Staub grumbled. "I'm reading it over. Okay, well, there's not much here. The Midstream Fellowship is nonprofit, but privately funded through a grant from MPD Shipping and Mining Corp. of Canada, a sole proprietorship of Maurice Paul DuPree. It doesn't solicit donations in the U.S., so that's all they know about it in Albany at the tax department. The Stewart Fund—let's see—it's a nonprofit charity, incorporated in Widows Cape, N.Y. Capitalized through a trust fund in the name of Marshall Stewart, but it also takes in private donations. Got a list here of contributors—Dunleavy, Knox, MacKenzie, Porter, another Porter, Stevenson, MacKenzie again— all residents of Widows Cape. That any help?"

"I don't know," I said. "It proves that DuPree controls the Fellowship's purse strings, but we already figured that. The names tied in with the Stewart Fund are all tied in with Castle House, except for Stevenson. That's the college president. I haven't met him yet." I paused for a beat. "What about the other information I asked about, J.D.?"

"I should have a copy of the state police file on the Castle House investigation by tomorrow morning. An acquaintance of mine at state police HQ says he'll get to it after

186

hours tonight, when there's computer time available. Same deal for the backgrounder on this Jack Rose character. Tony's got a guy doing a cross-reference on the old criminal court records and the state prison logs. Call me around noon here at the office and I'll review what we've got."

"Great."

"Meanwhile, I'm going to discreetly run some of this by an FBI guy I know up at the federal building in Rochester. See if he knows what the hell's going on."

"Very discreetly, J.D.," I cautioned. "I've still got some digging to do up here and I don't want any Bureau types easing me out of the picture with some bullshit about 'national security.'"

Staub snorted. "You just take care you don't dig so deep you can't climb back out again."

CHAPTER 25

THE residence of the Clampett College president was situated just off campus on a wide patch of lawn overlooking the school's athletic fields. The house was a tall brick colonial with a two-story portico across the front.

Rita and I arrived at about a quarter to eight, walking over directly from the Interfaith Chapel after attending a nondenominational service for Liam Dougherty, where several dozen somber mourners had listened to a generic eulogy from the school chaplain, followed by someone playing "Ode to Joy" on a pipe organ. Most of the same faces were now turning up at Dr. Stevenson's for the reception for Professor Janezek's replacement. The gathered company was subdued at first, but that didn't last any longer than it took to stroll across the large living room to a temporary bar that had been set up adjacent to a Steinway baby grand. By the time the initial round of Manhattans and dry whites had gone down, the guests had slipped into their party faces with no more effort than it takes to loosen a tie.

All but the guest of honor, Professor Terrance Alston. He stood beside Dr. Stevenson in the foyer, shaking hands with the new arrivals and glancing furtively from side to side like a cornered rat, an image compounded by a narrow face, long nose, and wispy moustache.

Rita made the introductions when our turn came. "Dr. Stevenson, I'd like you to meet Timothy Sheridan."

I exchanged a firm handshake with our host. He was medium tall and white-haired and had about him a marginally distracted air that, along with elbow patches and argyle sweater vests, seems common among academicians.

"A pleasure, Mr., um, Sheridan, is it?" Stevenson said hesitantly, before gesturing to his left. "And this is, um, Professor Terrance Alston, the new chairman of Clampett's history department. Professor, this is our lovely town library director, Miss Tonelli, and, um, Mr. Sheridan."

I gauged Alston to be around forty-five, although the washed-out gray eyes seemed older. He acknowledged us with a curt nod and recited, "I'm pleased to make your acquaintance. Good of you to come."

It was so slight, I almost didn't register it: a mild brogue that hinted at Celtic origins and immediately brought to mind the coarser urban Irish patois of Desmond Day. And the second-generation blarney of the late Liam Dougherty. All at once, like adjusting the contrast knob on the family Zenith, I was able to bring a set of once fuzzy images into sharp focus.

"I detect a trace of the old sod, professor," I said, smiling benignly.

Alston bobbed his head. "I hail from Donegal originally, 'though I've been in Boston many years now."

"The professor comes to us from Boston College, you know," Stevenson explained, his eyes rolling up toward the ceiling as he regurgitated the new man's curriculum vitae. "Excellent credentials down there in the areas of Western Civilization and American History. He did his undergraduate work at Trinity College in Dublin and also did his first teaching stint there before emigrating. We are very pleased to have him at Clampett."

"I can imagine," I said, returning Alston's flat gray stare.

189

"What made you decide to trade in Boston for Widows Cape, professor?"

Alston gave his shoulders a barely perceptible shrug. "I was raised in a little country village. When I was offered a chance to return to the small-town life—and to chair a department, mind you—I couldn't resist."

"And we couldn't be more pleased," Stevenson repeated. "It seems almost fated, how well things worked out."

"Oh?" I said. "How so?"

"As it happens," Stevenson explained, "Professor Alston was a guest at a Fellowship forum last winter. He and Professor Dougherty struck up a friendship. When it came time to organize a selection committee, Professor Dougherty remembered that Professor Alston had expressed an interest in relocating." His face sagged abruptly. "Dear Lord. Poor Liam. Now we'll need another selection committee, I'm afraid."

I wanted to press Alston on his relationship with the late Liam Dougherty, but Rita began squeezing my forearm like a student nurse searching for a vein. When I glanced down at her, she directed my attention to a clutch of people moving in behind us. In the lead were his honor the mayor and his wife. Both were staring at me, he with barely controlled fury and she with dismay. Behind them came a smiling Judge Robert Burns Dunleavy and a slight, well-dressed man in his late middle years. His face was angular and handsome, if somewhat severe, his expression placid but for a tiny Mona Lisa-like smile. This had to be Maurice DuPree. The giveaway was Claude Beauchamp, who hovered just behind the man's right shoulder, scanning the room through dark glasses.

Rita still had a grip on my right forearm, which made it all the more awkward when MacKenzie took hold of my left elbow and began tugging at me.

"I want a word with you, mister," he hissed.

Between the petite librarian and the diminutive mayor, I was beginning to feel like Gulliver under siege by the Lilliputians. Unfortunately, Rita was the first to let loose

190

and I allowed myself to be hauled into a corner by Mac-
Kenzie.

"Just who the hell do you think you are, barging into my
home like that," he seethed. "Telling my wife I gave you
permission to interview my father. That was a shitty—"

"I didn't tell your wife any such thing," I said as I pulled
my arm back. "I said I'd talked to you about interviewing
your father, which I did."

"You counted on her ignorance—"

"Just like you do."

He stared daggers up at me, his little ears as red as Karl
Marx. "Don't you dare threaten me, you son of a bitch.
This is my town, not yours." The carefully modulated
voice was inching up. "You fuck with me or my family or
my friends one more time and you're gone. Hear me?
Gone."

"That's funny, Mr. Mayor, but that's what your father
said you advised him about the girl."

MacKenzie backed up a step. "What—? I don't know
what you're talking about."

"Sure you do. You told Angus that he and the others
should've gotten rid of the girl. Emily Trevain."

If the eyes really are the windows to the soul, then Mac-
Kenzie must've had the shades drawn. His ice blues gave
off nothing but loathing.

"I'll tell you how it is, Sheridan," he said, his voice now
menacingly calm. "I tried to be civil, but you wouldn't
have it. You invaded my home, terrorized my wife, and
bullied my father. Now you're slandering our good name.
Immediately after this reception, I intend to file charges of
trespass and battery with Chief Turnbull."

"I didn't terrorize or bully anyone—"

"Tell it to the judge, Sheridan," he said. "We'll see
which of us he believes, hmm?"

With that as his parting shot, MacKenzie wheeled and
strode away in his miniature Bostonians. Before I could decide whether to go after him, I was joined in my corner of
the foyer by Dr. Knox and a lovely blond woman who he

191

introduced as his wife. She was wearing a shimmering black sheath dress, the kind that makes most women look like either a pencil or a sausage. On her, it merely underscored the gentle slopes and curves of her body. She shook my hand and smiled warmly.

"Sorry if we, er, interrupted anything—" Knox began to say, glancing from me to the retreating MacKenzie, but his wife jumped in.

"Oh, we're not really sorry at all," she said gaily. "I dragged Jimmy over here because you two looked so intense. It occurred to me a referee might be in order. Frankly," she said conspiratorially, "our little mayor can be too overbearing for words sometimes."

"Thanks for rescuing me," I said.

"Our pleasure. Besides, I for one had an ulterior motive." She turned to her husband. "Jimmy, didn't you say Mr. Sheridan is the writer who's been visiting your Mr. Johnson?"

"Yes, I did, dear," Knox said.

"Well, then, I'm sure he'd want to know, wouldn't he?"

"Know what?" I asked, suddenly dreading the answer. "Something's happened to Howard?"

"I'm afraid so," the doctor said quietly. "He's developed a severe bronchial infection. We couldn't cope with it at the facility any longer. Between the need to monitor his heart functions and the respiratory machines . . . we had to put him in the intensive care unit at House of the Samaritan Hospital in Watertown. He's barely holding on."

Mrs. Knox, reading my face, said kindly, "I'm so sorry, Mr. Sheridan. I understood you and Mr. Johnson were just casual acquaintances."

"Yes. Yes, that's all we are really," I said, surprised myself at my reaction to the news. It wasn't as if I hadn't known how sick the old pirate was—or that he didn't know himself, lying there in his bed with the funeral home brochures on his lap. "Is he able to have visitors?"

"That would be up to the attending physician," Knox said, "but I doubt he'd object. I can give you his name and the hospital's number, if you like, and you can check."

"Thanks," I said, fishing my pen and notepad from the inside breast pocket of my sportcoat. Knox recited the information, then downshifted into the cautious tones he no doubt usually reserved for his aged charges' next of kin.

"I must tell you, Sheridan," he said. "As of ten this morning, Howard was only semiconscious at best. What with the antibiotics and the painkillers . . . well, it's doubtful he'll even know you're in the room."

I thanked him again and went to find a telephone, MacKenzie and the others momentarily forgotten. As I was making my way across the packed living room, I spotted Rita next to the piano, hemmed in by Claude Beauchamp.

"Sheridan! There you are!" Rita sidled around the Frenchman and linked her arm in mine. Her smile was brittle around the edges and I had a feeling her impromptu display of affection was mostly for Beauchamp's benefit. "This is Claude. He's with the Fellowship," she added, trying a bit too hard to sound matter-of-fact.

"We've met," I said. "Sort of."

Beauchamp's smile belonged on a crocodile with a good dental plan. It was both beguiling and malicious, a perfect complement to the hooded eyes that skewered me from behind his tinted glasses.

"I must congratulate you on your taste in women," he said. "Good things come in all shapes and sizes, eh?"

Coming from him, it sounded like a dirty French postcard. I decided to change the subject. "Where's your sidekick Des? Home feeding the doggies?"

"Ah, you remember Peppy and Arabelle. But, as you may already know, the animals are only one of Desmond's passions." The Frenchman's predatory grin evolved into a moue. "He is off indulging one of these other passions— une affaire d'amour—and without his friend Claude, who taught him all his tricks." The pout disappeared in a burst of shrill laughter that galvanized the crowded room. Heads turned to stare in our direction, one of them belonging to the man I took to be Maurice DuPree. He looked at Beauchamp with ill-concealed displeasure, but quickly turned his attention back to his companions.

I'd heard that sort of manic laugh before, often in collusion with a wired grin and sunglasses worn at night. Beauchamp was a doper or a psychopath or both. I shook off the shiver that ran through my shoulders and turned to Rita.

"I need to find a phone," I said to her. Then, as much for Claude's ears as for hers, I explained about Howard Johnson's collapse. We left Claude by the piano, Rita leading me to a large, plump woman who was introduced as Dr. Stevenson's wife. She took us to a book-lined office off the living room, sliding closed its pocket door when she returned to her guests.

"I understand your concern, Sheridan," Rita said as she watched me cross to a handsome cherry rolltop desk and begin dialing the phone. "But it's kind of late to be calling the hospital now, isn't it?"

"I'm not calling the hospital." That had been my original thought, but Beauchamp had changed my mind for me. Now my immediate concern was Kara. Widows Cape was a small town. When it came to "affaires d'amour," there weren't many options for a brutal creep like Desmond Day. The phone buzzed three times before Kara's voice came on the line. I started to speak, then realized I was listening to her recording machine. I waited anxiously for the beep, then began my message.

"This is Sheridan. If you're there monitoring this call, please pick up the phone. This is very important."

I started over again, willing her to come on the line, when I heard a click, followed by a man's voice.

"Sheridan?" It was Alan Betz.

"Where is she, Alan? Why didn't Kara answer?"

"Christ, I'm glad you called. I didn't know what to do. She left with that Desmond guy. I couldn't stop her."

I muttered a curse. "What happened?"

"He tried to get in the apartment. Said he had money and wouldn't take no for an answer." Betz hesitated. "She didn't want to, but she was protecting me. She didn't want him to find me . . . so she talked him into taking her out to the island."

"Oh, Christ." My first impulse was to phone the police, but then what? Turnbull was MacKenzie's man, and Craven? He'd have too many questions; questions for which I had no time and too few answers. I hesitated for a heartbeat before telling Betz, "I'll pick you up in twenty minutes. We're going on a boat ride."

CHAPTER 26

EVERYTHING seemed magnified out on the river. The cool September evening air was sharper, the steady lap of the current louder, the pinpoints of stars more brilliant.

"After you drop me off, you'll pilot the skiff around to the west end of the island and head in toward the dock," I instructed Betz, who was scrunched down in the bow, wearing my Yankees cap. "You can handle the boat okay, Alan?"

"I think so, yes."

"Good. Review the rest of the plan for me."

"I look for the dogs to come out," he recited, reaching down for the greasy paper bag at his feet. "Then I pull in close to the dock and start tossing them the burgers."

"One at a time," I reminded him. "Then what?"

"I stay close, distracting the animals for as long as possible. If Desmond comes out, I move the boat out to the mouth of the cove and sit tight."

"Right. You sit tight until you see my signal, then you pick us up back at the drop-off point."

"Got it." We were silent for a moment. Then Betz said, "It isn't much of a plan, is it, Sheridan?"

I grunted. "Short notice. It'll have to do."

The three-quarter moon lit up the southern shore of the island, making it easy for me to pick out the old collapsed dock that had once served the Trevain farm. I concentrated on guiding the boat toward it, trying to stay as calm as the night, but feeling oppressed by urgency and guilt. It had been my bright idea to stash Alan Betz at Kara's apartment until we could figure out how to get him off the hook with the police. It seemed like a good move at the time—particularly since Kara had told me MacKenzie was planning to keep away from her for a few days. I figured it would keep Betz out of harm's way and also give Kara what she wanted, a piece of the action, without actually putting her at risk. Instead, I had maneuvered her right into the grasp of a man who had already proved himself a bullying sadist and who was most probably a killer as well. I had blown it big, and now there were no more thoughts of an investigation or a story or anything else. There was only the girl, and my private vow to get her off that island with mind and body intact.

I had hurried out of Dr. Stevenson's, leaving Rita behind to casually spread the word that I had been called to the hospital for a final visit with a dying friend. I stopped off at the diner in town and collected a dozen hamburgers, then picked up Betz at the apartment. By the time we reached the rented boat in its slip behind the general store, I had explained what I wanted him to do. I was glad he hadn't asked what would happen if the diversion didn't work, if the two Dobermans had been too well trained to be distracted by the food. I didn't have an answer.

I wristed the small outboard into neutral and let the skiff bump gently against the weathered pilings of the old dock. Quickly, I double-checked the pitiful arsenal stuffed into my pockets—a jackknife, a tube of Mace taken from Kara's apartment, and a flare gun with a single cartridge that had come with the boat. Then I climbed onto the rickety dock and waited for Betz to position himself at the outboard.

"It's nine-ten," I said as we both checked our watches.

197

"In fifteen minutes, you move in on the Castle House dock and start chucking burgers."

The Castle House sat regally atop its knoll, ringed on three sides by silver maples and larch and pine. A well-trimmed lawn circled the place like a green moat, a buffer between the looming trees and the house.

I was lying on a hillock in the pines at the rear of the grounds, some hundred feet from the building, studying the place for signs of life. It had taken me ten minutes to cross the island from the dock near the old farm, rejecting the direct route down the macadamed roadway for the safety of the woods, stopping every few minutes to listen for the dogs. A porch light glowed above the back door and I could see lamplight through cracks in the drapes at two of the windows. Other than that, the only illumination was concentrated at the front, where the bulky facade of the Castle House looked out at the river.

A moment earlier, I had thought I could hear faintly the distinctive purr of the rented boat's outboard. Now, as I lay on my stomach breathing in the rich loamy odors of the woods, I heard the staccato barking of the dogs. Without hesitation, I pushed myself upright and ran a beeline down through the trees, across the no-man's-land of lawn to the southeast corner of the house. From there, I could just make out the far end of the T-shaped dock stretching out into the cove and two dark smudges—the Dobermans—darting back and forth, frenzied.

A voice shouted harshly from somewhere at the front of the house. A command to the hysterical dogs. Then, when they didn't respond, a blocky figure crossed my line of sight, heading down toward the commotion.

Desmond. And he was carrying a rifle.

I put up a silent prayer that Betz would be prudent enough to motor out of range, then I beat it around to the back door.

"Shit." It was locked. I ran back to the corner of the house to check on Desmond. He was still making his way down to the dock, ambling along, too macho to hurry. Good for him. I slipped around to the south side of the house and onto a flagstone terrace. Two sets of French doors presented themselves, one set emitting soft lamp-light, the other dark. I tried the dark one first. Success. The handle turned smoothly and the door swung inward. I gently closed it behind me and paused to let my eyes adjust.

It was an office, or, more correctly for an English-style manor house, a study. Rich oak paneling, niches with built-in bookcases, a marble fireplace, and a pair of leather wing chairs. A room Henry Higgins would feel at home in, except for the personal computer and related peripherals all strung together on top of a huge library table.

For a moment, my reporter's instincts took hold. I went over to the PC. Beside it was a small storage case containing a dozen or so three-and-a-half-inch minidisks. About half were labeled as program disks. I ignored those and scooped up the rest—file disks labeled in some sort of alphanumeric code—and slipped them into my sportcoat pocket with the flaregun. Across the study was an interior door, a sliver of light showing at the bottom. I moved over to it and listened.

Silence.

I eased the door open and found myself looking out at a large foyer with a wood parquet floor and a wide stair-case leading to the second floor. Across the way was an archway leading into a huge living room. To my right was a corridor leading to the back of the house. I remembered what Kara had told me; that she had seen the office with the PC on her way to Desmond's and Claude's room.

I headed down the corridor, careful to stay on the Oriental carpet runner to deaden the sound of my footsteps. There were four doors leading off the corridor, all of them closed. One was tucked away behind the stairwell and had to lead to the basement. The second was a swinging door with a small round window. Access to the kitchen. The third door, at the end of the corridor, was the back entry that I had tried earlier. I slipped back the deadbolt lock, planning to use that exit when I had the girl, and moved to my right, to the fourth and final door.

I put my ear to the panel. I heard a forlorn mewing sound, like a kitten caught in a tree. I pushed the door open. The room was shadowy, its only illumination coming from a ginger jar lamp on a nightstand between a pair of twin beds. Lying on one of the beds, her bare legs curled up, her hands strapped to the headboard with leather belts, was Kara.

She was sobbing, her eyes wide and wet and unfocused. Her short dress was bunched at her hips, the bodice torn away, exposing her breasts. An ugly bruise marred her cheek. When I sat on the edge of the bed, she shrank away.

"It's okay, it's okay," I soothed her as I unfastened the belts from her wrists. "It's me, Kara. Sheridan. It's going to be all right."

"Sheridan?" She stopped pushing away and blinked up at me until the words tumbled out in fractured bits. "Oh, God, Sheridan! They're going to kill me . . . Desmond caught me working the PC . . . thought he was still in the shower—"

I gently folded my arms around her shivering body. "It's okay now, we're getting out of here." I took off my coat and slipped it onto her. "Come on, Kara, get up."

I got her to her feet. She was unsteady, but her breathing was beginning to come under control. I looked around the floor for her shoes. Suddenly, she stiffened beside me and screamed.

I ducked instinctively, felt a forearm glance off my shoulder, and threw myself backward, knocking Kara onto the bed beneath me. Someone came at me out of the shadows. I brought my knee up, catching my attacker in the stomach, his stale breath blowing over me in one great exhalation. I bounced up off the bed and threw my left arm around his neck, pounding at his face with my right. He tried to pummel my ribs, but he was weak and panicky, struggling for air. I tightened the headlock and ran him across the room, slamming his head into the wall, once, twice, until he went limp and crumpled to the floor.

I was breathing raggedly as I stared down at the unconscious body at my feet. It was Jamie Velez, Liam Dougherty's surly young student assistant. It took about two seconds for my battered senses to realize what that meant.

"Let's go," I said, turning toward Kara, still sprawled across the bed. "We've got to—"

A lightning bolt shot through the back of my head and the floor came up hard and fast. A fog began to settle over my brain and through it came a disembodied voice, taunting and cruel, like bad dialogue from a B-movie.

"Welcome to Castle House, boyo."

Fade to black.

When I came to, Jamie was sitting on the one twin bed, gingerly massaging his temples. Kara was curled fetally on the other bed, my jacket wrapped around her, her eyes dull. Desmond was surveying the scene from the doorway, caressing a pump-action shotgun. One of the Dobermans sat on its haunches beside him, staring stupidly at me.

I was still on the floor, on my side now, a stalactite of drool hanging from the corner of my mouth. For some reason, my first words were, "Is that Peppy?"

"Arabelle," the blocky Irishman said, smirking. "Peppy's out on patrol, should your friend in the boat have a mind to come visitin' again."

I wiped my shirtsleeve across my mouth and sat up slowly, painfully aware of the dull ache at the base of my skull and the dog's sullen growl. I looked up at Desmond, noticing for the first time the pistol stuffed into the waist band of his jeans. A SIG P-201.

"You must get those things wholesale," I said.

Desmond smiled thinly. "Better still, I get 'em free of charge. You just have to know the right people." He pointed with the barrel of the shotgun. "You crawl on up there beside the whore, while Jamie gets his wits back. I think you concussed the poor bugger."

201

I got up, still groggy, and sat on the bed with Kara. Jamie kicked out at my leg as I went past, but he was too weak to do any harm.

"I'm gonna kill you, motherfucker," he said.

"Shut it, Jamie!" Desmond ordered. "You had your chance to kill the bastard and you cocked it up, din'tcha? He nearly did you instead." He looked back to me and shook his head. "You just can't get good help nowadays."

I commiserated. "It's the schools. Not enough emphasis on the basics. Obviously, you're not a product of the American school system. Northern Ireland, right?"

At first I thought he was going to let his silence speak for him, but then he showed his yellowed teeth.

"A blighted little corner of Belfast known as Turf Lodge," he said casually, the grim smile cemented in place. "Beirut with rain and Catholics, y'might say." He leaned against the door jam and let the gun barrel drop to his side. Shotguns were superfluous with Arabelle around.

"So you came to the States for a change in the weather, is that it?" I asked. "I'd've guessed it was more in the nature of a business trip."

Desmond frowned and shook his square head from side to side. "Still nosing around, eh, right up to the bitter end? You think this is some fuggin' television program? The villain of the piece blathers on about his dirty deeds while our hero plots a daring dash for freedom?" He laughed. "I'll tell you this much; your next boat ride isn't likely to be as pleasant as the one that brought you here."

I glanced at Kara. She was staring without seeing, fear having stolen her senses. Maybe that was a good thing. I said to Desmond, "DuPree might have other ideas."

He sniggered his contempt. "DuPree's ideas don't count with me, Sheridan. I thought a genius like you'd've sorted that out by now."

I started a reply, but Desmond silenced me with a wave of his hand. "Shut it. I hear Peppy yippin', Jamie. The others must be back. Here, take the shotgun and watch these two while I go down to the dock."

202

The kid didn't look too enthusiastic, but he didn't argue, either. He teetered unsteadily when he came off the bed, then righted himself and took the shotgun from Desmond. The Irishman told the mutt to stay, then he left the room. Jamie said "Good dog" to Arabelle, who ignored him, and glowered at me. The overall effect was heightened by the still-glassy look in his eyes and the darkening abrasion where his face had met the plaster.

"I oughta blow you away right now," he said, sounding more glum than hostile. The pouty set to his mouth reminded me of a five-year-old who'd wanted to play ball with the big kids, only to learn that big kids play rough.

There wasn't anything else to do, so I did what comes naturally. I started asking questions.

"Does it get easier, Jamie? Blowing people away?" I asked. "When you murdered Liam Dougherty, did you—"

"I wasn't even there!" The kid lowered the barrel of the shotgun toward the floor. "Nobody even told me what was goin' down. Des and Claude—" He brought the scowl— and the shotgun—back to bear. "Just shut the fuck up, man. I don't need your mouth runnin' at me right now."

"I suppose you're gonna tell me you had nothing to do with Professor Janezek's murder, either, huh, Jamie?"

"That's right! I was only there to drive the car." He shook his head. "That was just . . . an accident, anyway, running into Janezek. He came walkin' down the street all of a sudden. Almost bumped right into Des and the other Mick." The scowl deepened. "Besides, he was a nosy son of a bitch, just like you. He was asking for it."

The other Mick.

I thought I had it then; or at least enough of it to hammer together a reasonable working theory, as J.D. Staub would say. The first nagging bits had come together at Dr. Stevenson's reception, when I'd met Terrance Alston. The Irish connection had grown too strong for coincidence. Add to it the basic premise—that the Fellowship was using Castle House as a front for some sort of smuggling activity—and the answer came up Irish terrorists. Money and guns for the Cause funneling north to Widows Cape from places like Boston and New York City; zealous expatriots like Alston and sympathetic radicals like Liam Dougherty working the American connection while Desmond Day keeps an eye on things for the leadership back home and handles any dirty work that might come up.

The other Mick.

Jamie could've been referring to Terrance Alston, but I didn't see it. Not when set side by side with the events that had happened in Washington on July Fourth. Rita had told me that the Fellowship had held its most recent "symposium" that weekend. A perfect smokescreen to slip someone into the States—and back out again—over the course of a four-day holiday. Alston was already in, a respectable college professor at Boston College. No. If my theory held water, the "other Mick" was someone too hot to bring in by conventional means. A specialist of some kind, imported to handle a specific assignment in Washington, D.C., on the Fourth of July.

Like blowing up a politician's limousine?

But if that was the reason Jamie Velez and Desmond Day and the other Mick were in D.C. that day, what was the point? What did Irish terrorists have to gain by assassinating the governor of Puerto Rico?

The long silence and the sudden frown that crossed my face had further unnerved the kid. He jerked the shotgun up level with my nose.

"Don't get any stupid ideas, man," he said, his voice quavering. "If this thing don't finish you, the dog will."

Kara made a sniffling sound and moved closer to me, wrapping herself in the crook of my arm. I patted her hand reassuringly and looked up at Jamie Velez. We stared at each other for a moment, then I decided to take a flyer.

"You claim you were just along for the ride, Jamie, but it doesn't wash," I said. "Velez is a Hispanic name. You Puerto Rican, Jamie?"

"What of it?"

"Know what I think? I think the whole Washington operation was your party. I think it was some kind of quid pro quo; Desmond and his Irish friend paying you back for your help by eliminating the governor of Puerto Rico—"

Jamie's piercing laughter threw me off. It wasn't the reaction I was expecting.

"Oh, that's real good, smartass," he said. "Like I'm some kinda Puerto Rican freedom fighter, right? Forget it, man. Me? I'm just like DuPree, a businessman. The only cause I got is cash."

"But, then, why kill the governor?"

"Who said he was the target?"

"Who else—," I started to ask, but then I knew. "It was the congressman they were after."

Before Jamie could respond, a door slammed shut somewhere at the front of the house. Desmond returning with DuPree and the others, I assumed. But when Desmond came tramping into view, his only companion was Rodney MacKenzie, who had turned a whiter shade of pale since I'd last seen him a couple of hours earlier.

"I'm telling you, we're in trouble!" he said, on the edge of hysteria. "Maurice says to destroy the computer files and dump all the weapons and plastique out in the channel."

"And how'm I supposed to do all that?" Desmond said, surprisingly calm in the face of the little mayor's panic. "Wave a bloody magic wand over the whole shipment?"

"Wait a minute," Jamie cried, his eyes bright. "What happened? Where's Mr. DuPree anyway?"

"On his way to Watertown with a carload of federal agents," MacKenzie snapped, grabbing at Desmond's sleeve. "Now, would you get your goddamn Mick ass moving!"

CHAPTER 27

DESMOND'S right hand shot out and grabbed the knot of MacKenzie's tie. He jerked the smaller man the rest of the way through the doorway and slammed him backward into the side of a highboy dresser.

"Nobody talks to me that way, especially no slimy little Scots fuck like you." He gave the tie one more good tug for emphasis, then let loose. "Now, tell me exactly what went down at that bloody social."

MacKenzie tried to reconstruct a bit of his dignity, but he couldn't pull it off. Fear wouldn't let him. It oozed out through his trembling hands and contorted face. Not that he had cornered the market. I had huddled closer to Kara on the bed, my arm around her shoulders, feeling the tremors caused by her sobs and my own quaking nerve ends. Even the kid, Jamie, looked as if he was about to lose his lunch. Only Desmond and the mutt, Arabelle, staring at me from the foot of the bed, seemed oblivious to the terror that suffused the crowded room.

"I told you. The FBI. They came at us on the sidewalk when we were leaving Stevenson's," MacKenzie said haltingly. "Said they wanted to question Maurice and Professor Alston. I wanted to go with them—I'm his legal counsel, after all—but Maurice said I was to—"

`"What about Beauchamp?" Desmond growled.

"He . . . tried to run. He had a gun. One of the agents shot him down right there on the sidewalk—"

"He's dead?"

"No, I . . . don't think so. They took him away in an ambulance."

"Bad luck," the Irishman said shortly.

MacKenzie stammered, "We . . . we've got to . . . to remove the weapons . . . clear everything out of the house that could incriminate—"

Desmond cut him off. "Too much bother. The operation's blown now, might just as well blow the rest. It's a good thought I had a contingency plan ready for just such an occasion." He glanced over at me. "I've wired the basement with incendiaries, y'see. History does have a way of repeatin' itself."

"No!" MacKenzie grabbed onto Desmond's arm. "That's not necessary! Maurice's orders were to—"

Desmond shook him off. "Maurice don't give the orders. Just because he bought you, counselor, don't be thinkin' we're all in his pocket." He pulled the Swiss automatic from his waistband and glanced at Jamie. "Watch this pair," he said. "While the honorable mayor and me go down to the basement."

MacKenzie pushed backward against the heavy dresser, his hands held out in front of him. "I'm not going anywhere with you. DuPree paid for all this. It's his operation. You Irish bastards think you can just take over—"

I didn't see Desmond bring his arm up and I didn't immediately register the sudden flat popping sound. It was like staring at a still photo. All in one moment, the pistol was shoulder high and MacKenzie was slumped down in the wedge between the wall and the dresser, a dark red hole in the center of his forehead.

Kara screamed and started to come off the bed, but I pulled her back. The dog began growling maniacally, excited by the smell of blood. Desmond commanded it to cease.

"You killed him!" Kara said, her voice thick.

207

"So I did." Desmond glanced down at the body. "He was a sorry little man at any rate. A rebel without a cause, y'might say. Just a money leech."

"And because you've got a cause," I said evenly, "that justifies all this? You think you're helping Ireland—"

He brought the pistol around and aimed it at my face. "Not a bloody word about Ireland from you, hear? You and your Irish-American bullshit make me sick. Drinkin' your green beer on St. Paddy's Day," he sneered. "When the time's right we'll kick the fuggin' Brits out of Ulster and the fuggin' Church out of the Republic and the fuggin' IRA fossils out of both, and then we'll begin to build a united Socialist Ireland. And parasites like you will have to find somewheres else to spend your holidays."

Up until he'd begun spouting off about parasites and a Socialist state, I had assumed Desmond was fronting for the provisional wing of the Irish Republican Army, a nasty enough bunch in their own right. But now I remembered news accounts of an even more radical faction; a Marxist splinter group called the Irish National Liberation Army.

"Jesus, man," Jamie whined just then, squeezing the shotgun nervously. "We don't have time for this shit." He looked down at MacKenzie's body. "We gotta get outa here."

Desmond stared daggers at me for another moment, then moved into action. "Right. On your feet, Sheridan. Get the whore up, as well. We're all goin' down to the basement. Arabelle, patrol!"

The mutt padded out of the room instantly. I got off the bed and pulled Kara to her feet and put an arm around her waist to steady her. She leaned against me and cried softly.

"Oh, God, I'm sorry, Sheridan, I'm sorry," she whispered over and over, like a canticle.

"It's okay, it's okay," I soothed her.

She was still wearing my sportcoat and, as I guided her toward the bedroom door, I remembered the flaregun. As we moved out into the corridor, I slid my hand down Kara's side and into the pocket. Desmond was ahead of us, his back turned, holding his pistol at his side with one hand while slipping a key into the cellar door with the other. Jamie was behind us, still slightly unsteady from the pounding I'd given him, holding the shotgun haphazardly with the barrel angled toward the floor.

"All right, guests go first," Desmond said mockingly as he swung open the door and began to turn.

I pulled the flaregun free and, in the same motion, threw myself forward, shoulder tucked, catching Desmond on the hip. He let out a bellow as he fell back and tumbled into the black abyss of the doorway, his cries ending abruptly as his stocky body crash-landed at the bottom of the dark stairwell. I was on all fours, gathering myself to go at Jamie, when a blast roared through the narrow passageway and bits of ceiling began raining down. Through the plaster dust, I saw Jamie and Kara struggling for control of the shotgun. He knocked her aside and brought the barrel around, desperately trying to pump another shell into the breach. I rose on one knee and fired the flaregun. The flare shot like a tracer bullet across the few feet that separated us, hit the gun stock, and ricocheted into the side of his jaw, knocking him to the floor in a shower of flames. When I got to him he was half-conscious. I canceled that half with a kick to the side of his head.

I scooped up the shotgun and barked at Kara, "C'mon! We're getting out of here."

The flare lay in the corner, orange flames licking at the baseboard trim, catching at the fringe of the carpet runner. As Kara moved in beside me, I grabbed the inert Jamie by the belt and dragged him toward the back door.

"Get the door, hurry!" I urged Kara. "We've—"

A low growl brought me up short. Letting loose of the kid, I turned halfway toward the sound. The Doberman was at the end of the corridor, poised and taut, baring its pointy yellow teeth. Too late, I tried to pump a shell into the shotgun's chamber. The animal suddenly bounded down the passageway and leaped for my throat. I threw up my arm, felt the powerful jaws clamp down near the elbow, the teeth begin to push through my shirt and into my flesh.

"The Mace!" I yelled at Kara, as the weight of the dog began to pull me down. "In the coat pocket!"

It took a five-second eternity for Kara to find the canister, while I clubbed at the Doberman, its jaws still stubbornly locked onto my elbow, the teeth digging deeper. Then I heard Kara yell and I turned my face away, squeezed shut my eyes. There was a long hiss and a yelp. The pain in my arm eased as the dog let loose. When I opened my eyes, Arabelle was writhing on the floor, whimpering frantically, her front paws clawing at her snout.

"Outside!" I ordered Kara. She yanked open the door and ran out. The flames had caught on the baseboard and were licking at the wall. The wool carpet runner was burning at one end like a candle wick. I switched the shotgun to the crook of my damaged left arm and grabbed Jamie's belt, dragging him across the threshold and down the steps of the tiny porch, depositing his limp body on the gravel path at the rear of the mansion.

Kara was kneeling on the ground by the stoop, gulping down air. She was beginning to recover from the shock, but her movements were still sluggish, like a swimmer caught in a heavy current. I used the lull to work the pump on the shotgun, chambering a live round.

"What are we doing?" she asked, confused, as she watched me. "Can't we use the phone? Call somebody?"

"It's not safe. That maniac's still in there, who knows in what condition, and he's got an armory stashed in the basement." I looked right and left as I spoke, swinging the barrel of the gun like a talisman to ward off evil. "For all we know, Desmond could blow the building—"

I saw a dark blur fly around the corner of the house. I'd forgotten about Peppy. He ran straight at me, but this time I was ready. I waited until he was within six feet, about to spring, and I fired the shotgun. He let go a piercing, agonized yowl as the blast blew him off the path. Then he lay still, a lifeless lump in the tall, cool grass.

Kara didn't need any more convincing. "Which way?" she asked, as she jumped to her feet.

I hesitated. We could head for the Castle House dock and take one of the boats. If the keys were on board. And if Desmond didn't spot us out on the brightly lit front lawn. But that was two ifs too many. Better to make our way across the island to the drop-off point, the old farm dock, and pray that Betz was waiting offshore to take us away.

"C'mon," I said, turning east.

Kara didn't ask for an explanation and I didn't offer one, saving my breath for the half-mile run. We cleared the lip of the lawn and found the macadamed service road and settled into a steady jog. The base of my skull throbbed where Desmond had slugged me, and my elbow felt like it had been fed through a Cuisinart, but I didn't care. The pain was a sweet reminder—we were still alive.

We followed the road through a long tunnel of overhanging maples and Norway pines, Kara keeping pace at my side. I sucked in the chill night air and stared myopically at the path ahead, willing the farmhouse to come into view, eager as a kid on his first trip to Disney World. Finally, the trees began to thin out and I could see open pasture and, farther on, bathed in shadow and moonlight, the rusted tin roofs of the farm buildings. Kara saw it too and, without a word, we each began to pick up the pace.

"Oh, shit!" Kara fell back just as we cleared the trees. It took me three more strides to stop, then I shuffled back to her. She had thrown a shoe and now she was sitting on the pavement, pulling on the wayward sandal and cursing, my sportcoat hanging off her like a set of drapes.

"Goddamn things," she muttered, puffing as she jerked at the backstrap. "'Bout as handy as a fucking pair of snowshoes."

I started to laugh.

"What's so damn hilarious, Sheridan?"

"Your vocabulary," I said. "You're back to normal."

"I guess so," she smiled, then frowned quizzically. "You hear something?"

211

"What—?" I listened, at first hearing nothing but the wind. Then something foreign; a steady, low-pitched whir. I looked back down the road and saw a pinpoint of light, a headlamp, moving toward us. Suddenly there was a flash back beyond the farthest trees and a heart-stopping thunderclap. The sky to the west appeared to be on fire. Oblivious, the single headlight kept coming.

"Desmond blew up the mansion," I said. "He's coming after us in the golf cart."

We turned and ran. Another fifty feet and we were onto the farm proper. The old graveyard reposed in a field to our left and, to our right, a gradual decline angled down to the river and the rickety dock.

I pulled Kara to a stop with my left hand, wincing at the pain in my elbow. "Get down to the dock," I said between shallow breaths. "Wave your arms, signal Betz to pick you up. If Desmond gets here first, get in the water. Swim if you have to."

She began to protest. "But what about you?"

"I can't let him corner me out there." I held up the shotgun and smiled grimly. "These things don't work too well under water. Now, you go. Now!"

She went. I didn't hang around to mark her progress. Instead, I ran to the left, over a ditch and into the graveyard, searching anxiously for something substantial to hide behind. The plots were overgrown with bramble and sedge, most of them marked only with low stone slabs or thin, worn headstones that were canted or knocked completely flat. But there were two headstones huddled together at the edge of the pathetic little cemetery, either one large and solid enough to give me cover.

I dove behind the closest one, then got to my knees and peeped over the top. The golf cart was in view now, a hundred yards from the clearing. I sat back on my heels, fighting to control my breathing, staring absently at the headstone in front of me. It took a moment for the inscription to register.

Emily Hart Trevain. 1918-1967. RIP.

I stole a glance at the other stone. Thomas Muncie Trevain. Loving Father. 1885-1937.

Under other circumstances, I might've laughed—or maybe cried—at the irony. After all my nosing around into the Castle House affair, I end up sharing a gravesite with the woman who had all the answers. But there was no time.

I stood up behind the gravestone and aimed the shotgun. Desmond was almost opposite my position, less than fifty feet away. He was looking toward the river, his right hand steering the electric cart, left arm dangling uselessly at his side. Must've broken it in the fall, I thought, but where was his gun? I couldn't see any weapon, couldn't bring myself to shoot him in cold blood.

I brought the shotgun down fractionally and called out. "It's over, Desmond! Stop right there!"

He jerked his head around, spotting me, and simultaneously lifted his foot off the accelerator. The cart rolled to a stop almost immediately.

"Step out and lie face down on the ground," I ordered.

"You're the boss." As his leg came down to the macadam, he rolled his hip, his right arm disappearing from view. Then, in one clean move, he was out of the cart, knees bent in a shooter's squat, the left arm still hanging at his side, the right swinging up toward me, gripping a pistol.

We both fired.

We both missed.

Desmond's bullet fragmented a corner of the gravestone, the pop of the SIG lost beneath the shockwave blast of the shotgun. My shot had gone wide, taking out one of the cart's tires.

Desmond came at me, snapping off shots on the dead run, while I chambered another round. At twenty feet, he stopped, dropped into a crouch, began to aim. I brought the shotgun up and fired. Desmond screamed as a crimson stain spread across his thigh. Then he looked at me, his eyes wild with rage, and started firing again. I crashed

213

down behind the gravestone, heart pounding, and pumped the shotgun.

Nothing.

I pumped it again, and again.

No use. It was empty.

I propped myself on one knee behind the cold stone marker and gripped the shotgun like a Louisville Slugger, the barrel warm in my hands.

And waited for Desmond.

CHAPTER 28

T HE mind can play tricks at a time like that.

Tired and sore and mentally drained, I held my position in the damp shadow of the gravestone for . . . five minutes? Ten? I couldn't say. The firing had long since stopped, but I knew the resilient Irishman was still out there. Reloading, dragging himself around to a better firing position, doing something intended to make me dead.

Then . . .

There came the thwump, thwump, thwump of a rotor blade whipping the air. Startlingly, a brilliant light burst through the noise and glided across the grave markers and tussocks of dry grass until it found me. For a moment, memory carried me back in time and I saw myself at nineteen, lying in a jungle clearing, clutching my radio and calling in the evac choppers to the LZ.

"Sheridan!"

A familiar voice broke the spell. Using the shotgun as a prop, I struggled to my feet and threw up my arm to shield my eyes from the glare of the search beam. A figure stepped into the circle of light.

Ellis Turnbull, a .38 police special in his hand.

I blinked at him and started to shift the shotgun to a

215

more agreeable position, but he misread the move and leveled his revolver at my chest.

"Leave it, Sheridan!" He barked. Then, softer. "Take it easy. Desmond is dead, Sheridan. It's over."

Two more figures moved into the light. Curly and Moe.

"Special Agent Twilly, FBI," Curly called to me, holding out a leather ID case.

I let the shotgun fall to the ground and then, suddenly dizzy, I joined it.

A mild case of shock, the doctor said, compounded by the blow to the back of the head and the traumatic run across Coffin Island. Nothing a good night's sleep wouldn't cure.

He was right. By morning, I was feeling rested and almost whole again, with nothing more than a bandaged elbow and a tender spot on the back of my head to show for my troubles. They'd kept me in the hospital overnight for observation. A necessary precaution, the attending physician had said, after closely examining both my skull and my Blue Cross coverage. I didn't argue.

As I lay on the bed, feeling foolish in the hospital gown, I paged back to the previous evening, sharpening the focus on what at the time had seemed like a waking dream.

The feds had airlifted Kara and me from the island in a Huey they had commandeered from the army at Fort Drum. As we rose high over the river and banked to the south, we could see the burning remains of Castle House below, glowing like a funeral pyre. Curly—Special Agent Twilly—had ridden with us while his partner and Ellis Turnbull stayed behind to sort out the mess. The kid, Jamie, was on board as well, strapped to a gurney in the chopper's aft compartment.

"We found him wandering in a daze at the back of the property after the house went up," Twilly had explained, shouting to be heard above the racket of the rotor. "The place blew just as our team landed at the dock. We were lucky we didn't lose anybody."

"And Desmond?" I asked him.

"Dead as a mackerel when we got down there."

"But my shot was low—"

"Caught him in the thigh," the FBI man nodded, his face impassive. "Tore open the femoral artery. A wound like that, shock sets in within thirty seconds, death about five minutes later."

We didn't talk much after that. Kara and I were too exhausted to do anything but sit there in silence. When we touched down at the airport outside Watertown, we were ushered into a nondescript Ford by a pair of equally nondescript federal agents and driven into the city, down Washington Street to House of the Samaritan Hospital, where we were led our separate ways.

Kara had been examined and released that night. I had found that out from the pretty nurse who had brought my breakfast. I would probably be released later that morning, she said, after the doctor had a chance to look me over.

Now it was near ten o'clock and I was still waiting. I climbed out of the bed and opened the closet. My clothes, including the sportcoat I'd lent Kara, were hanging there. I shuffled off to the bathroom. The shower's hot needles eased the tension at the back of the neck, but did nothing to lessen my melancholy. I leaned against the tiled stall, holding my bandaged elbow away from the spray, and felt my knees quiver as the realization hit me full force.

Only a few hours before, I had killed a man.

It's supposed to be easier the second time. I couldn't recall where I'd heard that—probably in a John Wayne oater. The first time had been in a jungle clearing, a recon patrol near Da Nang. Six of us boonierats and an S-2 spook who never explained his presence. I was the radio man, my M-16 slung across my back as an afterthought. We were pinned in the clearing, the ground rocking from the blast of Charlie's B-40s, one man already dead. I'd called in the Hueys and we were just lying there, waiting to be extracted, when the familiar popping sound of a Kalashnikov opened up to my left. The kid manning the M-60 screamed and went down. I unslung my rifle and rose up to my

217

knees, spotting the guerrilla's head and shoulders as he charged through the tall grass. Letting go a two-second burst and seeing that head and those shoulders turn to pulp. Ending his forward progress forever, simple as squeezing a trigger.

And now that same feeling had come back, of being shaken and somehow angry. I'd had no choice when Charlie had come charging out of the jungle and no choice when Desmond Day came at me in the graveyard. Maybe that explained the anger. Desmond had forced me to kill him, and in killing him, I'd been reminded again just how mortal we all are; how frighteningly easy it is to die.

When I came out of the bathroom, the doctor was waiting for me. So were Ellis Turnbull and Special Agent Twilly. Twilly had ditched the fishing togs in favor of a three-piece blue pinstripe number, transforming himself from Curly Howard to Daddy Warbucks.

"Where's Moe?" I asked the FBI man.

"Who?"

"Your partner."

"Agent Garcia," Twilly said, as he sat on the edge of the unused bed opposite mine. "He's down on the next floor, interrogating Jamie Velez. So far, he's the only one who's been willing to talk." He ran his hand over his shaved scalp and frowned. "All in all, Sheridan, things would've gone a lot smoother if you'd taken the hint from Chief Turnbull and butted out."

"Maybe if you guys had been upfront with me, I would have." I looked at Turnbull. He was wearing his tan double knits and a neutral expression. "Why didn't you just tell me you were working with the feds?"

Before he could answer, the doctor took over. "Sit on the bed, please, so I may examine you. I have a schedule to keep, gentlemen."

I did as the doctor ordered. He was dark and stocky and spoke in a singsong accent that sounded like Peter Sellers doing Nehru. His name tag read Dr. Jaglish. He probed the back of my skull, then gently gripped my jaw.

"It wasn't my idea," I heard Turnbull say as the doc and I stared into each other's eyes.

Twilly chimed in, "At the time, we didn't want to expose our investigation to anyone, particularly a journalist. We hoped the chief here could dissuade you, so to speak, without giving away the store."

Doctor Jaglish shone a pen light in my eyes, then grunted his approval at whatever he'd seen there. "Very good. Nothing to worry about, Mr. Sheridan."

"I can go?"

He nodded. "After you've signed the proper releases."

We watched him hurry out, then I moved over to the closet and removed my notepad and pen from my jacket. "I've got a few questions," I said, as I sat back on the bed.

Twilly looked bemused. "You muck up my whole plan and then you expect me to brief you?"

"We've covered this ground already," I said. "You should've let Chief Turnbull clue me in. Besides, I don't see how I messed anything up. You've got DuPree and Beauchamp in custody and the kid Jamie's talking."

"It'll take more than that punk's testimony to make the case," the FBI man said, his round fleshy face turning pink. "We could use some physical evidence, which we might've gotten if that lousy Mick hadn't firebombed the Castle House. Which he wouldn't have had a chance to do if you hadn't been out there poking around."

I held up my hand. "I'm not the one who caused Desmond to torch the place. He decided to do it after MacKenzie showed up with the news that you guys had picked up DuPree and the others. You should have sent your team out right on MacKenzie's heels."

He began to sputter. "We had to wait for a court order before we could—"

"Besides," I cut him off, "who says all the physical evidence was lost in the fire?"

"The goddamn place is an ash pile." He arched his eyebrows quizzically. "Unless . . . you found something?"

I smiled. "Here's the deal. Private press briefing, just the three of us."

Twilly glared at me for a moment, then sighed. "What've you got?"

I looked at Turnbull and gestured toward the closet. "Inside right pocket of my sportcoat."

He went to the closet, a trace of a grin softening his face, and dug out the floppy disks. Twilly hopped off the extra bed, hurried over beside him, and snatched the disks away like a spoiled five-year-old under the Christmas tree.

"What's on 'em?"

"I don't know," I said. "But MacKenzie was awfully eager to see that they were destroyed."

"Well, we'll soon see." Twilly, smiling broadly, slipped the disks into the pocket of his suit. As he brought his attention back to me, the smile turned sour. "Okay, Sheridan. I'll give you what I can, but it all goes down on deep background, understand? No quoting me until after the official press briefing at the federal building on Monday. My boss'll have my butt otherwise."

"Understood," I said, my pen poised. "Now, what exactly was the Fellowship up to and how'd you get tuned in?"

"Okay. First, I'm with the Bureau's antiterrorist division, assigned last July to investigate a car bombing in D.C. that killed five people, including the governor of Puerto Rico and an Ohio congressman named Griggs. You're aware of the incident, right?"

"Right."

"Our best lead was a Hertz rental we believed had been used by the terrorists to get in and out of Washington. The car was found abandoned on a side street here in Watertown. That led us to conclude that the bombers had gotten out of the country into Canada somewhere along the St. Lawrence. In the course of our investigation, we ran across a parallel Bureau investigation into Maurice DuPree and this Fellowship setup. Nothing hot, just a couple of local agents assigned to check out some long-standing rumors concerning the man and his varied business operations."

I interrupted. "Rumors indicating that DuPree's shipping company might be involved in a smuggling operation?"

Twilly nodded. "We suspect DuPree has been working the margins for quite a while, using the Coffin Island property and this Fellowship jazz as a front, but there wasn't enough to build a case. Several years back, he was indicated in a scam to bring undocumented workers up from Central America and slip them into the States. After that, his name came up in connection with embargoed arms being shipped out of the U.S. for various flash points in the Middle East. In both cases, the Bureau had suspicions, but no solid evidence.

"Anyway, we decided to take a harder look at DuPree and the Midstream Fellowship, see if he might tie in with the D.C. bombing. Along the way, we got a tip from a, uh, brother agency, concerning one Terrance Alston."

"That brother agency being the CIA?" I asked.

"No comment," Twilly scowled. "We have to observe certain protocols. So, where was I?"

"Terrance Alston," I prompted.

"Right. This brother agency had Alston's name on a short list of Irish nationals living in the States that were thought to be tied in with the Irish National Liberation Army—a bunch of Marxist whackos. MI-6—British intelligence—got wise to the guy first and passed their suspicions along. The scenario was that Alston was cultivating Irish-American groups, raising money that was supposed to be for some Northern Ireland children's relief fund but was actually going to buy arms for the INLA. When our guys in the other agency found out Alston had been hired to replace another professor at Clampett College, they got real curious."

I interrupted. "So the CIA—or whoever—inserted a search program into various Washington databanks, looking for more information on Alston. When it hit on a reference to Clampett College in the D.C. police case file on the Janezek murder, bells went off."

"I don't know about any computer moles," Twilly said, adopting a disingenuous stare. "Let's just say someone sent

221

along a suggestion that we look into the Janezek file. Once we did, we got onto the notion that Janezek's mugging might have had deeper implications. We also recognized that the target of the car bombing might not have been the governor, but Congressman Griggs. As it turns out, Griggs had been pushing a bill up on the Hill that would strengthen an extradition treaty between the U.S. and Britain, making it easier to extradite suspected Irish terrorists back to Britain for trial.

"Anyway, this all took time to develop. By the time we got clearance to come up here and set up a surveillance on the Castle House, we find out from Turnbull here that a writer named T. S. W. Sheridan had beaten us into town and was doing his own snooping."

I said to Turnbull, "I take it Agent Twilly was the mysterious phone tipster who called in the gunshot at Dougherty's place and who subsequently told you that I showed up after the shot was fired."

"Actually, it was Garcia," the chief constable said. "He was following the two caretakers. Followed 'em right to Dougherty's door. A few minutes later, Alan Betz showed up and the shot was fired. Garcia called it in on his car radio, then he hung back and watched what developed. He saw Day and Beauchamp come out of the apartment house, followed about five minutes later by a dazed-looking Betz. A few minutes later, you turned up."

"So you knew all along that Alan Betz probably wasn't the shooter. Yet you sicced Craven and his state cops on his trail anyway."

"Betz was a material witness to a murder and he was missing," Twilly interjected. "That in itself justified putting out an APB." He stuck out his index finger for emphasis. "I was with Chief Turnbull when we got Agent Garcia's radio report. I requested that he keep the investigation away from Day and Beauchamp for the time being, until we were ready to move on the whole bunch. If Garcia and I had stepped into things at that point, it could've screwed up everything. It was my call all the way, and I make no apologies for it."

I considered Twilly for a moment, then shook my head and turned back to Turnbull.

"And the threats you made about me being with Kara in my room?" I asked. "I figured MacKenzie had told you."

Turnbull shook his head. "Twilly here saw the girl arrive and drew the obvious conclusions. You think they ended up with the room next to yours by accident?"

I pivoted back to Twilly. "You two guys had me staked out all along?"

"Not really. Just keeping tabs," he said shortly. "Now, you want to hear the rest of this or what?"

"Yeah," I said. "What made you decide to move on Du-Pree last night?"

"We finally turned up solid evidence—thanks to the Royal Canadian Mounted Police—linking DuPree to a character named Charles Briand. You familiar with the name?"

I indicated that I wasn't, even as I wrote it down.

"He's a French-Canadian like DuPree," the FBI man went on. "Briand attended college in Paris back in the seventies and got himself involved with several radical left groups. When he returned to Montreal, he fell in with the Free Quebec Society, which in turn led him to DuPree. According to the dossier we received from the Mounties, Du-Pree apparently got turned onto the idea of an independent Quebec back in the sixties, when de Gaulle came over and stirred up all the French-Canadians with that inflammatory speech of his. At any rate, DuPree started using his smuggling expertise to help the FQS further its agenda to force a split from English-speaking Canada. When the movement began to lose momentum in the late seventies, he lost some of his zeal for politics, but not for money. He took Briand on as a partner and, using Briand's connections with various terrorist groups, the pair of them went into arms smuggling in a big way. This eventually got them tied up with the INLA."

"Okay," I said, looking up from my notes. "But I'm still unclear on how DuPree's connection to this Briand led you to move on DuPree and the others when you did."

A self-satisfied grin spread across Twilly's moon face. "Charles Briand is calling himself Claude Beauchamp these days. Agent Garcia and I had taken several long-lens photos of both Desmond Day and Beauchamp, some of which we sent on to the RCMP when we asked for their help on DuPree. They identified Briand and told us he was wanted up there in connection with several FQS-related crimes that had taken place in the seventies. That was all the pretext we needed at that point to move on the whole bunch."

I like to think I'd've seen the Briand-Beauchamp connection a little sooner if I hadn't been nursing a bruised skull. Perhaps as a way of compensating for my dull-wittedness, I decided to round out Twilly's narrative with a few conjectures of my own.

"So," I said. "DuPree rebuilt the old Castle House to use as a conduit for his smuggling activities, which in turn led to his involvement with the Irish National Liberation Army. The INLA connection proved to be very lucrative, but risky. That's where the Fellowship comes in; it was established to provide a cover story for any unusual traffic that DuPree might have going through the place. The INLA assigned Desmond Day to run the operation and keep DuPree in line. Then, last July fourth, the Fellowship uses the excuse of a four-day seminar to sneak an INLA explosives expert into the country to assassinate a troublemaking congressman. Unfortunately for Stefan Janezek, he sees Desmond Day on the street in D.C. that morning. Desmond may already have been aware of the professor's investigation into the Castle House and his suspicions regarding the Fellowship. In any case, he decides to kill Professor Janezek on the spot."

"That's how it adds up," Twilly nodded. "By the way, we think Day's real name was Desmond Hurley, an INLA trigger man. We're trying to verify that with the Brits. We're also trying to identify the explosives man, but we figure he's long since back in Ireland someplace, laying low."

"What about the other Fellowship members?" I asked.

"Dr. Stevenson appears to be clean," Twilly said. "Didn't have a clue. MacKenzie was in it for the money, same as DuPree. Dougherty was a natural; your basic radical chic dilettante who gets his jollies raising money for the IRA and the Sandinistas. He was brought in to help keep Stevenson in the dark and to liaise with Terrance Alston, who was busy raising money and buying arms. We figure Dougherty ended up panicking when things got hot, so they eliminated him. Only Desmond and Claude made a mess of it." Twilly shook his head. "Terrorists aren't too good at being subtle."

"And the kid, Jamie?"

"He was basically a gofer, to hear him tell it. A Cuban who was raised in Miami and speaks fluent Spanish. Briand recruited him to help with the smuggling operation back when they were transporting illegals up from Central America."

"What a can of worms," I said.

"Snakes is more like it," Twilly said, as he checked his watch impatiently. "Look, I've got an investigation to get back to. Save the rest of your questions for the briefing on Monday, Sheridan. Let's go, chief."

After they left, I sat there ruminating on Desmond Day. St. Patrick was supposed to have driven all the snakes out of Ireland. Another myth shattered.

CHAPTER 29

"WHAT do you think you're doing?"

"I think I'm putting on my shoes."

"Well . . . shouldn't you be in bed?"

"Not according to the doctor, although my cranium is petitioning me to get a second opinion."

I had been sitting in a side chair near the window, trying to ignore a slight dizziness as I bent forward to tie my shoelaces. Rita Tonelli had bustled into the room with a nosegay of crysanthemums in her hand and a cheery smile affixed to her face, all psyched to console an ailing friend. Now the smile wilted into mild embarrassment as she looked from me to the fistful of flowers and back again.

"I picked these for you from my windowbox," she said, coloring. "They're a little droopy this late in the year."

"They look just fine to me," I said, rising from the chair. I took the small pink and white bouquet from her and kissed her cheek. "Just what the doctor ordered." She let me put the flowers in a water glass on the nightstand before the veneer of normalcy she'd been affecting slipped away.

"Don't you try that phony insouciance routine with me, Sheridan," she scolded me. "I come from a big Italian family, remember? I know macho posturing when I see it." As if to prove her ethnicity, she began waving her hands in the air. "My God, you could've been killed out there. You all could've been killed. And Ellis! He's just as bad as you are." Her lips trembled. "I couldn't sleep last night, thinking about what might've happened outside Dr. Stevenson's. When that awful Beauchamp pulled out that gun and everybody started shooting, and Ellis caught in the middle of everything." She blinked at me, the green eyes misty. "Lord, Sheridan, I thought . . . I thought I was going to lose him . . . that we'd never—"

I went to her and put my arms around her and held her close. After a moment, I moved an arm's length away, still gripping her shoulders. "This world can get pretty scary sometimes, Rita," I said. "You can't always plan everything, expect it to conform to some preconceived notion. Sometimes you just have to go with your instincts—let your heart take you where it will."

"Yes." She looked up at me. "I've been unfair with him, haven't I?"

I dropped my hands and shrugged. "You read him a lot better than I did—particularly when you let your instincts take over. You knew he couldn't've been a party to all this Castle House business."

She smiled demurely. "I went with my heart that time, didn't I?"

"You most certainly did," I agreed, adding, "Now, how'd you like to show me the way out of here?"

We followed a long corridor to a bank of elevators—Rita leading the way and chattering about the sensational developments involving DuPree and MacKenzie and the rest—and rode down to the first floor. Alan Betz and Kara caught up with us outside the discharge office. Kara was dressed in white painters' pants and a cable-knit pullover. Except for the mouse under her eye, her outward appearance was none the worse for the previous night's ordeal. What was happening on the inside was anyone's guess, but the signs were good.

She and Betz were on me like a couple of mother hens, pestering me about my injuries while simultaneously pumping me for information. I got them to stop talking long enough to introduce Rita and Kara—they were cautiously cordial at first, like a couple of foreign diplomats meeting at a peace conference—and then I suggested we slip into the adjacent coffee shop and grab a table. I had a lot I needed to do, but I knew I owed them all an accounting and, truth to tell, I was still a bit unsteady on my feet.

After the four of us settled down with mugs of steaming coffee, I related my conversation with Special Agent Twilly. Alan kept saying "I knew it, I knew it," as I explained the real purpose behind the Midstream Fellowship. When I was finished, he related his own adventures out in the little rental boat, from the moment Desmond showed up on the dock brandishing the shotgun to the part where Betz picked Kara out of the water near the old farm just as the cavalry swooped down in the chopper.

"There's one thing I can't figure," Alan said when story hour finally wound down. "What is it that Jan discovered in his research that made him suspicious of the Fellowship in the first place?"

"That's one question that we'll probably never have an answer for," I said. "Something highly incriminating about Dougherty, I'd say. Maybe he made a slip of the tongue in front of Professor Janezek." I shrugged. "Whatever it was, it went up in flames with the professor's notebook."

"Jeez, don't mention flames," Kara said, frowning. "That reminds me of that creepy mansion and I don't ever wanna see that place again."

"That was a damn foolish thing you did," I scowled at her.

"And very brave," Rita chimed in. It may have been mere diplomacy, but it had a salubrious effect. For the first time, these two young women, so different from one another, regarded each other openly across the table top. A mutual accord had been reached.

"You know how it is," Kara said, mimicking a western drawl. "Sometimes a girl's gotta do what a girl's gotta do."

"That's very true," Rita nodded, then pushed away her half-filled cup of coffee. "And what I have to do, I'm afraid, is get back to the library. Saturdays are very busy and we're understaffed, as usual."

We said our good-byes, Rita planting a sisterly kiss on me. After she had gone, Betz took up the thread of conversation with a shy sideward glance at Kara.

"You know, you really are a very resourceful person, Kara," he said as he nervously pushed his glasses up the bridge of his nose. "You could do a lot of things—"

Her cheeks turned a deeper shade beneath the heavy applications of rouge and her eyes sought me out. "I know, I know." She sighed. "Last night, in that room? Then us running like hell across that island, it really started to sink in, Sheridan." She grinned ruefully. "I mean, maybe I didn't give waitressing enough of a chance. Hey, maybe with a pair of sensible shoes—?"

I rested my hand on her wrist. "And it'd only be for a couple more years, until you had your degree, right?"

"Right," she nodded, emphatically. Then, "I guess you'll be going home soon, huh? Now that you've got your story?"

"Soon."

Betz inspected me closely, then shook his head and chuckled. "So why do I have this nagging feeling you're not done with all this yet, Sheridan?" He held up his hand. "Never mind. I've had all the adventure I can handle for awhile. And so have you. Besides, we came by to give you a lift back to town, not to chew your ear off."

"I could use one, if you don't mind waiting around for a half an hour or so," I said. "I need to make a couple of phone calls, then I want to see if they'll let me in to see Howard Johnson. He's upstairs in the IC unit."

They decided to wait for me over second cups of coffee and slices of coconut cream pie. I headed out to the lobby and a bank of pay phones. My first call went to Karen De-Clair in Geneva. Karen was the managing editor of the *Finger Lakes Daily News* and an old friend. We spoke just long enough for me to tell her I had an exclusive to file in the next day or so and to convince her to arrange a deal for me with one of the wire services.

My second call was to Geneva as well; the Quincy County sheriff's department. As promised, J.D. Staub had the information I'd asked for in front of him; a computer printout of Captain Lester Tinderlay's original case file on the Castle House investigation and the backgrounder on Jack Rose, including the old prison records from Dannemora.

"Could you check the Castle House file for the estimated time that Fire Chief Porter and his men arrived at the scene?" I asked J.D. "And, if it's in the report, any known associates of Jack Rose that Tinderlay questioned during the investigation."

"Yeah, that's in here somewhere. Just a second," J.D. said. I could hear him shuffling through the printout. "It says here that the fire was spotted at about eleven-twenty P.M., 31 December, 1937, and that the Widows Cape volunteers got out there twenty-five minutes later, at eleven forty-five. That any help?"

"It could be," I said. "What about the known associates of Jack Rose?"

J.D. shuffled some more paper and read off a short list of names. When he finished, I said, "That's it? Tinderlay didn't question Howard Johnson?"

"Not according to this," J.D. assured me. "Wait a minute, Howard Johnson? I saw that name someplace. Here it is, in the prison records on Jack Rose."

I felt the back of my neck stiffen like a high-tension wire. "What's it say?"

"Hold your horses," J.D. groused. "Well, basically, this Jack Rose ended up doing an extra six months in stir because he and another inmate tried to make an escape while outside the prison on a work detail. The other inmate's name was Howard Johnson."

My mind began racing as more and more pieces of the puzzle began dropping into place. "That's great, J.D. Look, I've got to go now. I've—"

"Wait, there's more, Sheridan. This Howard Johnson? A guard gunned him down during the escape attempt. The man's been dead since May 11, 1934."

I didn't bother to get a visitor's pass at the hospital's reception desk and I didn't wait around for an elevator. Instead, I consulted a building directory in the lobby and took the stairs two at a time to the second floor and followed a bright green floor stripe to the intensive care unit. Unlike the rest of the hospital, the rooms in the ICU each had a small window mounted in the door. I zigzagged my way down the corridor, glancing into each room, trying to locate Howard. I had checked about half the rooms when a door opened at the end of the corridor and two men came out. One was a gaunt, stooped fellow wearing a long white smock. The other, dressed in an impeccable gray suit, was Dr. James C. Knox.

"Dr. Knox," I said breathlessly. "I have to speak to Howard. Is he able to—"

Something in his eyes stopped me in my tracks. He shook his head slowly. "I'm sorry, Mr. Sheridan. Howard Johnson died an hour ago. His heart simply gave out."

I looked questioningly to the other doctor, but his face was a professional mask.

I turned back to Knox. "Is he in there?"

"Yes. Doctor Brillstein and I were just—"

I brushed past him and went into the room. It was small and austere, a single bed surrounded by the electronic miracles of modern medicine: bulky machines, wires and IV lines, cathode ray tubes—everything disconnected or switched off.

Howard lay on the bed, the sheet pulled up to his neck, the one eye still covered with a black patch, the other closed. I stood at the foot of the bed and stared at the legless lump hidden beneath the sheet and tried to sort out the tumult of emotions that pounded at me. Knox slipped into the room and walked over beside me.

"We did our best—" he began, but I didn't want to hear it.

"Tell Judge Dunleavy I'll be out to see him tonight at his place," I said evenly. "Eight o'clock."

Knox exhaled wearily. "The last two days have been difficult for him, for all of us. I'm not sure—"

"Tell him I have a story to tell. A true story."

CHAPTER 30

THE entire ground floor of my cottage in Mohaca Springs would fit neatly into the main living room at Glenaire. The walls were covered half in golden oak paneling and half in green and gold brocaded wallpaper. Tall Palladian windows offered a view out over the deep front lawn to the river and, invisible now in the gray dusk, Coffin Island. The ceiling was high enough for the New York Knicks to run layup drills.

The five of us stood around in front of a cavernous marble fireplace, obligatory sherries in hand: Judge Dunleavy, Dr. Knox, the realtor Fred Porter, Ellis Turnbull, and myself. It had taken only two words to convince the chief constable to accompany me: job security.

"I'm not sure why I let myself be talked into this, Mr. Sheridan," the judge was saying. "At a time like this, I should be with Estelle and Angus. No matter what Rodney got himself into, the MacKenzies are like family to me."

Porter chimed in petulantly, "If you think this is going to be an interrogation, Sheridan, think again. We've all been questioned by the FBI and we've been cleared of any involvement with Rodney and his scheming friends in the Fellowship."

"I don't doubt you were all ignorant about what the Fel-

233

lowship was up to," I said. "MacKenzie merely used his influence with you—and what he knew about the Castle House tragedy—to see that the town and the college would give its vocal support to the Fellowship, while tacitly agreeing to stay out of its affairs."

"And just what is it that you think Rodney knew about the Castle House tragedy, Mr. Sheridan?" Dunleavy asked. He tried to sound skeptical, but he missed. The previous forty-eight hours had taken a lot out of him, including most of his bluster and nearly all of his guile.

"That's the story I promised you, judge." I downed the last swallow of sherry and set my glass on the mantel. "Why don't you all take a seat while I tell it."

There was some grumbling as they settled in, Turnbull and Porter choosing a pair of wing chairs, while the judge and Dr. Knox occupied opposite ends of a long leather sofa. I held forth in front of the fireplace and began the tale.

"New Year's Eve, 1937. Lumber baron Ernest Castle decides to ring in the new year with a party at his vacation retreat out on Coffin Island and he enlists the services of his caretaker, Tommy Trevain, and Trevain's daughter Emily. Into the picture steps Jack Rose, a local petty thief and ex-con who also happens to be the secret lover of Emily Trevain. Jack figures this is his chance for the big score. After selling Emily on the plan, he enlists the aid of Big John Cawley, a simple-minded brute. Cawley would provide the muscle, in case any of the partiers got out of line.

"Everything started out well. After laying out the buffet dinner, Emily fakes illness to get herself excused from the party. On her way out the back, she lets Jack and Cawley in and points them in the right direction, then she heads home to the farm to establish an alibi. The two thieves, their faces covered, surprise Castle and his guests in the dining room and begin stripping them of their valuables. But then, Tommy Trevain recognizes Jack and calls out his name. Cawley shoots Tommy. The guests and Tommy Trevain's body are hustled down to the basement and locked up in the wine cellar. Rose and Cawley gather up

234

the loot and head back to the Trevain farm, where their car is stashed."

I paused a moment. The faces that stared back at me were impassive, except for Turnbull, who was taking it all in with unmasked curiosity.

"Jack tells Emily what happened to her father and she becomes numb with guilt. Meanwhile, Cawley is beginning to panic. He wants to drive across the ice to Canada. Jack—an experienced river man—knows better than to attempt the channel crossing in a heavy sedan that early in the season, but he also knows better than to argue with Cawley. So he gives Cawley his half of the valuables and lets him go. Predictably, the car breaks through the ice and Big John meets his maker. Emily, meanwhile, tells Jack she doesn't ever want to see him again. But Jack loves her and he figures she'll eventually forgive him, so he leaves part of the take with Emily and heads south, planning to relocate somewhere and send for her when things cool down and she's had a chance to reconsider. Only it never happens. He tries to contact her a few months later, but she doesn't come, doesn't answer his letters. To make matters worse, the newspapers are filled with stories about the Castle House holocaust and Jack learns that he's the number one suspect.

"Afraid to return to Widows Cape, Jack joins the merchant marines under an assumed name. A few years later, during World War II, Jack's ship is torpedoed in the Atlantic and he becomes a cripple, for years shuffling from hospitals to convalescent homes, a prisoner of his disabilities and his criminal past. With nothing better to fill the time, Jack sends for old news clippings from the Castle House case and begins to figure out the truth behind the fatal fire. Then, in 1967, he learns that Emily Trevain has died, frozen to death out there on Coffin Island—just the sort of sad, gruesome 'human interest' story that might make it onto the wire services on a slow news day. He figures his life couldn't get much worse, so he takes a chance and begins writing letters to certain influential people in Widows

235

Cape, threatening to tell what he knows unless they bring him home and take care of him. The gamble pays off. Jack is brought back to Widows Cape to live out his days in relative luxury at the Riverside Nursing Home, where everyone knew him by his assumed name, Howard Johnson."

I paused again. This time, Judge Dunleavy filled the silence, but just barely, his voice subdued.

"That's quite a leap of the imagination, Mr. Sheridan," he said. "But what evidence do you offer—?"

"In a moment, judge. The story isn't finished."

I started in again. "While Jack Rose was pulling off the robbery, four young men were returning to Widows Cape from Watertown, drunk as lords. At least two of the young men were not in much of a party mood, however. Earlier in the week, they'd had some sort of spat with their girlfriends, Alice and Victoria Spicer. Maybe the trouble began because the two beauties had been invited to Ernest Castle's party. Their beaus, in a fit of adolescent jealousy, refused to take them, so they went on their own. Now, as the four young men drove back to Widows Cape, someone suggested they drive across the ice and crash the Castle House shindig.

"Everyone agreed this was a good idea, so off they went. Only, when they got to the mansion, the place seemed to be empty. In a rage, the young men began trashing the house—throwing the food around, dumping out the booze. Inadvertently, in the midst of the drunken mayhem, a fire broke out—a candelabrum overturned, a whiskey-soaked carpet caught fire, whatever. Maybe they tried to put it out at first, but it soon got out of hand and they fled outside. Eventually, as the blaze grew, Fire Chief Manfred Porter and his volunteers showed up. The young men told Porter what they'd done and he acted immediately, taking them aside, assuring them he'd keep them out of it, ever mindful of the boys' rich and powerful parents. Porter's actions proved especially timely when, a few hours later, it was established that Castle and his guests had perished in the wine cellar. And, thanks to a message scratched into a

236

foundation stone by one of the unfortunate victims, a convenient villain had been provided to take the blame for the tragedy. Jack Rose."

Judge Dunleavy, ashen, stared into the cold fireplace while Dr. Knox's eyes flitted nervously from my face to Chief Turnbull's. Only Fred Porter chose to put up a defense.

"This is slanderous, Sheridan. You can't prove any such thing ever happened!"

"We have Howard Johnson's body and a set of Jack Rose's fingerprints from his old prison records," I said. "That will prove Johnson and Rose were the same man."

"That doesn't prove your allegations against my father and the others," Porter said.

"There's more. Circumstantial, maybe. But overwhelming. Learning Howard Johnson's true identity was the key. When I found evidence earlier today that Howard was really Jack Rose, everything began to fit together. For example, Howard told me that the robbery had been planned for ten o'clock, when Castle and his guests all would be gathered in the dining room for the buffet. The time jives with what Emily Trevain told the police at the time, that she had gotten sick and gone back to the farmhouse sometime before ten. But witness testimony and police files state that the fire was sighted around eleven-twenty that night, over an hour after the robbery was to have occurred. Of course, Howard Johnson, in relating a secondhand account, could've gotten the time wrong. But Jack Rose wouldn't, because he was there."

Ellis Turnbull had listened quietly, but now his policeman's training was taking over. "So if Rose and Cawley pulled the job at ten, they would've been out of there by ten-thirty at the latest. Which means they weren't around to start a fire sometime after eleven."

"But the four young drunks were," I said. "It's the only scenario that fits the evidence."

"Maybe," the chief said skeptically.

"Look, the way I see it, Emily spotted the fire long after

Jack left. She hurried back to the mansion and ran into Dunleavy and the others standing around half in the bag. She figured out what they'd done and, horrified, she told them about Castle and his guests locked away in the cellar.

"The boys tried to get back inside—Marshall even burning his hands in the attempt—but it was too late." I looked at the judge. "Now, you had to deal with Emily and what she had seen. But it was a Mexican standoff. She was as guilty, in her own mind, as anyone. So you all arranged to buy her silence—or blackmail her into it. Probably with the complicity of your parents, since you would've had to go to them with the story in order to get the money to take care of Emily. That would explain the formation of the Stewart Fund after Marshall committed suicide. Maybe it really was meant to be a tribute to the boy, but it was also a convenient device for paying Emily Trevain's bills, seeing that she stayed out on the island, alone with her guilt and her secrets."

I switched my gaze to Fred Porter. "Insuring the silence of Fire Chief Porter was less of a problem. The price was a partnership in the MacKenzie family's real estate business." I ignored Porter's blustery denials and turned back to the judge. "And then, when it all seemed to be going away, Jack Rose came back into your life and you had to buy him off, too. So you and Dr. Knox's father and the others arranged to pay Howard's—or Jack's—nursing care expenses with the tried and true method, the Stewart Fund."

When Dunleavy didn't respond, I continued on. "You made a mistake, judge, when you told me that you had known Howard Johnson back in the early days, when he used to pal around with Jack Rose. I found it curious that another Johnson—Sonny Johnson, the newspaperman, who himself was born and raised here—had never heard of a Howard Johnson. Even more curious, Captain Tinderlay, in questioning Rose's known associates, hadn't interviewed a Howard Johnson. Now we know why. Because there never was a Howard Johnson."

No one burst forth with a dramatic confession, but no

one denied anything, either. They simply sat there like an unholy trinity—Dunleavy, Knox, and Porter—each man's face a study in remorse. Then Dr. Knox broke the spell.

"It became part of our legacy, Fred's and Rodney's and mine. To guard the terrible secret of Castle House, protect our fathers' reputations," he said, calmly staring up at me from the couch. "Don't judge them too harshly, Mr. Sheridan. They weren't really bad men."

"I know," I said, watching the judge. "It would've been simple for them to eliminate Emily Trevain and make it look accidental, rather than maintain her out on the island. And later, when Jack Rose came back as Howard Johnson, an invalid in a nursing home? Easier still to kill him off."

Dunleavy looked up just then, his eyes liquid with memory and anguish. "For half a century, Sheridan, I've been trying to atone for one rash, unforgivable act."

I said, "You once reminded me, judge, that we've all made youthful mistakes. And that charity includes the ability to forgive. You were right about that."

Fred Porter asked apprehensively, "What will you do now, Sheridan? Now that you have your story."

"My story is the Fellowship," I said. "Nothing more."

The judge exhaled, a long, ragged sigh. "Thank you. I'm in your debt."

"No," I said, shaking my head. "But, there is one favor I'd like to ask."

CHAPTER 31

A CHURCH bell pealed somewhere far off. I stopped digging a moment and absently stared across the river toward Widows Cape, squinting to pick out the steeple.

"St. Jerome's," Ellis Turnbull drawled laconically. "Eleven o'clock mass." He was sitting on a fossilized boulder, elbows on knees, watching me sweat.

Sunday morning. Warm for September. Already, I had stripped off my shirt and the long handle of the shovel had become slick from my moist palms.

"I guess the judge still has some juice," I said as I pushed the shovel's rounded blade back into the hard earth. "Getting someone to issue an exhumation order that fast."

"He's got friends on the county bench, all right." Turnbull pulled at a clump of weeds. "I hope this isn't a waste of time, Sheridan."

"Me, too."

"So why do it? I mean, why here of all places?"

"Just playing a hunch," I grunted, shifting the dirt.

"Seems like a pretty wild hunch," Turnbull said. "Not that I'm betting against you. Not after the way you put the rest of it together."

"Dunleavy didn't actually come out and confess to anything," I reminded him. "Not in a legal sense."

"No, but you had 'em. All three of them. It might be tough to prove in a court of law, but I have no doubts that it all went down pretty much like you said."

I tossed another shovelful of earth onto the pile. "You going to pursue it, chief?"

He didn't hesitate. "Nope. Like I was saying, it'd be tough to prove in court. Besides which, I don't see how justice would be served. The others are all dead, except for Angus MacKenzie, who's as good as. And Dunleavy, well, I just think whatever debt he owed has been paid. The man's done a lot of good in this county over the past fifty years."

I nodded. There are those who would argue that a crime was a crime, and that time and good deeds didn't supercede society's right of retribution. But I wasn't one of them.

"By the way," Turnbull said. "Craven got back to me with the ballistics report on the pistol that killed Dougherty. He and Professor Janezek were both shot with SIG P-201s, all right, but not with the exact same gun."

"Not surprising," I said. "I imagine Desmond tossed the first one somewhere in D.C. after he murdered the professor, then replaced it when he got back to Castle House. Weapon of choice," I shrugged as I resumed shoveling.

"Yeah, I suppose professional shooters are married to their tools the same as carpenters or auto mechanics," Turnbull said. "Speaking of the Castle House, there's a couple points you could clarify, just to satisfy my curiosity."

"Such as?"

"Last night when you were detailing the robbery, you said Cawley had shot Tommy Trevain. What makes you think it wasn't Jack Rose?"

"I just don't believe he was the type, even though Howard told me it was Jack Rose—meaning himself—who had done the shooting. He was just going along with what everybody had been led to believe, I think. Also, in a weird way, the old pirate relished the idea of being this legendary outlaw." I smiled. "The fact is, everyone I spoke to except Howard said Jack Rose was just a small-time sneak thief.

On the other hand, Howard himself, in one of our interviews, referred to Cawley as 'that murdering moron.'"

"Could've gone either way, I guess," Turnbull said. "Something else that bothered me, though. This Jack Rose masquerading as Howard Johnson. Wouldn't somebody have recognized him, even after so many years?"

I laughed. "You never actually met Howard, did you?"

"No, I never did."

"Well, take my word. After losing most of his hair, one of his eyes and both legs, he'd've had a hard time recognizing himself. The poor old guy was a real mess."

Just then the shovel clanged against metal. Turnbull hopped up from his rock and stood behind the headstone belonging to Tommy Trevain and peered over expectantly into the two-foot-deep depression I'd made in the old gravesite.

"You've found something?"

"We'll know in a second," I said, as I dropped to my knees and clawed at the loose dirt, perspiration dripping off the end of my nose. "Thank God she didn't go too deep. I'm not in shape for this kind of work."

In another moment, I had the object free. It was a round metal tin, the type grandmothers use to ship cookies for Christmas. This one had once been red and gold, with a scene of some sort painted on the cover, but oxidation had long since turned the container rusty brown. When I shook it, I heard a muffled rattling sound. I dug my fingers in under the lip of the cover and pulled.

"Rusted tight." I rapped the tin against the blade of the shovel a couple of times and tried again. This time, just as my fingernails were about to tear out, the lid came free. Inside was a folded piece of oilcloth. Ceremoniously, I peeled back the folds and held the tin out in both hands.

Turnbull whistled. "I don't believe it. Christ, will you just look at that stuff!"

The 'stuff' sparkled in the morning sunshine. Half a dozen gold rings, some with diamonds and other gems mounted in them, assorted wristwatches and cufflinks, a heavy silver bracelet, a jade brooch, a string of pearls, a glittering diamond necklace with matching earrings. The last of Jack Rose's Castle House take.

"I don't believe it," Turnbull said again.

I grinned up at him. "Like I said, just a hunch." I glanced over at the adjacent headstone, the one that marked Emily Trevain's final resting place. "It didn't register Friday night, when I was sprawled there waiting for Desmond to finish me off," I said. "But later, when I was lying in the hospital, replaying the whole thing in my head, I remembered a remark Judge Dunleavy had made. He commented on how ironic it was: The bodies of the Castle House victims were in such bad shape that they all had to be cremated. Including Tommy Trevain. That planted the seed. Then, when I asked him about it again last night, he remembered that Emily had requested that her father's ashes be scattered on the river. So I had to ask myself, why would Emily place a headstone on a piece of barren ground?"

"That is truly weird," Turnbull said, shaking his head. "It's like she was pulling some morbid practical joke."

"Yes. That poor girl. The jewelry symbolized a romantic dream that suddenly became a horrible nightmare. So she buried the dream and marked the place in memory of a man who, both in life and in death, had imprisoned her on this island. The final irony came with the inscription. 'Thomas Muncie Trevain, Loving Father.' An empty sentiment for an empty grave."

I suppose what came next could be called a moment of silence. Anyway, we both just stood there, not speaking, staring off at some private horizon. Eventually, I handed the treasure tin to Ellis.

"I guess you'll need to inventory this stuff."

"Yeah, I guess. I'm not sure just what the procedures are on a recovery like this." He shook the tin like a forty-niner panning gold. "Survivors might have some claim on it, maybe an insurance company or two. Then, of course, the state will want a healthy chunk."

"I imagine so."

"Still, Sheridan, even if all you get is a recovery fee, you'll end up with a tidy little bundle."

"Enough, you think, to pay for a couple years' tuition at Clampett?" I added quickly, "Not for me, chief. Don't worry, I'm not sticking around. And if I was, I still wouldn't be any threat to you."

"That's finally been hammered into my thick head," he said, grinning sheepishly. "Rita and I did a little soul-baring over a late supper at the Gazebo last night."

"That's good."

"Yeah." He frowned. "But who's the tuition . . . oh. The girl?"

I nodded. "I figure she's due a fresh start."

He glanced into the tin again. "I'd say you'll be able to cover that and have a good chunk left. Got anything else on your wish list?"

"Just one thing," I said, thinking about a satin-lined, carved mahogany casket.

THE MEASURE OF A MAN
IS HOW WELL HE SURVIVES LIFE'S

BOLD NEW CRIME NOVELS BY
TODAY'S HOTTEST TALENTS

CAJUN NIGHTS
D.J. Donaldson
A rash of weird, violent murders haunts New Orleans—and each new clue to the perpetrator leads investigator Kit Franklyn deeper into a world of bloody revenge.
_____ 91610-8 $3.95 U.S. _____ 91611-6 $4.95 Can.

MICHIGAN ROLL
Tom Kakonis
Four quirky—and very dangerous—strangers show up in Traverse City, Michigan. Seduction, drug-dealing, death—it's certainly more than gambler Timothy Waverly bargained for.
_____ 91684-1 $3.95 U.S. _____ 91686-8 $4.95 Can.

SUDDEN ICE
Jim Leeke
A lonely Ohio farmhouse goes up in flames, killing two...or so it seems. Then the county Sheriff learns the hapless couple were killed before the fire started...
_____ 91620-5 $3.95 U.S. _____ 91621-3 $4.95 Can.

Publishers Book and Audio Mailing Service
P.O. Box 120159, Staten Island, NY 10312-0004

Please send me the book(s) I have checked above. I am enclosing $_____ (please add $1.25 for the first book, and $.25 for each additional book to cover postage and handling. Send check or money order only—no CODs) or charge my VISA, MASTERCARD or AMERICAN EXPRESS card.

Card number _____

Expiration date _____ Signature _____

Name _____

Address _____

City _____ State/Zip _____

Please allow six weeks for delivery. Prices subject to change without notice. Payment in U.S. funds only. New York residents add applicable sales tax.

M STREET 5/90